"There Now," He Whispered, "You're Safe Now."

The roar of the rain against the tin roof sounded deafening. Jesse caught Darcy to him and held her tightly. She felt so good in his arms. Each part of her body molded naturally into his own.

Minutes passed along with the storm, but they lingered in the warmth of their embrace. She felt his broad, firm chest and the steady comforting beat of his heart. The all too familiar desire began to rise in her. Her pulse raced but no longer from terror. Slowly she lifted her chin and their eyes met.

"Darcy," he moaned, "don't tempt me so."

For an answer she pulled his head down for her kiss. At first their lips met shyly then as Jesse gave way to the overpowering emotion that racked his body, he pulled her to him and kissed her almost roughly.

Darcy met his passion. Her touch was driving shafts of fire along his nerves. Almost against his will he lowered his head and again claimed her lips. With a low moan Jesse knew the last of his resolve had crumbled and the molten fire of need coursed through his veins.

Dear Reader,

We, the editors of Tapestry Romances, are committed to bringing you two outstanding original romantic historical novels each and every month.

From Kentucky in the 1850s to the court of Louis XIII, from the deck of a pirate ship within sight of Gibraltar to a mining camp high in the Sierra Nevadas, our heroines experience life and love, romance and adventure.

Our aim is to give you the kind of historical romances that you want to read. We would enjoy hearing your thoughts about this book and all future Tapestry Romances. Please write to us at the address below.

The Editors
Tapestry Romances
POCKET BOOKS
1230 Avenue of the Americas
Box TAP
New York, N.Y. 10020

Embrace
the
Storm

Lynda Trent

A TAPESTRY BOOK
PUBLISHED BY POCKET BOOKS NEW YORK

This novel is a work of historical fiction. Names, characters, places and incidents relating to non-historical figures are either the product of the author's imagination or are used fictitiously. Any resemblance of such non-historical incidents, places or figures to actual events or locales or persons, living or dead, is entirely coincidental.

An *Original* publication of TAPESTRY BOOKS

A Tapestry Book published by
POCKET BOOKS, a Simon & Schuster division of
GULF & WESTERN CORPORATION
1230 Avenue of the Americas, New York, N.Y. 10020

ISBN: 0-671-46957-6

First Tapestry Books printing April, 1983

10 9 8 7 6 5 4 3 2 1

POCKET and colophon are registered trademarks
of Simon & Schuster.

TAPESTRY is a trademark of Simon & Schuster.

Printed in the U.S.A.

To John and Annell McGee
for East Texas mud, old houses,
and a skunk.

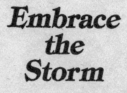

Embrace
the
Storm

Chapter One

"DARCY! DARCY MAYHEW!" THE STRIDENT VOICE called loudly in a complaining tone. "Where are you!"

The young woman straightened her aching back and let the wet dress she held slither down the galvanized ridges of the washboard. "Out here, Aunt Petra," she called out as she brushed a bead of perspiration from her brow with the back of her wrist. Behind her the day's wash snapped as the wind tried to tear the sheets from the line. Darcy's arms felt leaden from the hours of scrubbing, but only her aunt's dress and a few undergarments remained in the large wicker basket.

"There you are!" the elderly woman exclaimed as she emerged from the back door. "Why didn't you answer me, girl?"

"I did, Aunt," Darcy replied. She wasn't sure if her aunt was hard of hearing or if the old woman merely feigned deafness as another excuse to chastise her.

1

"No back talk, Miss! When you finish there, come to the parlor. I have an errand I want you to run." The old woman frowned down at her grandniece, then turned with a rustle of iron-gray taffeta and returned to the cooler recesses of the house.

"Yes, Aunt Petra," Darcy said automatically as the screen door closed behind the woman's ramrod-taut figure. She tucked an errant strand of dark brown hair back into the severe bun she wore and glanced at the height of the sun. Midafternoon, it was. Unless the errand was a short one, she would really have to hurry to be back in time to finish the supper. Fortunately, the stew meat was already simmering on the stove. She bent once again over the washboard, and as she quickened her pace she tried to ignore her protesting muscles.

Hard work was not a stranger to Darcy Mayhew. Orphaned at the age of seven, she had known little else as she was shuffled from one of her kinfolk to another. She had a vague, happy memory of her parents—not much older than she herself was now—and the lush, green fields of their Pennsylvania farm. But that had all ended thirteen years before, and now, with her parents' faces hazed and faded in her memory, she no longer felt the agonizing sorrow of their deaths. As Darcy had grown from a child whose wide brown eyes had seemed too large for her face, she had flowered into a beautiful woman. So beautiful, in fact, that those kinfolk with sons and the ones whose husbands had a roving eye no longer wanted her around. The reason for her lack of a permanent home was unknown to Darcy. She knew only that she had been sent to Plymouth to the last of her relatives, her Aunt Petra Garfield.

Aunt Petra, who was in fact her father's aunt, had had no use for Darcy's mother. She felt the young woman had been the cause of her nephew's unpopular decision to leave Plymouth and become a farmer. Aunt Petra was right. Darcy had the dubious fortune of resembling her pretty mother, and for this Aunt Petra could never forgive her.

Darcy rinsed the dress she was washing in the second tub of water and hung it dripping on the line so the weight of the water would pull out most of the wrinkles. The faded blue dress she wore was spotted darkly with water and her voluminous white apron whipped in the wind as she pushed the wooden pins over the fabric. At this rate the clothes would be dry in no time.

When the basket was empty and the clothesline full of flapping garments, Darcy poured out the wash water, being careful to stand uphill and not muddy her shoes. Then she upended the tubs to dry against the wall of the washhouse and hung the scrub board on its nail. Drying her reddened hands on the apron and using the tail of it to wipe the sweat from her face, Darcy headed for the house.

Like her aunt, the house was tall and very proper, with its predominant color being an uncompromising gray. It was a narrow house, three stories high, with small porches on the front and rear and an iron widow's walk on the roof. Darcy's room was tucked into one of the high pitched gables that overlooked the backyard, and beyond that the distant sea.

Knowing better than to pass through her aunt's parlor in her disheveled state, Darcy chose the stairs in the back of the house, which had been built for the use of servants.

At the top of the last flight of the close, dark stairs, Darcy turned to her room on the right, the room originally intended as the governess's quarters. Across the hall were the rooms that had been occupied by Aunt Petra's two children, who had long since grown up and moved away to houses of their own. Darcy had met Aunt Petra's younger daughter once—a replica of her mother except that her hair was more brown than gray—but the visit had been brief and the only one during the past year.

Darcy closed her door and took a clean dress from her chest. She slowly unbuttoned the soiled one and hung it on a nail to dry. As she pulled the pins from her hair, it tumbled past her waist in thick waves of sable glory. She brushed it in long, sweeping strokes that made it gleam as it lightly touched her pale skin, then recoiled it into a decorous bun at the nape of her neck. She washed her face and sponged down the rest of her body, waiting a few minutes to air-dry and cool off before dressing. She slipped the clean pink dress over her head and smoothed it down past her tiny waist. The dress fit her snugly and molded her full breasts and slender arms. A bit of white lace softened the severity of its lines at her wrists and at the high, rounded neck. She fluffed the cotton skirt over her petticoats and hoped she looked presentable. With no mirror she wasn't certain.

When Darcy knocked at the parlor door and

entered, Aunt Petra looked up at her over the rims of her spectacles. The old woman was going over her household accounts, which she kept in a small secretary. As usual she sat perfectly straight with her back the correct four inches from the ladder back of the chair. Darcy found herself wondering if Aunt Petra ever relaxed enough to lie down at night.

"I was going over the mail," Aunt Petra said. "I had expected a letter from my daughter today. Is this all that came?"

"Yes, Aunt." Then Darcy added impulsively, "Perhaps the letter is only late. You know how the mail is. I'm sure Cora meant to write . . ."

"No doubt the letter will arrive tomorrow. However, I shall drop her a note to reprimand her for her tardiness. Punctuality is a hallmark of good breeding, Darcy. Never forget it."

Despite the woman's sharp words, Darcy saw the envelope tremble ever so slightly in the old fingers. Instantly she went to her aunt and lay her hand on her thin shoulder. "Everything is all right, I'm certain. Cora's lying-in is near and she may have forgotten to mail the letter. Please don't worry. If all were not well—"

Aunt Petra jerked away and stood rigidly, holding the chair in a steel grip. "How dare you mention that subject to me! No lady ever talks of such a matter. Your low breeding ever presents itself no matter how hard I try to properly instruct you."

Darcy pulled her hand behind her as if she had been burned and looked up at the taller woman. "I'm sorry. I only meant to reassure you."

Aunt Petra's eyes narrowed. "Reassure me? Or ingratiate yourself with me? Listen well, Darcy Mayhew. You may live out your days in this house but you will never be mistress here. Upon my death this house will go to my children. Not to you!"

"But I never meant—"

"Of course you did! You're as grasping as your mother ever was!"

Darcy's eyes darkened with anger but she bit back her retort. "You had an errand for me to run?" she said coldly.

"Yes. Take two of those jars of berry jam you put up last week and a loaf of bread over to Widow Pennington. She's down with the grippe and the ladies of my church group are doing for her until she can get around again. Then go by the freight yard on your way home and ask why the highboy I ordered for Cora hasn't been delivered. Walk briskly, mind you, and don't dawdle." Aunt Petra turned her back in dismissal.

Darcy didn't bother to answer, but left the room. As she went down the hallway and out to the building that contained the kitchen, she was fuming. To think that Aunt Petra would take her words of kindness and twist them into something evil. As if she would even have the house if it were offered to her! Darcy took a basket from a peg on a rafter, lined it with a linen dish towel and put in two jars of jam. She lay the loaf of bread between them so they wouldn't roll together and break, covered them with the ends of the dish towel and stepped out into the sunlight.

Widow Pennington lived on one of the small side streets that ran down to the sea. Her late husband had been a ship's captain and the tiny house was as far inland as he had ever cared to be. As Darcy walked up the short walk she felt the cool sea breeze on her cheeks and tasted the bite of sea salt on her lips. Overhead three gulls circled, and she could see the rigging and masts of a tall ship. She mounted the three steps and crossed the porch to knock on the front door. This was the sort of house Darcy dreamed of owning one day: small and neat with bright blue clapboards and white shutters.

When the elderly maid opened the door, Darcy smiled and said, "Aunt Petra sent over a basket for Mrs. Pennington. Is she feeling better, Eva?"

The maid sniffed depreciatingly. "As well as can be expected for one of her years. Go on up to her bedroom, Miss Darcy. You know the way." She took the basket and favored Darcy with a thin-lipped smile.

Darcy went up the stairs and down a short hall. At the closed door she hesitated, then knocked softly lest Widow Pennington should be asleep.

"Come in," a voice called.

Darcy opened the door and smiled at the tiny woman who lay bundled in the large bed. "Are you feeling better today?"

"Why, Darcy, how good to see you again," the elderly woman said as she tried to push herself upright in the bed. A spasm of coughing shook her and she lay weakly back down.

"You lie still," Darcy scolded. "If Eva hears you

coughing she will be up here with more of that vile medicine she concocts."

The woman grimaced childishly and replied, "That woman is a termagant. Watches me like a chicken hawk, she does. It's a miracle she lets you come to visit me at all."

Darcy smiled, pushed a fat yellow cat off the chair and sat down. Widow Pennington had complained about Eva for as long as Darcy had known her, but the two were inseparable. "Your color is better today."

"Thank you, sweet. I believe I'll likely shake the grippe again this year. No credit to that horrid medicine, though." She looked hard at Darcy and said, "You look peaked yourself. Is Petra working you too hard?"

"No, of course not," Darcy lied. "There is a lot to be done in properly running a household."

Widow Pennington snorted. "Not as much as Petra Garfield will have you doing if she can get away with it."

"Really, it's not so bad. By the way, she sent you a basket of bread and jam."

"Give her my thanks, child. Though we both know who baked the bread and made the jam."

The yellow cat jumped up in Darcy's lap and she absentmindedly stroked his thick fur. "I have nowhere else to go," Darcy answered. "And she has no one else. Not really. Cora and Dorothy are both married and have families of their own. She needs me."

"Child, don't fool yourself," Widow Pennington

said. "Petra needs no one but herself. Don't bury yourself there as her servant. That's how she treats you, as you well know. Why, if I told Eva to do half the work you are expected to do, she'd leave me without a by-the-by."

Darcy's hand stilled on the cat's broad head and felt the tremor of its purring. "What else can I do? I haven't the wherewithal to set myself up as a governess and I know nothing at all about a trade."

Another racking cough shook the frail old woman. When she could get her breath, she said, "There will be a way, child, you'll see. There will be a way."

The door opened and Eva came into the room. In one hand she held a bottle of dark, syrupy liquid. In the other was a large spoon. "I heard you coughing clear down in the parlor. Open your mouth." Without giving her mistress time to argue, Eva poured a generous dollop of medicine into the spoon.

Widow Pennington obediently swallowed the medicine but grimaced. "You see how set upon I am?" she complained to Darcy. "This woman is a tyrant."

Eva merely glanced at her mistress, then said, "Can you stay for supper, Miss Darcy? We have a stewed chicken and fresh beets."

"Is it getting as late as that?" Darcy exclaimed. "I had no idea I'd stayed so long. I must leave right away." She clasped the Widow Pennington's dry, small-boned hand and tried not to notice the fever she felt there. "You behave yourself now, and mind Eva. I'll drop by again in a day or two."

The old woman returned Darcy's smile but her

9

eyes were becoming vague as if she had other matters on her mind.

As Darcy followed Eva back down the stairs, she asked in a low voice, "Tell me truly, she is getting better, isn't she?"

Eva shook her head sadly. "No, Miss. She rallies for a spell, then sinks again. I've never seen her so weak. She would be angry, though, if she heard me say so."

Darcy nodded. "I understand. I'll not mention it to anyone. You'll get word to me if . . . if there's need?"

Eva paused, her work-worn hand on the front doorknob, then nodded silently.

A brisk breeze billowed in Darcy's skirt as she hurried up the street and across the docks to the freight yard. Like Eva, Darcy felt the odds were slim for her friend's recovery and her heart was heavy.

With little difficulty, Darcy found the man in charge of the freight yard and delivered Aunt Petra's message. He replied that the shipment that undoubtedly contained the highboy in question had been delayed by bad weather but was expected any day. Darcy thanked him and left. As she was about to start home, an advertisement nailed to the office wall caught her eye. Even though she was already late, Darcy stopped to read what it said.

"Brides wanted. Must be healthy, of good character, and single. Matrimony is guaranteed to clean, decent men now living in the territory of Colorado. For more information, write Simon Peabody, Esq., Plymouth, Mass."

Darcy read the circular through twice. She had heard of so-called "mail-order brides," but she had never seen an advertisement for them. The women in Aunt Petra's church group called them scandalous and shameful. Yet Darcy's lively imagination had embellished them as adventurous pioneers. What would it be like, she wondered, to see a real mountain? Would it be higher than Potter's Hill near the farm where she had once lived? And did the rivers really flow gold from all the gold dust they carried? Were gold nuggets lying in the streambeds like goose eggs, just waiting to be picked up? She pictured the clean-cut, decent young men striding over mountain tops and along riverbeds, harvesting the gold.

A distant rumble of thunder pulled Darcy back to reality, and she blushed when she thought how she must look, standing in a freight yard reading a circular for mail-order brides. Aunt Petra would be mortified if she ever heard of it. Another growl of thunder rolled ominously in the darkening sky.

Since her childhood, Darcy had been frightened of thunderstorms. Uneasily she began to walk home, the circular forgotten.

That evening as Darcy finished the dishes, dried them and put them away, Aunt Petra made one of her numerous surveys of the kitchen. Aunt Petra had become convinced over the years that every servant she had ever employed had conspired to steal all her belongings. She viewed Darcy as being of the same ilk.

"There should be more of the pickle relish,

Darcy," she said accusingly as she adjusted her steel-rimmed spectacles to peer into the deep cupboard. "Where's the rest?"

"We're running low," Darcy answered dutifully. "I'll put up more this summer."

"Put up more indeed! And the elderberry jam. Wasn't it on this shelf?"

"Yes, Aunt, but we ate it all last week." Darcy carefully put a china platter in the stack on the shelf and reached for a plate.

"How could the two of us possibly have consumed two dozen jars of jam?" Aunt Petra demanded.

Darcy had no answer for the rhetorical question and replied, "I have no idea. I suppose we were hungry for jam this year."

Aunt Petra grabbed Darcy's arm to chastise her and the plate slipped from her fingers to crash on the floor. "Look what you've done! My grandmother brought that set from England!"

Before she could trust herself to answer, Darcy drew a deep breath. "I'm sorry," she said in a carefully controlled voice, but sparks of anger deepened her dark eyes. She and her aunt glared at each other for a long moment; then Aunt Petra stepped back, breaking the tension. Darcy knelt to clean up the shards of glass.

Believing Darcy's silence to be a sign of fright, Aunt Petra delivered a stinging lecture on clumsiness. Darcy ignored her with a considerable effort, and she found her thoughts returning to the circular at the freight office.

Colorado! An entire continent would lie between her and Aunt Petra's nagging. Of course, she would never actually agree to such a scheme, Darcy told herself, but it wouldn't hurt to get more information. She threw the remains of the broken plate away.

Chapter Two

FOR SEVERAL DAYS DARCY HAD GONE TO THE POST office to watch for the mail. Not, she told herself, because she really intended to follow up on the mail-order bride information, but because of Aunt Petra. If the letter should fall into Aunt Petra's hands, Darcy would at best be put out to starve in the streets. She shuddered to think what an enraged Aunt Petra might do at her worst.

At last the day came when the postmaster handed Darcy a letter addressed to her. She looked at it hesitantly, as if even contact with the envelope might somehow elicit a commitment. The man waiting in line behind her cleared his throat impatiently, and with a start Darcy took the envelope and stepped away from the mailroom window.

The circular posted on the opposite wall caught Darcy's eye and she paused. It was identical to the one she had seen in the freight yard. She looked from the poster to the return address of Simon Peabody, Esq., and fought back a blush. The idea of all this made her feel a little guilty, yet at the same time, exhilarated. No one Darcy had ever known had dared do such a headstrong thing. Of course she wasn't going through with it, but even holding the unopened letter gave her a thrill of excitement.

At the trash bin by the door, Darcy paused, the letter hovering in her fingertips. What would the reply say? she wondered. Curiosity made her pull the letter back and walk hurriedly from the post office. She would read it first, she decided, then throw it away.

Darcy walked down to the nearby sliver of beach where she often came when she wanted to be alone to think and sat down on a large driftwood log. The sea wind pulled at loose tendrils of her hair and she squinted slightly in the brilliant sunlight. She had rarely received any mail, so she took her time in opening the envelope. The letter inside was very official in appearance and was worded such that she had to reread it twice before she understood its meaning.

It said the prospective grooms were known to be decent, upright men with high moral standards and a desire to settle the wilderness. Due to the scarcity of women and the time and expense of the men returning east for a more conventional courtship, the men had contacted Simon Peabody, Esq., to supply them with suitable brides. Any woman desiring to wed one of the brave pioneers must be of impeccable moral structure, thrifty, hard-working, between the ages of nineteen and thirty-five and willing to remain as consort to the groom of her choice.

In order for the prospective bride to become acquainted with the candidate grooms, a list with five names, the respective physical description of each man and the location where he might receive mail was included. Once the bride had decided which groom she wanted, she was to send his name and her passage money to Simon Peabody, Esq. He would arrange matters from there, including a proxy marriage prior to the journey west.

Passage money. Darcy smiled wryly. Even if she were so foolhardy as to really consider the venture, she couldn't afford it. How odd, she thought, that the wealthy young men couldn't pay for their brides' passage with one of their golden nuggets. She shrugged and tucked the letter into her skirt pocket. If Simon Peabody, Esq., was charging passage money from both ends of the line, it was none of her business. She had no intention of leaving Plymouth.

Darcy strolled along the crescent of pale beach. To her left grassy knolls jutted over the sand and rolled up to a forest of thick oak trees. On her right the gray-green waves tumbled and broke on the sand. Sea gulls wheeled over her head and shrieked for food, but she ignored them. How tall *were* mountains? she wondered.

Reluctant to return home to the ironing that awaited her, Darcy walked slowly through the streets toward Widow Pennington's house. She had had no time to look in on her friend the day before, and she was worried over the old woman's failing strength. As she turned down the short street, she was almost bowled over by a boy running at breakneck speed.

"Rob! Slow down! You nearly knocked me off my feet!" Darcy exclaimed as she recognized the son of the Penningtons' manservant.

He gasped for breath, his eyes wide with the import of his news. "I been sent to fetch you!" he choked out. "Miss Eva, she said to run get you as quick as I could!"

The dreaded news sunk in and Darcy felt her skin grow clammy with apprehension. "Come on!" She lifted her long skirts and ran down the street, not caring who might see her and report her indecorous flight to Aunt Petra.

Without waiting for Eva to answer the door, Darcy rushed into the house and ran up the stairs to the doorway of the bedroom at the end of the hall. Eva stood at the foot of the bed, a handkerchief pressed to her large nose. The manservant and his wife waited awkwardly at the far wall and a middle-aged man with a black bag and a somber expression stood beside the bed. The air was still and close as if it, too, were waiting. The Widow Pennington lay very still in the featherbed, her harsh breathing seeming far too loud for such a tiny body.

All Darcy's energy drained from her and she slowly entered the room. Eva looked up and dabbed at her red-rimmed eyes. "She took bad early this morning," she whispered. "It's good you came so quickly."

Darcy went on numb feet to the bedside and took the old woman's hand. The skin was loose and dry, as if it no longer associated itself with life, and the fine-boned fingers lay limp in Darcy's own strong ones. Surprisingly, the old woman opened her glazing eyes.

"Darcy? In the box, child. The red box."

"She means her sewing box," Eva whispered. "Her mind must be wandering."

But Darcy lifted the japanned lid of the wicker sewing basket and looked back at Widow Pennington for further instructions.

"Under the pincushion," came the weak gasp. "No thief would look under a pincushion."

Darcy pulled the pincushion from its nesting place and caught her breath. Five gold coins lay neatly stacked in the hole beneath the ball of sawdust. "But I can't—"

"It's yours, child. It's freedom." The old woman's voice trailed away so that the last words were scarcely audible. Her labored breathing filled the room, faltered, then ceased altogether.

Unable to believe her friend was gone, Darcy looked from the doctor to Eva, who was sobbing at the end of the bed. Without speaking, the doctor folded the still hands upon the unmoving chest.

With all the supper chores behind her, Darcy sat on the edge of her bed and tried to come to terms with all that had happened that day. On her lap was the Widow Pennington's sewing basket, the treasure once again hidden beneath the pincushion. The gold had apparently been safe there for some time and Darcy knew of no better place. Besides, Aunt Petra would never covet the worn sewing basket of a dead woman she had considered her social inferior. Darcy ached with loneliness for her only friend, yet her large eyes were dry in her misery. The tears could come later, after Aunt Petra had gone to bed.

Slowly Darcy reached into her skirt pocket and drew out the letter from Simon Peabody, Esq. Widow Pennington had said the gold coins were to buy her freedom, but what would she have said if she had known about this letter? Somehow Darcy doubted that a woman as proper as Widow Pennington would have looked kindly on such a daring venture. Besides, she thought, would life as a stranger's wife be preferable to her life as Aunt Petra's servant? She could be going from bad to much, much worse.

Resolutely she put the letter in the sewing basket between the padded lining and the wicker side. Tomorrow, she told herself firmly, she would take it to the trash bin and burn it.

Suddenly she jumped as Aunt Petra summoned her by ringing the bell that was attached to her wall. Darcy sighed tiredly. She had had a long and draining day. Another of Aunt Petra's endless tasks was the last thing she wanted. She laid the sewing basket on the floor beside her bed and touched her hair to be sure it needed no attention. Going down the two flights of stairs, Darcy brushed the folds of her skirt into place and straightened the lace collar of her white cotton blouse.

With a natural grace, she crossed the foyer to the parlor door, rapped discreetly and entered. Aunt Petra stood with her hand on the bellpull to ring for her again. With her was a portly man with mutton-chop whiskers and a bulbous nose. His nose, like his cheeks, was rosy with tiny red veins and his eyebrows bristled wildly. When he saw Darcy he did a double take and smiled as his pale eyes seemed to undress her.

"Darcy, this is Cousin Marcus Dobson, a relative of ours. This is my niece, Marcus. Poor Phillip's child."

"Delighted, I'm certain," he said with a barely discernible lisp. "I knew your dear papa well when he was a lad."

Darcy inclined her head slightly to acknowledge the introduction. "Did you also know my mother, Mr. Dobson?"

Aunt Petra sniffed. "Certainly not. That was long before our Phillip made his *mistake.*"

Marcus Dobson looked uneasily from one to the other and tried to smooth matters by saying, "I've only just arrived from Boston. All the talk there is of the gold strike out west. I suppose you've heard all about it."

Sudden interest lit Darcy's eyes. "What news have you heard? We get information so much later here in Plymouth."

"There's a new mine, called the Comstock, that everyone's raving about. Seems the gold goes on forever in it."

An eager smile transformed Darcy's pretty face into true beauty. "It's all they say it is? The gold strike, I mean?"

"Apparently so, though, of course," he said with a laugh to Aunt Petra, "I've no knowledge of what you've heard. It's the Promised Land, for sure."

"What nonsense, Marcus," Aunt Petra interrupted reprovingly. "The Promised Land is nowhere on this sinful earth, and certainly not in the heathen West! Darcy, show Cousin Marcus to the guest room. Then you may retire for the night."

"Yes, Aunt," Darcy replied. "This way, Mr. Dobson."

Marcus picked up his battered portmanteau and followed her from the room, his eyes fastened hungrily on her rounded hips. "Good night, Petra. I'll see you in the morning."

Darcy led the way to the small front bedchamber, then groped her way familiarly across the room to light the bedside lamp. She was aching to hear more about the gold fields and what sort of men worked them, but she wasn't sure that Marcus's bedroom was the most proper place to chat.

Lowering his portmanteau to the floor just inside the doorway, Marcus looked around approvingly. "Well, well. Petra has added some nice touches since my last visit. This will do nicely, indeed. I will be very comfortable here."

"You'll be staying with us for a while?" Darcy asked hopefully.

"Yes," he said, swinging his gaze back to her.

"Possibly for several months. I'm rather at, well, loose ends at the moment." He stared at her well-rounded breasts. "I may possibly even settle in Plymouth permanently."

Uneasily, Darcy stepped away from the bed and lit another lamp on a reading table. The extra light made the room seem less intimate, but unless Marcus moved away from the door, she could not pass by him and into the hall. "I hope you will like Plymouth, Mr. Dobson."

"Please, call me Cousin Marcus, as my other young cousins do. Or better yet, only Marcus when we are alone." He licked his thick lips and came farther into the room.

Before Darcy could make a quick exit, he closed the door behind him. "Come here, Darcy, and let's be friends. I've heard a great deal about you. Your mother was an actress, wasn't she?"

"For a very short while," Darcy said with growing apprehension. "When she met Papa she gave up the stage."

Marcus wet his lips again. "I've heard a great deal about actresses. Tell me, do you say you take after her, or after your father? I can't seem to see a bit of Phillip about you to save my soul." As he spoke he moved slowly toward her.

"Cousin Marcus, please. I shouldn't be in here alone with you. Whatever would Aunt Petra say?" She edged around the room and tried to keep a chair between them.

"We needn't tell Petra. Her room is on the other end of the hall."

"It's a very short hall, Cousin Marcus, and my aunt has perfect hearing," she lied uneasily.

He dropped his voice to a gravelly whisper. "Then we must make very little sound." With surprising speed for one of his poundage, Marcus crossed the room, grabbed her arm and pulled her to him. Before she could scream, he clamped his mouth down upon hers, his teeth bruising her lips.

Darcy struggled as he clasped her to his soft belly. His breathing was loud on her cheek and his pudgy hands were kneading her breasts. With no compunction at all, Darcy kneed him in the groin; and as he bent double in surprised pain, she shoved him backward with all her strength. With a yell, Marcus fell over the chair and thudded to the floor.

"Marcus! What on earth!" Petra exclaimed as she hurried through the door. Her mouth dropped open as she saw Darcy standing there, her hair disheveled, her lips bruised. "Darcy! What are you doing here!"

"He wouldn't let me pass!" she cried out in a trembling voice. "He tried to take liberties with me!"

Aunt Petra's face drained of all color and she looked as unyielding as a statue. "What are you saying!"

Marcus had scrambled to his feet and was trying to stand erect, though he kept one hand placed low on his stomach. "She apparently misunderstood my meaning, Petra," he said in a placating tone. "I meant merely to bid her good evening as any relative would do to a young cousin, and she flew at me like a wild thing."

Aunt Petra's glare snapped from Marcus to Darcy. "Apologize immediately! I'll not have such behavior shown to a guest in my house!"

"Me apologize? Never!" Darcy gasped as righteous anger swept away her fear. "He was all over me! Kissing me and pawing at me!"

"Darcy!" Aunt Petra drew herself up to her greatest height. "You forget yourself!"

"Now, now, Petra," Marcus broke in soothingly. "No harm was done. Not really. The girl is young and headstrong." He turned to look at Darcy. "We have plenty of time to get to know each other. Before you know it, Darcy and I will have ironed out our little differences and be the best of friends."

Even through her anger, Darcy recognized the clear threat in his eyes. She could not possibly avoid being alone with him indefinitely, and he had already said his stay would be a lengthy one. With a look that clearly showed him she understood his threat, Darcy turned and walked to the door. "I wouldn't count on us ironing out anything, Mr. Dobson," she said in clipped tones. "Nothing at all."

"Darcy!" Aunt Petra exclaimed.

Without a backward glance, Darcy left the room and went upstairs to her attic. As soon as she reached its comparative safety, she locked her door and pulled her bed against it for good measure. Her face was set in determined lines as she took the letter from her sewing box.

With bold strokes she penned a response to Simon Peabody, Esq., requesting passage west to marry— She glanced at the list of five names, closed her eyes and stabbed one with her finger. Jesse Keenan, of Elk Hollow, in the territory of Colorado, she wrote with a steady hand.

Chapter Three

DARCY DREW HER SLEEVE ACROSS HER DAMP FORE-
head and gazed behind her at the panorama of
mountains she had already crossed. Because the way
had become steep, she and the three other women
who rode on her wagon had to walk, as did their
driver. The yoke of patient oxen leaned into their
harnesses and the covered wagon lurched up the
incline behind them.

On Darcy's left hand gleamed a narrow band of
gold, the symbol of her marriage by proxy to a man
she had never met. Most of her traveling companions in the wagon wore an identical band, all provided by Simon Peabody, Esq. To many of the women,
the wedding band symbolized a previously unhoped
for dream come true. These were the ones who were
plain of face or uncomely of figure, or those who had
tarried too long in the race for a mate only to
discover reticence's reward was spinsterhood. One
or two of the new brides, like Darcy, were head-

strong girls who had run away from home for one reason or another. The other, smaller group of women were older, with hard and knowing eyes. They were going to Colorado with another purpose in mind. In the eastern cities they were considered old and jaded; in the womanless territories they could ply their ancient trade with little competition and be as sought after as any eighteen-year-old.

Darcy had followed the other brides' example and had made no contact with these low-moraled women, but she had watched them throughout the long trip with concealed interest. She couldn't help but wonder at the logic in this. Was she not going two thousand miles to live with a total stranger? Darcy fastened her eyes on the mountains ahead and told herself that as Mr. Keenan's legal wife, what she was doing was very different.

One of the women assigned to Darcy's wagon fell in step beside her and a slight frown furrowed the older woman's brow. "We'll be there tomorrow," she said uneasily. "It's there in that valley ahead."

"You look worried, Clara. Are you not feeling well?"

"Sure, sure. I'm never sick." The woman walked along silently for a time, one strong hand holding her long skirts aside as she strode up the slope. Then she said, "Tell me, Darcy, do you think they will hold us close on the promises we swore to on that sheet of paper? I mean, if you stretched the truth—only a bit, mind you—do you think aught would come of it?"

"I don't know," Darcy replied. "I guess it just depends on what it was."

Clara sighed and narrowed her pale eyes to study the valley of their destination. "Well, say on the part about our age."

Darcy suppressed a smile. "I doubt anyone will be too concerned about that. After all, you're a young woman still, and in obvious good health, else you couldn't have made it this far. I wouldn't worry about it."

Clara grunted a nonverbal reply and flicked at a pesky fly buzzing around her head. After several minutes she said nonchalantly, "What about the other part?" A dull blush stained her high cheek-bones.

Darcy glanced at her and said carefully, "You mean the part about us being untouched?"

"Yeah. That's the part. How particular do you reckon they'll be about that?" She let her eyes roam the horizon as if she were only discussing the weather.

"I guess that depends on your man," Darcy answered slowly. "If he's happy with you, it's no-body else's business."

"Maybe so. Now I don't want you thinking I'm like those hussies in the back wagon," Clara said firmly. "I was engaged to be married a year ago. He was a fine man. A bit older than me, but a good person."

"What happened?" Darcy asked softly when Clara's speech broke off in her abrupt manner.

"He got himself killed in a robbery. Some men broke into his dry goods store and he was shot."

"I'm sorry."

"Yeah, I was, too. He was a good man. Loved me, too. But I'm over it now. Otherwise I wouldn't be on my way to be a wife to Hiram Rabin. Trouble is, though, we jumped the gun a bit."

"I see." Darcy had never before talked to an admittedly fallen woman, and somehow Clara Rabin, with her capable hands, large frame and weathered face, didn't look the part. "Does Mr. Rabin know?"

"Not yet," Clara said with what was meant to be a carefree grin. "Not yet," she repeated more quietly.

That night when the women gathered around their campfire, Clara was silent and thoughtful. Darcy tried to act as if this were only another night in what had become an all too familiar routine of the trail. The other two women, a very plain one named Elsie and a very young one named Crystal, did the dishes and then came to sit by Darcy to watch the embers glow and slowly die. The day's walk had taken them to a higher altitude and the fire was welcome in the chill night.

"We'll be there tomorrow, I heard Tom say," Crystal said, nodding toward the fire where the drivers sat in male companionship.

"I wonder what mine will be like," Elsie said in her low voice. "By this time tomorrow we'll be married women for sure."

29

"You shouldn't talk that way," Crystal scolded nervously.

"It's true," Elsie replied dogmatically.

"That may be, but it's not a subject for discussion," Crystal said primly, tossing her dark curls.

Clara smiled without humor and continued gazing into the fire. She didn't care for Crystal and thought her ways were too highfalutin for a mail-order bride.

"Why did you come with us?" Elsie asked. "You're pretty enough to have found a husband back east."

Crystal sighed. "I'm running away. My father is such a tyrant I couldn't bear to be under his roof another day. I just didn't know how far it was to Colorado. How about you, Darcy?"

"I'm running away, too, I guess. I'm an orphan and none of my kinfolk wanted me around. I got tired of slaving away for my aunt about the time she got tired of having me there, so I told her I was leaving and I left."

"Just like that?" Elsie asked.

Darcy thought back to the horrid scene that had taken place between her and Aunt Petra the day after Cousin Marcus had accosted her in his bedroom. "Pretty much like that," she replied. "I couldn't possibly have stayed there any longer."

"What about you, Clara?" Elsie said.

"I'm here because I never saw a mountain," Clara said lightly. She took a stick and poked experimentally at the dying fire.

"Me, I'm here because there's a scarcity of young

men in my home town," Elsie volunteered. Self-consciously she touched her thin hand to her pocked cheek. "There just wasn't enough men to go around, I guess."

The fire crackled cozily and no one challenged her statement. In the blackness beyond the light, June bugs rustled in the high grass and an owl called triumphantly from the night-shrouded forest.

"I guess it's about time to go to bed," Clara said conversationally as she had every night since they had shared the wagon. "We're leaving early in the morning."

Darcy helped her kick dirt over the live coals and saw to it that the fire was well out before following the others to their bedrolls beneath the wagon. Most of the travelers were quieter on this night in anticipation of the big day to come and had turned in early. Only one small fire glowed nearby. Darcy looked around the group of pale mounds that were the other wagons and sighed. It was the last night of her maidenhood. She had not expected to spend it in the mountains so far from all she knew and with comparative strangers.

"Don't fret, Darcy," Clara's voice sounded softly at her elbow. "The marriage act isn't so bad." She grinned and her strong teeth gleamed. "I hear tell some even like it."

Darcy smiled faintly and bent to crawl under the wagon one last time.

The town of Bancroft was small in area, but the streets were far more crowded than any Darcy had ever seen in Plymouth. Houses with tar paper nailed over whatever lumber had been available were scattered about, but it was clear that most of the men lived in lean-tos covered with canvas or hides, or in tents. There was no pattern to the town. The sleeping quarters seemed to have been thrown up wherever the mood had struck the men. Only four buildings showed any semblance of sturdiness. One was the general store and assayer's office; the other three were saloons.

Darcy found that her mouth was dry and she was gripping the canvas of the wagon with a finger-numbing strength. Everywhere she looked were men, all shapes, sizes, and ages. And most were as mud encrusted as any beggar she had seen on the Plymouth docks. Her frightened eyes met those of her traveling companions.

"Well, I guess my plainness won't matter much here," Elsie said at last.

"Nor my age," Clara added.

Darcy and Crystal exchanged a long look. "It'll be fine," Darcy told her. Crystal nodded almost imperceptibly.

Within the hour, the entire town had gathered around the lead wagon where the wagon master had stood up to claim their attention. In a loud voice he called out the first man's name, and when one of the miners stepped forward, he introduced him to his new bride.

"It's like a slave auction!" Crystal exclaimed. "How degrading!"

Clara shrugged. "How else could they do it? We

knew all along there would be no niceties or court-
ing. At least the men are treating the women re-
spectfully."

It was true. Now that the introductions had
begun, the wild catcalls and scuffling had subsided
and there was an expectant hush as each bride was
handed down by the wagon master.

In what might have been an hour or an eternity
the wagon master climbed up on the seat of Darcy's
wagon and led Elsie forth. She was blushing furiously by the time an equally red-faced young man, hat
in hand, came forth to claim her. Crystal was
introduced to a tall man in the tanned leather
garments of a trapper and was led away. Clara's
husband turned out to be the owner of the general
store and by the awed look on his face, Darcy knew
Clara's worries had been for naught.

Her head held high, Darcy joined the wagon
master and looked out at the sea of strange faces.
Her knees felt weak and her entire body was trembling, but she allowed herself to show no fear.

"Jesse Keenan!" the wagon master bellowed.

The men looked from one to another, but no one
came forward.

The wagon master cleared his throat and again
consulted his list of grooms. "Jesse Keenan!"

"If he ain't here, I'll take her!" cried an anony-
mous voice from the crowd.

"Hush up, man," he was quieted at once, "she's
somebody's wife!"

Darcy felt a blush stain her cheeks as the name
was called again to no avail. She wished she could

creep away and cry at her betrayal. She had come all this way and no one was waiting for her! All the other brides before her had been claimed and gladly escorted away. Only one other wagon was behind her and she could feel their pitying eyes on her back. She lifted her head higher.

"Anybody know this Jesse Keenan?" the wagon master snarled.

"I think he's got a claim up yonder on Wolf Creek in the high valley. I know for sure he's not a miner," a man in the front row volunteered. The man beside him nodded.

"Well, where is he?" the wagon master demanded.

"I don't have any idea. Those prospectors are an odd bunch. Could be he's moved on, could be he just forgot what day it is."

The wagon master looked at Darcy and frowned. This had never happened to him before. "I'm real sorry, ma'am. I guess you can stay here in the wagon a few days and see if he shows up. Otherwise, you're welcome to travel back east with us."

Darcy recalled the aching miles of toil that lay between Bancroft and Plymouth, the swollen rivers, the arid plains, the Indians they had seen occasionally. And the prospect of returning to Aunt Petra. "No," she said firmly. "I won't be returning with you."

He shrugged and tipped his hat. "As you please, ma'am."

She watched him swing down from her wagon and go on to the next one. Then she went back inside the shade of the canvas and sat on the driver's trunk. With the other women's belongings removed, the wagon was nearly empty. Almost roomy. There was enough space for her to sleep there all night rather than to try and make her bed on the rutted lane. But there was no way to barricade the entrance against any miner who might decide to join her in the night. She thought of her companions and sighed. Crystal and Elsie had been taken away to parts unknown and Clara would have enough potential problems with her lack of virginity and an unsuspecting groom. Even if Clara did have a place for Darcy to sleep, which was unlikely, she wouldn't need an overnight guest on her wedding night. No, she would have to take her chances in the wagon.

By the time the other brides had been claimed, long shadows were reaching toward the wagon. Slowly the men disbanded and made their way to the saloons where the painted women were already gathering. Bits of rowdy songs drifted to Darcy as she spread her pallet on the dusty floor of the wagon. A dark figure blocked the light and she started back with a cry.

"Pardon me, ma'am," the wagon master said as he pulled at the brim of his hat. "I didn't mean to startle you. Me and Tom will be sleeping under your wagon tonight. These miners are a wild lot and I'd feel better about being near if you should need me."

"Thank you," Darcy said with relief. "I appreciate your thoughtfulness."

Nevertheless, she slept fitfully, and somewhere in the night she decided on her course of action.

Chapter Four

THE LAST OF THE WIDOW PENNINGTON'S GOLD COINS bought a bedroll, some provisions, a pack mule and a buckskin mare with the saddle and bridle thrown in for good measure. Darcy mounted her new horse and turned it toward the mountain that loomed beyond the town. The mare splashed daintily across the broad shallows of Wolf Creek and, with the laden pack mule in tow, began to ascend the mountain.

Behind her, the ever-present noise of the mining town began to fade and the road that had been a muddy rut in town was covered here with wild grasses. Darcy skirted the yellow-red mouth of an abandoned mine. The heavy timbers had been scavenged from it for use in more promising locations, and a raw gash of collapsed earth marked the path the mine had taken toward the interior of the mountain. For fear that she was even now riding over some of the unsupported tunnels, she urged her mare to the tree line, where thick limbs laced above her and equally thick roots spread in the earth below.

Following the small river, Darcy let herself wonder about the practicality of her plan. Supposedly her unknown husband had staked his claim on the banks of Wolf Creek, but the assayer in the general store had been uncertain of the claim's exact location. She only knew it was located in a high valley—unless he had pulled up stakes and moved on. With the secrecy employed by prospectors in their highly competitive search, it was not unlikely that just such a thing might have occurred. The only description of the claim was that it stretched from Wolf Creek to a big, misshapen pine, to an outcropping of granite, and back to the river. Even now she was passing an oddly shaped tree and there was another one already in sight.

The rhythmic motion of the mare's steady climb lulled some of the worry from Darcy. High above her reared pines and cottonwoods in the vivid greens of summer. Wild flowers of every imaginable color covered the small meadows and the cerulean sky was broken only by the whitest of clouds. Butterflies, looking like flowers flying free, fluttered above the blooms or sunned lazily on the warm rocks that cropped out of the ground at intervals. The heady scent of the evergreens and grasses obscured the subtler fragrances of the flowers. All around her were the calling notes of birds that hushed on her arrival and continued at her passing.

The miners' camp was left far below by the time

she stopped to eat. The sun slanted in golden rays through the leaves and spangled the water beside her. Although she had grown accustomed to great physical exertion, Darcy found that the altitude robbed her of her breath and energy. Even the dun-colored mare and the red mule were breathing harder than their sedate pace had warranted.

Darcy ate a biscuit with a slice of fried sausage and watched twigs and leaves spin by her in the water on their headlong journey down the mountain. Already she was falling in love with the rugged beauty of the Rockies. Despite the rough terrain that had to be fought to be won, and could never truly be conquered, she felt at home here as she never had in the tranquil pastures or bustling cities of the east.

She forced herself to consider the possibility that she might never find the man named Jesse Keenan. It was an unpleasant possibility. But she was determined to stay in the Colorado territory, even if it meant living in the squalid mining camp for a while. Eventually more and more women would come west and their men would settle down to build real towns with schoolhouses, churches and real homes. The mountains would remain as they always had, essentially unchanged by the ravages of puny mankind, and the result would be as near heaven as anything Darcy could imagine.

But to survive here she would have to find a way of earning a living. Her first thought was that she might find work as a cook in one of the many tents that had been erected for that purpose, but that idea was repugnant to her. Still, it would be an income and in time she could save enough money to build an eating establishment of her own. At least she wouldn't have to return to Aunt Petra. The very idea of going back to her unloving aunt and the slobbering advances of Cousin Marcus made her skin cold. No matter what, she told herself firmly, she wouldn't go back to that.

Feeling more rested, Darcy mounted her horse and continued up the mountain. What little trail there had been at first had dwindled to nothing, and now only the rushing water on her left marked the way. Even the mountain peak was lost to her in the tangle of treetops.

The mare wound her way through a thick stand of aspen whose heart-shaped leaves shimmered in the breeze. The grass below the horse's hooves was emerald, lit with white star-shaped flowers of minute dimensions. In the near distance a doe, startled by Darcy's unexpected presence, lifted her head, then bounded away in graceful leaps.

Darcy left the aspen and rode out into another small meadow overshadowed by a lone, twisted pine of gigantic proportions. Feeling too tired to continue, she dismounted and let her horse graze as she wandered by the river. A huge rock, smooth and hollowed by wind and water, stretching far out into the river, looked inviting, so Darcy climbed out onto it and rested. Tiredly she pushed a loose strand of dark hair away from her face and sat down, arching her aching back to relieve the tenseness of her muscles.

Below her feet the water raged around the rock in

a series of small rapids. The roar of water boiling upon itself and coursing over stones and fallen logs obscured all other sounds from her ears.

When the man behind her spoke, Darcy jumped as if she had been stung.

"Come off that rock, ma'am, and be on your way." He was a tall man with broad shoulders and a lean waist and hips that molded into well-muscled legs. His hair was dark, as were his menacing eyes, and his skin was as tanned as any Indian's. His savage appearance was not lessened by his clothing, which was of soft leather, nor the long squirrel rifle he held in his large hands. The barrel was pointed directly at her.

For a moment Darcy was too stunned to move. Then she forced words out of her dry mouth and stammered, "You aren't going to shoot me with that, are you?"

He looked searchingly at her face. It had been a long time since he had seen a young woman, and even longer since he had seen a beautiful one. "Who are you traveling with?" he said gruffly. "And why are you on my land?"

"Nobody. I mean, I'm traveling alone. And I didn't know the land here belonged to anyone. There aren't any fences," she added as she swung her legs around and stood up. "Could you point that gun somewhere else?"

The man's eyes narrowed suspiciously and he kept the gun trained on her. "It's not likely you're telling the truth. Bancroft is a long way from here. A lot farther than a woman would ride for pleasure." His dark gaze raked over her appraisingly. "You don't look much like a claim jumper. Are you one of the saloon girls at Prairie Belle's?"

"Certainly not!" Anger at being taken for one of the scarlet women gave Darcy back her nerve. "I came up here to look for my husband. If you will step aside, sir, I will be on my way."

He grinned and his face became boyish. "He must have been crazy to run away from a woman like you." Slowly he swung the gun to a less threatening position, but he kept his left hand on the trigger.

"He didn't run away," Darcy said haughtily as she climbed down from the rock.

"What's his name? I know most of the men on this side of the mountain. Maybe I can help you find him."

She brushed the dirt from her skirt as she answered, "Keenan's his name. Jesse Keenan. He has a claim staked on Wolf Creek."

Unaccountably the man drew his breath in sharply and his eyes narrowed once more. "Who's that you said?"

"Jesse Keenan," she repeated, looking up in surprise at his unexpected reaction. "Do you know him?"

"Know him? I *am* him." The rifle pivoted back in her direction. "And, lady, I know for a fact I never married anybody."

Darcy's mouth dropped open. "You? You're Jesse Keenan?"

41

"Don't you think it's a mite strange for a woman not to know what her own husband looks like? Who are you, anyway!"

"I'm Darcy Mayhew. I mean, Darcy Keenan. I wrote to tell you I was coming in the wagon train. And besides," she said with a spurt of anger, "why didn't you come to meet me? I was mortified to be left standing like that."

"Wait a minute. Hold on there. You aren't making any sense whatsoever. Are you sure you're right in the head?"

"How dare you say something like that to me!" Darcy sputtered, her anger overriding her fear. She shoved the gun barrel aside and glared at him. "I came over two thousand miles by wagon train to be your bride and now you have the nerve to pretend you never heard of me?"

Jesse tilted his head to one side and stared at her. "You mean to tell me you're one of those mail-order brides?"

"Yes, of course. I don't know what you expect to gain by pretending not to know me, but I can assure you, I'm not amused."

"I'm not laughing too hard, either," he snapped. "And I sure as hell don't have any bride. And what's more, I don't want one!"

"It's a little late to change your mind, Mr. Keenan. I'm already here."

"Well, you can just go back again. I won't marry you."

"You already have! We were married by proxy in

Plymouth, Massachusetts. I have the paper to prove it!"

Jesse glared back at her. "Let me see that paper."

She went to her pack mule and fumbled in the canvas bag until she pulled out the document. "There!" she announced triumphantly. "Your mark is on the bottom line on the right. My signature is on the left. And here," she said with a flourish, "is my wedding ring!" She held her left hand in front of his face.

He glanced at the gold band, then grabbed the paper from her. Quickly he scanned the words, then exclaimed an oath as his name seemed to leap at him from the paper. "What kind of a joke is this!"

"It's no joke, Mr. Keenan. As you can see, we are legally married."

"That's not my signature," he growled at her. "It's just a mark. I can read and write, so why wouldn't I sign my name?"

"How should I know? You never wrote me a letter."

He stared at her. "Then how on God's green earth did you figure you married me?"

Darcy loftily explained the advertisement of Simon Peabody, Esq., and her decision, though not her reason, for agreeing to become the bride of a stranger. Jesse waited with growing impatience until she finished, then looked back at the damning mark on the paper.

"I don't know what's going on here," he said, "but I know for a fact I never sent off for any bride.

This mark was made by somebody else, not me." He glanced at the sky. "You'd best be going back down the mountain now. You can probably make it back to town before full dark if you don't dawdle."

"Back—" Darcy stared at him incredulously. "I'm not about to leave this mountain!"

He shrugged and shouldered his rifle. "Suit yourself. There's a deserted lean-to about a mile upstream. You can sleep there and be on your way in the morning. But where you think you'll get to is beyond me. There's nothing upstream but woods and nothing beyond that but tundra." He turned his back and started to walk away.

"Wait just a minute!" Darcy cried out, running to catch up with him. "You sent for me! I'm not leaving here!"

"I didn't do any such thing and you're not staying on my claim," he said firmly.

"I won't leave," she snapped, matching his long stride as well as she could.

"You seem to have a problem understanding me. I won't *let* you stay here." He pointed the rifle at her and frowned threateningly.

"Put that silly gun away," she commanded, shoving the barrel to one side. "I came across plains where mosquitos were big as June bugs, worried about Indians, baked in the sun and nearly froze at night. There is no way in the world that I'm going to curtsy and trot back to town just because you changed your mind!"

Jesse stared down at her. He was familiar with only two kinds of women: the overly proper ladies he had left behind in St. Louis, and the floozies at Prairie Belle's. This one just didn't fit either category. "I told you I didn't marry you. There's some mistake."

"There sure is and you're the one making it."

"But I don't want a wife, damn it!"

"Is your name Jesse Keenan?"

"Yeah!"

"Well, you've got one!"

They glared at each other. Darcy felt dangerously close to tears, but she fought them back valiantly. After coming so far, she couldn't bear the thought of it all being a mistake.

Jesse saw the moistness in her eyes and the barely concealed quiver of her chin. "All right," he said gruffly. "You can stay the night. Maybe after supper we can get to the bottom of this." He strode away before she could reply.

Darcy watched him walking toward a small cabin she had not noticed earlier. Then she hurried back to get her horse and mule.

"I've been thinking," Jesse said in his slow voice. "Somebody must be playing a trick on me. Nothing else makes any sense."

"Some trick," Darcy snorted as she dried the last plate and put it on the shelf. "Who would do such a thing?"

He shook his head in puzzlement. "I don't know. There's one man I wouldn't put anything past, but I haven't seen him in months."

"It's taken months for me to get here," she

reminded him as she joined him by the fire. She sat down in the other chair, her back to the low bed in the shadows at the rear of the cabin. The only other furniture was the rough-hewn table where they had eaten.

After a short while, Jesse nodded. "It could be him. Nathan Stoddard has a strange sense of humor like that." He gazed into the crackling fire.

Darcy watched him covertly. The golden light made his handsome face gleam like a bronzed god's and his unruly hair fell boyishly across his broad forehead. A small scar on his high cheekbone drew her attention and she had the strangest desire to reach out and touch him. His lips were sensuous and looked as if he might be of a pleasant temperament when he wasn't faced with an unwanted bride.

"You aren't, well, odd . . . are you?" Darcy heard herself asking.

"What do you mean by 'odd'?" he asked in surprise.

"You seem so adamant about not wanting a wife."

He laughed, and his even teeth gleamed in the firelight's glow. "You're the first woman that ever questioned that!"

She blushed and quickly looked away. "I'm sorry I said that. I never did have a great deal of tact. It's just that you haven't even touched my hand and after all, I am your wife . . ." Her voice trailed away. She felt embarrassed at having expressed such a brazen thought.

Jesse leaned forward in his chair and cupped her chin in his strong hand. His dark eyes searched the brown depths of hers. In the flickering light she looked as confused and vulnerable as an injured fawn he had once nursed back to health. A small pulse raced in the curve of her slender throat and the dark masses of her hair looked too heavy for her small head to support. Without speaking he lowered his face to within inches of hers. Her breath was sweet on his lips and her fine skin was as soft as peach down beneath his fingers.

Slowly he stroked the curve of her cheek and saw her eyes grow soft with longing. Then, taking his time, Jesse claimed her lips. They were velvety beneath his and he felt them part naturally as he kissed her. He let his other arm slip across her back, and he pulled her closer as she hesitantly raised her small hand to rest on his shoulder. Her kiss was innocent and her response automatic as he felt her sway toward him, only the distance of their chairs keeping their bodies apart. A curious dizziness spread over him as he kissed her and a fire kindled in his loins. It took all his will power to raise his head and break away from the spell of her kiss.

Darcy's lips remained parted and her head tilted up to his as she marveled at the unnamed emotion that shook her. A small muscle tightened in his lean jaw and his eyes seemed to burn into hers with a need she could not guess.

Abruptly, Jesse jerked away and got up from his chair. "Oh, no," he said harshly. "Not that. I'm your husband on paper, but as long as the marriage is not consummated, it's not binding."

Darcy's gaze faltered and she stared at the fire.

Consummated? She had only the vaguest ideas what this might entail. Her education in the rites of marriage had been sadly ignored. Yet only moments before he had been so gentle with her, so tender. She wished the moment could have lasted longer.

"You're leaving in the morning and that's final," Jesse stated in a firm tone. "I'll sleep outside on my bedroll. You take the bed."

"Why do you want me to go?" she asked softly. "Am I that unattractive to you?"

He paused in his pacing and glared first at her, then up at the ceiling. "Nothing about you is unattractive. That's why you have to leave as soon as possible."

"But why!" Darcy cried out. "All my life people have made me leave them. All I want is to belong somewhere. Anywhere!"

Jesse came back to her and stood behind her chair. It took all his strength not to touch the thick coil of her hair. How could he bear to have her here all night and not make her his own after the searing passion of her kiss?

"Why can't I stay here?" she whispered, still staring at the fire.

"Because I don't want to be tied down. I may move on tomorrow, for all I know. Or next week. In the winter it gets bitter cold here and even a man can hardly stand it. My life is rough and too harsh for a woman. I may find gold tomorrow or I may never find it. A wife means a family. What would I do with a houseful of children up here on a mountain in

Indian territory, whether I find gold or not? Besides, women don't last long in the wilds. You could die."

"That's the reason?" she asked, looking up at him. "Just that the life is hard?"

"It's not just hard, it's *damned* hard! I've seen strong men that couldn't make it!"

Darcy stood and turned to face him. "I'm tough, Mr. Keenan. I'm not used to a soft life. However hard it is here, it will be preferable to the life I left. As to my dying and leaving you with children to raise, I promise you I will do my best to stay alive." Amusement shone in her dark eyes.

"You don't listen very well, do you? I just told you why I don't want a wife."

She looked around the cabin. "Mr. Keenan, I can assure you I am not in the least interested in your worldly possessions. Nor do I particularly want to be married to a stranger. However, I do want a new life. Since you admit that your life is hard, I think it's only logical that you would welcome a helpmate. I'm willing to be only that. You gain an extra pair of hands and a strong back, I gain a new life and a home. It sounds fair to me."

Jesse looked down at her and wondered how such a slender back could possibly be a strong one as well. "That's the most ridiculous idea I ever heard," he told her, his fists on his hips.

"Nevertheless, I'm staying," she said firmly. "Now, if you don't mind, I would like to go to bed now." She waited expectantly for him to leave.

Jesse glowered at her, then turned with a growling sound and strode toward the door.

"By the way," she called after him, "I think I would prefer to call you Jesse. Do you mind?"

He stared menacingly at her, grabbed up his bedroll from the bed and left, slamming the door behind him.

Chapter Five

DARCY DRIED THE LAST SPOON AND LAID IT ON THE tin plates on the open shelf. She swept the floor and straightened the two chairs, then pushed a pot of water near the fire to heat in preparation for the next meal. Then she untied her apron and satisfied herself that the water drops that had missed the apron wouldn't show on her dark blue dress. She wanted very much to be pleasing in the sight of her strange new husband. With a touch to her dark hair to be sure no tendril had escaped her bun, she stepped out into the sunlight and pulled the cabin door shut behind her.

Jesse was down by the creek, kneeling patiently by a cradlelike contraption which he was rocking back and forth. Darcy wandered closer and sat on a nearby rock to watch him. When all the dirt had been washed through the screen mesh into the bottom of the wooden cradle, Jesse picked through

51

the rocks and pebbles, then lifted the tray up and dumped them out. Darcy leaned forward expectantly. Carefully, Jesse continued rocking the cradle while he probed the dirt in the bottom with his finger, his dark eyes intent on the search. Darcy stretched out farther and gazed eagerly into the slatted bed as the water carried the mud from one end to the other and then out. When nothing remained but a fine black powder, Jesse tossed the residue aside, and disappointment clouded Darcy's face.

"That's it?" she asked as he shoveled several scoops of gravel from the bottom of the riverbed into the sluice box and began the same washing motions again. "That's all there is to it?"

Jesse glanced at her as if he had only then become aware of her presence. "What do you mean?"

"I thought you hunted gold with a pick or something. All you're doing is messing around in the mud."

Frowning at her, Jesse refrained from answering. He searched the bottom of the cradle, then dumped it out to start again.

"Isn't there a faster way?" she asked after he had gone through the motions twice more.

"If there is I haven't found it."

"But in all the pictures I've seen, prospectors have picks and burros and go around chipping at rocks. Are you certain you're doing it right?"

Jesse straightened and snapped, "I have a pick in the box under the bed and you can pretend that red mule of yours is a burro if you want to branch out on your own."

"There's no need to get huffy. I was just asking." She spread her full skirt about her as she hugged her knees to her chest and rested her chin on them. "Wouldn't it be faster if you had someone to shovel for you while you wash out the dirt?"

"The idea is to find gold," he said tersely. "Not to fill the sluice with rocks or to dredge out the river."

"It seems to me that if you don't find gold here it would be smarter to go somewhere else."

"Gold's here, all right. I've already found enough to know that. It may be that my next shovel load will be full of yellow."

Darcy watched him go through the business of shoveling, washing and dumping for a while. The sun had shifted and a ray pierced the canopy of leaves to fall on his raven-black hair, making it gleam. What sort of man was he, she wondered. Did he dislike everyone, or only her in particular? And if he disliked her so much, why had he kissed her last night? She wished she had had brothers or male friends so she could have learned the odd ways of men.

Jesse glanced at her as he bent to toss more river mud into the trough. She certainly didn't fit in with his idea of a mail-order bride. He had heard stories about these women. They were either too ugly to get a husband in the conventional way, or they were running from a scarlet past. But one thing he knew for sure: Darcy was not ugly. He frowned at the water that curled through the wooden box. Yet she didn't look anything like the sort of girls who worked for Prairie Belle. Why, one of them even had a moustache and pockmarks!

"Why did you decide to become a mail-order bride?" he asked bluntly, then wished he had phrased the question more discreetly.

For a time Darcy was silent, watching the water roil over the large round rocks half buried in the streambed. "My parents died years ago and I ran out of relatives," she said at last. "The last one that took me in only wanted a servant and to be able to hear praise from her friends for her 'Christian charity.'"

"And you didn't want to work so hard so you came here? That wasn't very smart." He tossed the load of mud onto the ground.

"I guess I would have stayed there until one of us grew old and died," she continued as if he hadn't spoken. "And at the rate we were going, it wouldn't have been Aunt Petra. But then a cousin of hers came to visit. A man by the name of Marcus Dobson." Darcy's voice grew cold and her eyes narrowed at the memory. "He tried to force himself on me. When I told Aunt Petra, she called me a liar. She said Cousin Marcus was only being friendly and my wicked mind had drawn the wrong conclusion. There was a rather unpleasant scene and I told her I was leaving."

Jesse stopped work and looked at her. His eyes narrowed speculatively. "How did you pick me?"

She smiled sadly. "I just chose your name at random. All I could think of was escaping from that house before Cousin Marcus could try again." She gazed across the water to a grove of cottonwood trees. "Now you say my coming here was all a mistake."

He dumped a fresh shovelful into the cradle. "Aren't there other relatives you could go to?"

She shook her head. "I don't know what there is about me, but they all wanted me to go after a few months. It seemed as if the more I tried to be friendly and pleasant, the quicker I had to leave. I don't understand it."

Jesse looked over at her. In the bright sunlight her hair gleamed with deep sable highlights and her dark, almond-shaped eyes were like fathomless pools. A light tan had deepened her skin from ivory to cream, but no freckles marred her face. The wind pressed her long skirts against her legs and her full breasts strained against the bodice of her dress. Her waist was slender and supple, her hips rounded and graceful. Jesse looked quickly back at the sluice box. "I think I know the answer to that," he said wryly. If he were going to resist her, he had better not spend much time looking at her, he decided.

Darcy sighed. So he was displeased with her appearance. She had been a plain child and small for her age. Now he had confirmed her suspicions that she was equally plain as an adult.

"Well, it's been nice meeting you," he said firmly. "But I guess you had better be starting back down the mountain. Go gather up your things and I'll saddle your horse when I finish this tray."

"Back down . . . I thought we got all that settled last night!"

"It was late and I was worn out from bending over this sluice all day. I never agreed to let you stay." He poured out another tray of pebbles and stood up to dust the debris from his pants. Without looking at her he started up the incline toward the barn. "Go on, now, and get your things packed in your bed-roll."

As Darcy watched him go, her anger flared, and it was only with the practiced restraint of the many years she had spent in unquestioning obedience to one relative or another that she didn't scream after him. Five minutes passed before she came down off the rock. Another three passed as she struggled with her inbred training to accept that she was again unwanted and should prepare to move on. Then, with a determined toss of her head, Darcy reached down between her legs and pulled the back of her skirt through and tucked it into her waistband, making the billowing material into bulky culottes. With a glare at the barn, she pulled off her shoes and stockings and waded out into the river.

The water was cold and the current was much swifter than she had expected. Beneath her feet the smooth rocks were slick and dark with patches of river moss. Darcy put the shovel in the muddy strip Jesse had been working and scooped up a handful of pebbles. Instantly the river snatched it away before she could lift it out of the water. Realizing there must be more to this than she had assumed, Darcy tried again. This time she lifted with the current as she had seen Jesse do and she came up with most of her shovelful intact.

She poured it into the top of the sluice box and began rocking it as he had. To her delight the water washed the mud and debris through the sieve just as it was supposed to do and left a clean tray of pebbles for her scrutiny.

By the time Jesse returned with her horse and mule, Darcy felt proficient at her new trade.

"You haven't even started getting ready to leave, have you?" he accused.

She looked up at him, then back at the pebbles she was beginning to wash. "No, I haven't. You know, this is fun, isn't it? To see all these little rocks so shiny and clean looking. Chances are that nobody in the world ever saw them but me." She flashed him a smile. "It makes you think, doesn't it."

"No, it doesn't. Now get out of that river and leave my sluice alone."

Instead of answering, Darcy sat on the sunny rock and sorted carefully through the gravel. "I think you were going too fast," she commented. "I've noticed that a lot of pebbles are covered up with the larger ones and I can't see them if I dump the tray as quickly as you were."

He made a growling sound low in his throat and with great restraint said, "Lady, I've been prospecting this river for nearly two years. Don't tell me how to do it." He reached down to take her arm and help her to her feet.

"Look!" Darcy exclaimed suddenly. "It's gold! I found some!" She grabbed a gleaming nugget from the tray and held it out to him in her outstretched palm. The sunlight glittered off the angles and planes

57

and made the small nugget seem to pulsate with life on her pink palm.

"Let me see that," he said as he took it from her.

She scrambled to her feet and stood on tiptoe to watch more closely as he examined it. "It's real gold, isn't it?" she prompted eagerly.

"Yeah, it looks like it is," he said begrudgingly.

"How nice! It really isn't so hard to find after all, is it!" Darcy beamed excitedly as she jumped off the rock and took up the shovel again. "Let's find some more."

Jesse held the nugget out to her. "You keep this. You found it."

Darcy hesitated, squinting up at him in the sunlight. "I trust you to hold it for me. I don't have any pockets in this dress and I can hardly hold gold in one hand and dig with the other, now can I?"

"You have no intention of leaving, do you," he stated with resignation.

"None whatsoever," she replied amiably. "I propose that we become partners."

"Partners? That's crazy talk. I can't have a woman as my partner."

"Why not?"

"Well . . . because. That's why. No man I know of has a woman partner. Prospecting is hard work. It's dangerous, too, sometimes."

"You aren't going to start that again, are you? I told you I don't mind hard work and I can take care of myself."

"What happens when you get the vapors or something like that?" he countered.

She suppressed a smile. "I have never had the vapors in my life, Jesse Keenan, and I have no intention of starting now. I'm staying."

"What about in the winter when we get snowbound for weeks at a time? I can't leave my claim and take you down to Bancroft every time it starts to snow."

"I imagine it will snow in Bancroft as well," she replied, rocking the sluice back and forth.

"Sometimes it gets so lonely up here you can hear your thoughts echo."

She glanced up at him again. "Not anymore, it won't."

Jesse watched her work and tried to think of some argument that would convince her to leave. "Your reputation will be ruined," he announced direly. "You can't stay alone with a man on the side of a mountain and there not be talk."

"Jesse Keenan," she said with exaggerated patience, "everyone but you thinks we are married. It would cause a lot more talk if I *don't* stay. Besides" —she nodded toward the nugget he still held in his hand—"I may bring you luck."

Jesse looked back down at the gold. It was one of the largest ones the river had yielded. "All right. You can stay for a while. But just as my partner—not as my wife. I still don't want to get married."

"That's fine with me," she answered. "I'm as married now as I care to be."

He watched her working and again tried to fit her into a category, but failed. Had she indeed meant what her words might have implied? Maybe she was trying to escape a scarlet past. Again his jaw clenched as a memory of another woman in a far distant place muddled his mind. They are all alike, he thought grimly. At any rate, this one was as willing to work as anyone he had ever seen, and he had to admit that he found her intriguing. As his partner and not his wife, what difference could it possibly make if she were a fallen woman? As long as he kept to his own bedroll the marriage would remain invalid. Besides, he couldn't get her to leave. Jesse had always been one to know when to give over, so he waded out into the stream beside her.

"You'll need some heavy boots," he said. "Wading barefoot on sharp rocks will ruin your feet. Maybe I can make you a pair from a hide . . . Partner."

Darcy looked up at him and then smiled. "I'd be much obliged . . . Jesse."

Chapter Six

"HOW MANY DO WE HAVE NOW, JESSE?" DARCY asked as she stirred the pot of stew.

He sat at the table with a small scale and the gold nuggets they had taken from the river. "About two pounds. I have to admit, my luck seems to have changed in the past couple of weeks."

Darcy smiled at him over her shoulder but made no reply. She wasn't given to talking for the sake of conversation any more than he was and often their silences had been more meaningful than their words. "I like it here," she said after a while. "I was noticing earlier how the sun goes down at the end of our valley, right beyond that notched mountain peak. You couldn't ask for a prettier sight."

"Now there you go, Partner, sounding like a farmer instead of a prospector. We may pull up stakes tomorrow. You never know."

"I know," she replied. He reminded her of this so

often that she had begun to wonder who he was trying to convince. She ladled up two bowls of stew and sat down opposite him at the table. "Where does gold come from?" she asked.

He glanced up at her. "Well, it comes from veins in the ground. You know that."

"Then how does it get into the river?"

For a short while he chewed in silence. "It breaks off the vein and falls in, I guess."

"Then it seems to me that if we go upstream we should be able to find the vein."

"Don't you think I already thought of that? I didn't just put my stakes here because of the view. I went upriver and didn't find a trace. Not any color at all past that waterfall where the swimming hole is."

She leaned forward excitedly. "Then the mother lode must be right around here?"

Jesse finished half the bowl of stew before he answered. "Yep."

"Well, why don't we look for it? Why spend so much time in the river?"

"Partner, for a smart woman you don't have much sense. All the gold I ever found here was in the water. I've looked all over for that vein and I can't find a sign of it."

"Maybe it's under the water."

"Now that's fine. I'll lift up that river and you crawl under it and look." He grinned at her and pushed the pan of bread closer to her plate.

Darcy broke off some of the bread and chewed thoughtfully. "Some butter on this sure would be good. I know, I know. I sound like a farmer."

"I was going to say a city woman that time. Whoever heard of a prospector owning a cow?"

"I still say we should be able to find that vein if we really try," she said, choosing to ignore his rhetorical question. *"Could* it be under the river?"

He finished his stew while he thought. "Yeah, it could be. If it is I don't know how we would ever get it out. I've seen some places we could reroute the river, but around here the bedrock is only a few inches below the grass. Now, over behind the cabin the ground is easier to dig, but that wouldn't do us much good. As it is, the water's too deep and swift for us to do much excavating out toward the middle."

"What about in the swimming hole? Have you ever looked at the bottom? What's it look like?"

"Sure, I looked. It's just like any other pool. No gold down there that I ever saw."

"It has to come from somewhere," she said, absently stirring her stew.

"That's just what I decided. Got any more of this fine food?"

She nodded toward the fire. "It's there in the pot."

He waited for a minute and when she made no move to get it for him, he went after it himself. "Looks like you could at least serve a man his supper," he grumbled as he sat back down.

"Wives serve supper. Partners get their own food."

"It's no wonder you never got married," he muttered. "You're a mean-tempered woman."

She smiled sweetly at him.

For a time their eyes met and held. Then he broke the spell by saying, "You know, I've been thinking about putting in a garden out back next spring. Maybe plant some corn and some pole beans. Some squash, maybe."

"Don't plant anything too big," she teased. "We may pull up stakes any day now and I don't want to have to carry a crop of pumpkins to our next spot."

He scowled at her, wondering if she was making fun of him.

"Some apple trees might be nice, too," she said gently. "There's a dozen ways to cook apples, and then some."

"I'm not making any promises."

"That's fine, Jesse."

Darcy lay in the bed and gazed up at the roof rafters, which were silhouetted by the faint orange glow from the dying embers in the fireplace just beyond the foot of her bed. Occasionally, the aroma of wood smoke filled the room as an errant breeze blew back down the chimney. Outside she could hear crickets singing in the tall grass. A distant owl called dismally. The moon was full, but its light through the tiny window was blocked by the woolen blanket that separated her bed from Jesse's pallet. She moved restlessly.

"Partner? You awake?" Jesse called out just above a whisper.

"Yes," she answered after a time. "Can't you sleep, either?" His gentle, deep voice had sent a shiver through her that she tried to ignore. Of late she had been plagued with the memory of his kiss the night of her arrival. She wondered if he slept in his clothes or a nightshirt. The woolen wall always hung in place and she had never seen him other than fully dressed.

"No, I can't. Must be the crickets keeping me awake."

"Most likely," she sighed. She had noticed the crickets every night since her arrival, but only recently had they disturbed her sleep.

"Are you ever sorry you came here?" he asked quietly. "Things didn't work out quite like you planned."

"I haven't been sorry for a minute. I'm glad you're not a miner, though, or we would be stuck down in Bancroft." She laughed softly. "I can guarantee no cricket noises keep anyone awake there."

He chuckled. "No self-respecting insect would go near there. All that mud and jerry-built shacks and tents. Not to mention the miners themselves. I'll bet a grizzly bear would smell better than one of those miners."

"What about the saloon hall girls?" she said before she thought, then wished she could bite back her words.

He was silent a minute, then said, "Some of them smell like grizzlies, too."

Darcy felt herself blush in the darkness. "I . . . I didn't mean to say that. It's none of my business."

"I never thought I'd be lying here on the other

side of my woolen blanket discussing saloon girls with a lady," he said with amusement in his voice, "but now that you mention it, how do you know about Prairie Belle's girls?"

"There were some painted women on the wagon train. None of us wives had anything to do with them, but you can't travel that far with someone and not notice them." She tried to still her curiosity, but finally asked, "Did you go to Bancroft . . . often?"

Again the silence stretched out. "Not too often. Like I told you when you decided to squat on my claim, it gets real lonely up here. Awful lonely."

Darcy was surprised at the stab of jealousy his words produced. A log popped in the fireplace, sending a shower of vivid sparks onto the hearth. "I don't want to hear about it."

"Okay, Partner. You're the one that brought it up." Again she heard the amusement in his voice.

After awhile she said, "What about you, Jesse? Where do you come from?"

"I grew up in St. Louis. My father owns a bank, my mother is the head of the social register. Are you impressed?"

"No, but Aunt Petra would be."

He laughed. "I wasn't impressed, either. One day I decided I couldn't stand one more social or one more eligible daughter or one more meeting at the bank, so I put an end to it. My younger brother is a natural banker—smart, good with figures. He kept his face straight when I told him he was the new heir-apparent, but I could see he was thrilled over the prospect. Dad was pleased, too, since I never had been very interested in banking or anything that went with it. Mother nearly had a fit, though. At first she was sure I was going to be scalped before I got out of the state, but by the time I left she was resigned to my fate and was basking in the condolences of all her friends."

"Do you ever write them?"

"Sure. I send a packet whenever I hear of a wagon going east. Once in a while I get letters from them. Not often, though."

She picked at the hem of the sheet and wondered if he would write to them about her. She decided she would rather not know. But somehow his story seemed incomplete. Would a man come all the way to the Colorado territory simply because he didn't want to be a banker? "Do you miss living in town?"

"No. I guess some people aren't meant to live in cities. I get to feeling tight and nervous when I see strangers all around me—especially since I came up this mountain. Even going to Bancroft is a chore for me. I just hope nobody else decides to stake a claim up here. With just me here, no one figures there's any gold; but if one comes, they'll all come."

"Does this mountain have a name?" Darcy asked.

"Not as far as I know. The river is Wolf Creek and we look out on Elk Valley, but I never heard the mountain called by name."

"Let's name it!"

"You mean just like that? What for?"

"So it'll have one, of course." She sat up and reached for her shawl to cover her nightgown. "Come on. Let's go outside."

"Now? In the middle of the night?"

"Why not? There's a full moon and I'll bet it's as bright as day out there." She heard a scuffling noise as Jesse got up from his bedroll and the dividing blanket jerked as his elbow hit it.

"All right," he said, "but don't you ever tell a soul I went outside at midnight to name some fool mountain."

"Coming around," she called out in the signal they had arranged to protect their privacy.

"Come on."

She hurried around the end of the blanket as he finished buttoning up his pants. He wore no shirt and the moonlight gleamed whitely on his powerful chest and lean belly. The unexpectedness of seeing him so nearly naked made her gasp.

"You aren't getting the vapors, are you?" he teased. "It was your idea."

"I . . . I thought you slept in your clothes or in a nightshirt!"

He laughed at the expression on her face. "Partner, I haven't slept in a stitch since I was ten years old." He held out his hand to her. "Come on. Let's go get this old mountain named so we can get some sleep."

Cautiously Darcy took his hand as she clutched her shawl more securely around her. She let him lead her out of the cabin and into the moonlit yard. He was a giant beside her in the gray-blue light, a marvelous statue worked in silver and ebony. When he moved, muscles rippled beneath his smooth skin and the night spun shadows in his wind-tossed hair.

Jesse gazed down at Darcy and wondered if he had made a mistake in coming out here with her. Her skin gleamed with the luster of fine pearls. Her eyes were deep and searching. A man could get lost in their depths, he thought, and never find his way back. Her hair lay over her shoulder in a single braid as thick as her wrist and hung down to her waist. He had not realized it was so long. Nor had he noticed how tiny she was when she stood so close to him.

"You forgot to put on your shoes," he said protectively. "Don't step on a sharp rock."

She nodded mutely, her eyes gazing deeply into his soul.

"Are you cold?" he asked, unable to look away from her.

"No. Are you?"

"No."

As if the night wind wafted her toward him, Darcy swayed, locked in the embrace of his gaze. He reached out and touched her cheek wonderingly and found her skin to be smooth and cool beneath his fingers. Gently, as if she were infinitely fragile, he ran his fingers down her cheek to stroke her shadowy hair. A pulse fluttered in her throat above the collar of her prim nightgown and he caressed it tenderly, never taking his eyes from hers.

Wrapped in the blanket of silvery light, they stood almost motionless, as if afraid that any sudden movement might break the enchantment. Very slowly Jesse bent his head until he could feel her warm breath on his lips. Then he kissed her, gently at first; then more deeply, drinking in all the passion he felt her give and returning it in kind. His hands roamed across her back and down to the firm flesh of her buttocks as he pulled her closer and nuzzled the hollow of her neck. Her arms encircled him tightly, and as the warm globes of her breasts pressed tantalizingly against his bare chest, a low moan escaped his lips.

Darcy lifted her face for his kiss. His skin was firm beneath her hands and as creamy as satin. Never had she touched a man's bare flesh and she was excited by the difference between his hard strength and her own softness. As if the moonlight gave her license to do things the sunlight would deny, Darcy tasted the seductiveness of his lips and met his gently exploring tongue with eagerness.

Effortlessly he bent and swept her up in his arms, cradling her against his broad chest as she again kissed him. Darcy felt seared by a passion she didn't fully understand, but she knew instinctively that the feelings were good. She ran her fingers through the black silkiness of his hair and tilted her lips once more to his.

"Damn, woman. Do you know what you're doing to me?" he moaned as he nibbled her earlobe. Without waiting for her answer he carried her back inside the cabin and around to her side of the blanket.

Darcy opened her eyes only long enough to see that the glow from the fireplace had washed Jesse's skin to a molten bronze, then snuggled against his muscular chest where she could hear as well as feel the hammering of his heart. The familiar rustle of corn husks, as Jesse laid her on the bed and sat beside her, brought Darcy back to an awareness of her surroundings and she opened her eyes wide.

Jesse, too, seemed stunned as he gazed down at her inviting form, still lying in the circle of his arms. Slowly he drew back, never taking his eyes off her. He lifted a few silky strands of her hair and let them trail through his fingers and back down onto her shoulder. "We can't do this," he said in tones barely above a whisper, "not and remain partners." The sadness in his dark eyes was no less intense than the pain in his voice. "I want you so much I ache. But if I lie beside you now, nothing will ever be the same again."

"It might be better," she countered, gently touching his muscled arm.

He shook his head regretfully. "I've seen a lot of marriages, lady, but I've never seen one that looked really happy. If I make love with you now, I'll lose the best friend I ever had."

Silence enveloped them as they intently searched one another's soul for a different answer. Then Jesse got up from her bed and went back to his pallet on the floor. Only inches separated them, but the distance was insurmountable. Neither found sleep that night.

Chapter Seven

DARCY STOOPED TO DUCK UNDER THE LOW-HANGING limb of the aspen and brushed aside its emerald leaves. Beneath her feet the ground was strewn with tiny white wild flowers and purple woods violets amid the silken grass. A shower during the night had washed the leaves and left them shining, and the aroma of the fresh greenery was heady in the air. Bright yellow butterflies flitted here and there and a bird called cheerfully from a nearby treetop. Across the river the dark brown trunks of the cottonwood grove contrasted sharply with the yellow-green of their leaves.

Enjoying her break from work, Darcy wandered upstream, her linen towel and cake of yellow soap clutched under her arm. Usually she bathed in the shallow pool in the bend of the river just above the white-water cascades where they panned for gold, but today the woods were too beautiful to do the ordinary, so she had decided to go to the swimming hole.

She rounded the corner where the path turned back toward the stream and stepped out into the small glade that sided against the pool. Upstream a wall of gray-black rock formed a backdrop for a rushing waterfall. The water plunged some twenty feet into the large, green pool, but disturbed the surface very little. Darcy knew this meant the water was deep, but she intended to stay in the shallower area at the opposite end of the pool just ahead of the rapids where the river necked back within its narrow banks. She lay her towel and soap down on the grassy slope and began to loosen her hair from its bun.

Suddenly she saw a figure walk to one of the rocks alongside the pool and dive into the water. It was Jesse and he was wearing nothing at all. Her mouth dropped open at the unexpected invasion.

"Hey!" she called out as he surfaced. "I was getting ready to bathe in there!"

Jesse looked around until he spotted her on the bank, her hair loose and blowing in the slight breeze. "This is my place," he answered. "Go on back downstream and use the shallow pond where you always bathe."

"But I was here first!" she protested.

"Then how do you account for the fact that I'm in the water and you're on the bank?" he countered.

"If you were a gentleman you would have looked to see if I was around before just jumping in like that."

"If you were a lady you wouldn't be standing up there watching me," he said with a grin. "Besides, you didn't tell me you were coming all the way up here."

Darcy blushed and turned her gaze toward the waterfall where the sun had spangled the mist into a rainbow. "Nevertheless, I have just as much right to be here as you do."

"No, you don't. This is my own private pool."

She jerked her head back around to glare at him and shaded the sun from her eyes with one hand. "Since when do you get to have a private pool all your own?" she demanded.

"Squatter's rights. I've been coming here to bathe and swim since I started working this claim. It's too deep for you, anyway. I learned to swim as a boy, but I doubt you ever learned how. By the way, any time you want to move on downstream is fine with me."

Darcy watched him treading water for a moment, unsure how to respond to his logic. "How do you know if I can swim or not?" she challenged, deciding he could tread water a little longer.

"Can you?"

"I don't want to talk about it." She raised her chin defiantly.

Jesse laughed, the drops of water coursing down his face from his wet hair. "Look at it this way. You'll have your own private pool, too. It's just shallower than this one."

"It's also more inclined to be muddy." This had

never been a problem to her before, but she had no intention of letting him off so easily.

"You must splash around a lot to muddy up half a river."

"I see no reason to discuss my bathing habits with you, Jesse Keenan." She jerked her head haughtily, sending her hair billowing behind her in a dark cloud. She grabbed up her soap and towel and flounced back the way she had come. The farther she went, however, the angrier she became. "Who does he think he is!" she muttered as she slashed her towel at a clump of milkweed. "You'd think he owned the whole river!" She yanked aside a branch and strode through the bushes, tangling her long skirts in the tall dewy grass. " 'Too deep,' indeed! I'll show him!"

Darcy waited impatiently for what seemed to be a very long time; then she heard Jesse's melodious whistle. This was the signal that he was through with his bath and that he was heading back downstream. If she didn't call back that she needed more time to bathe, he would assume that she was finished and dressed, if not gone already. Darcy kept quiet and out of sight as he passed and waited until he had had time to reach the sluice. Then she hurried upstream to the swimming hole.

Quickly, before she lost her nerve, Darcy shucked off her clothes. The wind brushed her body, sending a sensuous shiver over her as she eased herself into the still water. The sandy bottom curled around her toes as she carefully felt her way. Within fifteen feet of shore, she was waist deep and, as she had expected, each step toward the waterfall took her deeper. Cautiously, she kept her distance from the falls and moved farther from the bank. About halfway across the pool, the slope increased sharply downward and she hastily backed up into the shallower water. She stood several yards from the bank, in water that reached just below her breasts. Behind her, her hair floated like a fan of umber seaweed.

Using the rationale that she was close enough to the shallows to keep from drowning, she took a deep breath and sank lower in the water to swim for shore. And promptly sank. She came up sputtering and fighting her fear. When her feet touched the reassuring sand, she stood up quickly. Undaunted, she tried again. This time when she pushed into the water she held her breath as well as moved her arms.

After she had fought her way to the bank, she doggedly turned and waded back out where the bottom began to drop. Then she took a deep breath and tried again. By the time she was halfway to shore she had managed two strokes in a row before sinking. Soon she learned to quit fighting the water and to trust it to buoy her. She swam five strokes and reached the bank.

Feeling a surge of accomplishment, she leaned on the grassy slope and caught her breath. She had done it! She had actually learned to swim! Not too far, she had to admit, but she had done it!

"So there, Jesse Keenan!" she muttered to herself as she reached for her soap and lathered her long hair. "And I didn't drown!"

Spurred on by her success in the swimming hole, Darcy waited every day for Jesse's all-through whistle, then slipped away for her swimming practice. As the days went by she became more and more confident in the water and even began to venture out toward the middle of the pool. She had been a little surprised that Jesse hadn't questioned her daily, unexplained absences, but then he had seemed preoccupied with his work of late. In fact, his lack of attentiveness might have irked her somewhat had she not wanted the practice time even more.

One day as she swam, she decided it was time to extend herself further and she struck out toward the waterfall. As she neared the plunging water, the pool became noticeably colder and she felt fingers of rushing water tickle against her legs. The fascination of the arching rainbow above her and the myriad of crystal drops that soared away from the main body of the falls caused her to pause.

Suddenly, strong arms grabbed her and she nearly choked in her astonishment as she felt her chin locked in the crook of Jesse's elbow. He began pulling her away toward the shore, the water splashing over her head in his effort to save her. Darcy panicked at the unexpected treatment and struggled to break his grip, but soon submitted to his advantage over her. As Jesse hauled her to the bank and swung her up onto the grass, pulling himself out beside her, he demanded anxiously, "Are you all right?"

Darcy doubled her fist and hit his shoulder as hard as she could. "Are you crazy!" she yelled. "You nearly drowned me!"

He was caught off guard by her anger and rocked back on his heels. "You were already drowning. I'm the one that saved you."

"No, I wasn't! I was swimming!" she sputtered. "I didn't start drowning until you grabbed me!" She coughed and shoved her heavy hair from her face.

Jesse stared at her in wonder. "Swimming? I didn't know you could swim!"

"Obviously." She glared at him and rubbed her stinging nose before coughing again.

"Swimming," he repeated incredulously. "How long have you known how to swim?"

"About two weeks," she replied huffily.

The water was clearing from her lungs now and she became aware of the wind on her bare flesh. "Oh!" she exclaimed, as she tried to cover her nakedness with her hands.

Jesse, finally calming enough to notice her lack of clothing, quickly handed her the towel as a deep blush colored his own cheeks. He turned his back hastily as she clutched the towel to her and grabbed for her clothes. To cover his embarrassment over his body's awareness of her, he pulled on the boots he had kicked off in his rescue effort. His thick socks were sodden, as was the rest of his clothing, and though he was uncomfortable, he was determined not to show it.

"You had no right to invade my privacy like that!" Darcy sputtered behind him. "No right at all! What do you mean by sneaking up on me like that!"

"I didn't sneak up on you!" he growled. "I was trying to save your life!"

"You nearly drowned me!"

Jesse scowled and turned to argue with her. Darcy stood there in only her chemise, the wet fabric clinging transparently to her damp skin. She gasped and both wheeled their backs toward each other.

"I couldn't find you and I got worried," he snapped to hide the pounding in his veins at the sight of her. "I called out, but I guess the waterfall was too loud for you to hear me. I'm sorry," he added.

Darcy sighed. What he said did make sense. After a moment's hesitation, she turned and reached out, touching his arm. "You really tried to save me?" she asked softly now that her fright was passing.

He turned and looked down at her. She was fastening the last button as she gazed up at him. Her skin was still pale from the cold water and beaded droplets hung on her long eyelashes. Her hair was plastered wetly to her head and looked heavy and unwieldy as it hung in dripping ropes down her back. He had never seen a more beautiful woman. "Yes," he said hoarsely. "Of course I tried to save you. Do you think I would ever do anything to harm you?"

She looked up into his tormented eyes and shook her head. "You'd not harm me. I know that. But you frightened me!"

He tore his eyes away and glared at the safer view of the mountains. "How was I to know you'd try some damn fool thing like learning how to swim all by yourself! It's a miracle you didn't drown!"

"I was careful. I never swam out from the bank, so I knew where the bottom was all the time. I'd wade out and then swim back. Besides, I figured if I did lose my footing I would be washed into the rocks there, and I can wade in water that deep."

"Now that's really dumb!" he exploded. "You'd be dead before that still water put you on the rocks, and besides that, those rapids would sweep your feet from under you."

She looked at the splashing white water. "It doesn't look all that deep to me," she said doubtfully.

"Well, it is! Even I have trouble wading out in that stretch of water! That's why we work the stream below here! In the spring thaw these rocks are dangerous even to a strong man, let alone a woman your size."

"Oh. You never mentioned that," she said. "I guess I should have told you I was swimming here."

"I wouldn't have let you. In fact, I recall telling you not to do it!" He frowned at her.

"I remember," she said haughtily. "That's why I did it."

They glared at each other; Jesse was the first to look away. "You're a hard woman, Partner. And mean to boot."

"And you're as mule-headed a man as any I ever met." She smiled. "We make a good team."

He glanced at her and found her smile infectious.

"I guess we are at that. Nobody else would ever put up with you." He rubbed his shoulder where she had hit him.

"Don't you be too sure of that, Jesse Keenan," she said primly. "One of these days somebody might just steal me away once word gets out that I can work a sluice *and* swim!" She tossed her head playfully and led the way back to the cabin.

Chapter Eight

DARCY DEEPLY SCORED THE SQUARE OF SALT JOWL and added it to the pot of beans she had bubbling over the fire. As it fell into the water and the aroma of supper filled her nose, she hummed a little tune. Life on the mountain was no harder to her than it had been at Aunt Petra's, only different. And, too, Jesse appreciated her efforts.

She glanced out the doorway to watch Jesse's broad-shouldered form at work down by the river and she smiled. It gave her pleasure to see his sure movements, the way sun glinted in his dark hair, the way his clothing molded to his body. The odd feeling began to rise again in her and she looked away. Lately the sound of his voice or an unexpected glimpse of him had started her pulse racing and made her feel giddy inside. She wasn't too sure why her body responded to him like this, but she knew it had a lot to do with the mysterious ritual called "consummation."

For a long time now she had been aware of her changing feelings toward Jesse. She had first admired him, then liked him as a friend. Now she knew she loved him. If he were to leave her now, his absence would deeply wound her soul. This knowledge was not reassuring. Not that he showed any sign of wanting to leave her, but he also showed no indication of wanting her to be his wife in all ways.

Often when she was busy washing dishes or tidying the cabin, she felt his gaze upon her and would look up as he was lowering his eyes. At other times when he was unaware that she was watching him, she noticed his expression seemed strained as though he were weighing a monumental decision, or so she hoped. Once she was almost certain he called out her name in his sleep, but when she asked him about it the next day, he had snapped that he had had no dreams at all, none at all. Although he stated firmly and often that he was pleased with their partnership and wanted nothing more, every sign showed her that he was becoming more and more fond of her—she hesitated to even consider it might be love. It was very perplexing.

Darcy washed the wild greens she had found growing in the woods and set them in another pot on the fire. She used the same wash water to clean the salt pork from the knife and to wipe clean the table top, then threw the water out the open door. As she took up a dish towel and dried the table and her hands, she wondered at the eccentricities of men. To her, it seemed so simple. She loved Jesse and maybe he loved her, and that removed the barrier of his marriage ban. Yet somehow, it didn't. She was beginning to wonder if this elusive "consummation" was something pretty terrifying in itself.

Suddenly, a low growl halted her thoughts in frozen silence. Slowly she turned her head toward the door.

A large bobcat, looking most uneasy himself, filled the doorway. As he lifted his head and sniffed the air, Darcy glanced warily at the slice of venison she had planned to fry for supper. Again he growled menacingly, sending shivers up Darcy's back to prickle the base of her neck, and took a step into the cabin.

With no apparent way out, Darcy acted instinctively. With a loud cry, she grabbed the heavy iron skillet and ran directly at the bobcat, banging the skillet on the wall to make as much noise as possible. The cat screamed, his growl rising above her own, and slapped at her, spitting like a huge house cat. Darcy knew he would jump at her if she hesitated, so she yelled louder and banged the skillet even harder.

The cat flattened his tufted ears and licked his lips uncertainly, then, with another shriek, he turned and ran. Darcy chased after him out the door and across the tiny porch, then threw the skillet at him as hard as she could. It missed by a wide margin, but as it clattered harmlessly on the rock-strewn ground, the cat increased his speed and raced for the woods.

At the first sounds of trouble, Jesse had started running to Darcy's aid and was halfway to the cabin before he heard the second scream. He stopped abruptly as the large bobcat bolted from the cabin, and his jaw dropped in amazement as Darcy threw the skillet after him. Seeing she was no longer in danger, he calmly strode to the skillet and picked it up. The long handle was broken half off, but otherwise it was undamaged. He turned it over to inspect the other side as he walked to where Darcy was leaning weakly against the cabin door.

"Hunting?" he asked casually, a gleam of laughter in his eyes.

She glared at him, still trembling inside.

"You dropped your skillet," he said politely as he offered it to her.

Darcy snatched it from him and considered throwing it at him next. Jesse looked in the direction the bobcat had taken. "Your weapon seems to pull to the right a bit," he said, keeping his voice even with an effort. "Next time aim more to the left and go for his ears."

"Very funny. Aren't you even concerned that he might have attacked me?" she demanded.

"Nope. He was running too fast to take time to bite." The suppressed grin spread across his face. "Besides, I figure you would have mentioned that right off."

Darcy waved the skillet under his nose. "One more word and I'll go for you next!" His levity had eased her fear considerably.

He laughed and took her weapon from her. "Come on down to the river and see what I found. Supper can wait."

She followed him down to the sluice, glancing once or twice toward the woods where she'd last seen the bobcat. She held out her hand for the nugget, and the size and weight of the gold on her palm melted the remainder of her tension. "Oh, Jesse, it's lovely. It's the best one yet!"

He nodded. "That vein must be a big one, but it beats me where it is. All I can figure is that it has to be under the river." He gazed at the rushing water and shook his head. "If it's out there in the middle I don't know how we can get to it."

"Well, while you're standing there thinking, I'm going to be panning," Darcy answered. "A fortune may be washing by us right now."

He chuckled. "Gold fever's catching. Looks like you got a double dose of it." Bending to his sluice box of pebbles, he poked them with his finger. As if to himself, and without looking at her, he murmured, "I've never seen a bobcat run so fast. I swear his fur was smoking before he reached the woods." He pretended to be engrossed in examining a shiny pebble.

For an answer Darcy flicked the pan of cold water at him. He dodged and grinned at her. She found herself returning his smile. When she turned back to the river her heart was singing.

Darcy picked through the rocks in the pan, then the silt, then scooped another pan full to start over. She was so intent on her search that the low rumble of thunder, barely audible over the roar of the river, almost went unnoticed. She looked up and frowned at the lowering sky. Low over the distant valley the sky was deepening to a bruised gray. As she watched, a crooked finger of lightning speared at the far mountain.

Darcy straightened and slowly wiped her hands on her apron as the sound of thunder rolled down the valley to her. Since childhood she had been terrified of storms, and in her excitement she had not seen this one building. A fresh wind touched her face, bringing with it the scent of rain.

Jesse glanced at her, then looked back. Most of the color had left her face. "What's wrong?"

"Nothing," she said abruptly. "I was just thinking I ought to go see about supper before long. I left the greens cooking." She darted a nervous glance back at the storm clouds as she knelt back by the stream and sloshed more water in her shallow pan. A threatening rumble bounced off the mountains and she closed her eyes tightly for a minute.

"Sounds like a potato wagon fell over," Jesse commented lightly. When she didn't answer, he sat back on his heels and looked closely at her. "Are you all right?"

"Yes!"

He rocked the sluice absentmindedly while his eyes followed her jerky movements. The wind was whipping her long skirt now and trying to pull her hair down from her chignon. As he looked out over the panorama of the valley to check the progress of the rapidly building storm, twin tongues of fire ripped from cloud to earth. The crash of thunder made the ground tremble. Jesse looked back as Darcy made a small choked sound in her throat and sloshed the pan harder until all the rocks flew out with the water.

Rain was beginning to slant downward in the valley below and the mounting wind lashed the trees as if an invisible giant hand combed their branches. As he watched in fascination, the rain approached the higher valley. Darcy jumped as another bolt of lightning seared the sky.

"You're scared?" Jesse said incredulously.

"No!" She heard her voice crack and felt perilously near tears.

"You are!" Jesse exclaimed, too surprised to notice the nearing rain. "You're afraid of storms!"

"I am not!" she snapped at him, her hands trembling.

Jesse stood and put his arm protectively around her as another crash shattered the air. She shrank against him and let him hold her as they ran for the cabin. Big, thick drops that plopped audibly onto the boulders and grass pelted them before they reached the shelter, and the wind that gusted against them made the trees around their clearing shudder. Once inside, Jesse pulled the door shut and fastened the latch. Even in that short distance they had been soaked, and her dress clung damply to her as she shivered with cold and fear.

"Well, I'll be damned," he said in a voice full of amazement. "You can come all the way across the country in a wagon to marry a stranger, teach yourself to swim in a dangerous pool and even chase a bobcat with a skillet, and you're afraid of a storm?"

She buried her face in her hands and cried out, "Don't you tease me, Jesse Keenan! I can't help it!"

Quickly he was beside her and holding her close. "No, no. I didn't mean to make fun of you, Partner. It's just that I didn't think you were afraid of anything." He brushed his lips across her forehead. "You just caught me off guard, that's all."

A blast of thunder that seemed to echo forever made Darcy throw her arms around him and hold tightly to his firm strength. He held her comfortingly until the last of the sound rolled away down the valley.

"You're soaking wet," he said with gentle tenderness. "You'd better get into some dry clothes."

The roar of rain against the tin roof sounded deafeningly in Darcy's ears and she nodded but didn't loosen her hold. The wind was whipping against the door now and the rain was running down the rough-hewn wall and staining a patch of the dirt floor.

"The window," she whispered through bloodless lips.

Jesse carefully untwined her arms and left her long enough to fit the windowpane into place. Instantly the glass was sheeted with water. He latched it securely and came back to her. Silently he took her cold hand and led her to the fire. Stoking it to flames, he swung the cooking pots away from the increased heat.

Jesse studied her as though he'd never seen her before. She was pale and her skin had a waxen sheen. The usual soft brown of her eyes had been replaced with a glittering blackness of unshed tears, as her pupils had fully dilated with her fear. As the thunder raged around them she trembled visibly and her breath was quick and shallow.

"Darcy?" he asked uncertainly.

She ignored his rare use of her name. "It was on a night like this that they died," she whispered. "My mama and papa had gone to bring the calves in out of the storm. They told me to stay in the house, but I was watching them from the window." Her large, staring eyes seemed to again be seeing the most horrifying event of her life. "They had fastened up the calves and were running back to the house when it looked as if the world exploded. There was a flash of light that nearly blinded me and at the same time it thundered as loud as I could hear it. When I could see again, Mama and Papa were just lying there! Just lying in the mud, not moving!" She swallowed dryly. "I wanted to go to them, but I couldn't! I just couldn't make myself go out in the lightning! They just lay there," she ended with a whisper.

Jesse caught her to him and held her tightly. He ached to heal the wound that must have lain raw and bleeding all these years. Somehow he knew she had never before told this to anyone. "There, now. Everything is fine," he murmured soothingly to the child she once had been. "You're safe now."

"Nobody ever knew I saw it," she said, her voice muffled against his chest. "When the neighbors came they said Mama and Papa had died at once. They found me hiding in the cellar and took me away. I never saw Mama and Papa again, not even at the funeral. After that I never had a real home." Her voice was strained now. "Everybody dies or sends me away. One of these days you'll make me leave, too!"

"No, no," he protested soothingly. "All that happened a long time ago. I'm not going to send you away."

The storm was already beginning to fade as quickly as it had come. With relief she buried her face against his chest and held him tightly as sobs racked her body. Jesse let her cry, knowing that tears were rare for her and hoping this would help ease her pain. Yet with each distant peal of thunder she trembled. She felt so good in his arms. Each part of her body molded naturally into his own. Her head barely reached his shoulder, and she was so slender that he was afraid he might hurt her if he hugged her too tightly.

Minutes passed along with the storm, but they lingered in the warmth of their embrace. Darcy rubbed her cheek against the softness of his shirt, still damp but warmed by his body heat. Beneath, she felt his broad, firm chest and the steady, comforting beat of his heart. The all too familiar desire began to rise in her, vanquishing even her fear of the storm. She drew in a deep breath, savoring the fresh scent that always clung to him. Her pulse raced, but no longer from terror. Slowly she lifted her chin and their eyes met.

As Jesse gazed down at her, she noticed a small muscle tighten in his jaw. Darcy hesitantly reached up and brushed her fingers along his smooth-shaven cheek. Gently she traced the hard line of his jaw and let her fingers linger on his lips.

"Darcy," he moaned, "don't tempt me so." Her rosy lips were parted slightly, revealing her even, white teeth, and her dark eyes were wide with wonder.

For an answer she ran her fingers through his thick hair and pulled his head down for her kiss. At first their lips met shyly; then, as Jesse gave way to the overpowering emotion that racked his body, he pulled her to him and kissed her almost roughly.

Instead of pulling away as he had feared she might, Darcy met his passion. Eagerly she ran her fingers through his hair and gloried at the texture of it as he kissed her into light-headed surrender.

"Jesse, Jesse," she murmured as he drew back to look at her. She saw the torment in the depths of his eyes and she spoke tenderly. "Don't turn away from me again. I want to be your wife in all the ways it can mean. I want to lie beside you at night and wake up by you in the morning."

He stared down at her and fought against his own ghosts of the past, against the memory that was so painful, still, that he couldn't talk about it, even to her. The memory that told him never, never to trust his love to another woman. But Darcy looked up at him with willing eyes of love, and her touch was driving shafts of fire along all his nerves. Almost against his will he lowered his head and again claimed her lips.

With a low moan Jesse knew the last of his resolve had crumbled and the molten fire of need coursed through his veins. "Have you ever . . ." he said hoarsely. "That is . . ."

"No," she whispered, her eyes melting into his. "There has been no one."

Jesse paused long enough to control his desires and tenderly stroked her cheek. "I won't hurt you."

She nodded trustingly. "I could never be afraid of you."

Jesse lifted his hands and slowly removed the pins from her heavy hair, letting it tumble into his hands. The dark, lustrous masses fell about her like a cape, and he caressed the silken strands wonderingly.

Again his lips lightly caressed hers as his fingers deftly loosened the buttons of her dress. He pushed the damp material back from her shoulders and eased her arms from the sleeves. He pulled back to look at her as the dress slid to a bundle around her feet. Slowly, taking care not to frighten her, he pulled off his shirt and wet boots, then knelt to remove her shoes and stockings. At last he pulled free the ribbon that held her thin chemise in place and ran his large hands along her shoulders to stroke away the straps. Beneath his fingers her fully rounded breasts were freed and lay bare to his gaze, the pink nipples already thrusting eagerly toward him. Jesse caught his breath at her beauty.

Her waist was slender, yet not too thin, and when he removed her lower undergarments he saw that the curve of her hip molded gracefully into her thigh. He ran his hand over the smooth plane of her stomach before letting his fingers trace the rounded curve of her breast. Darcy swayed toward him but let him feast his eyes on her nakedness.

She reached out and tentatively touched the swelling muscles of his chest, then stroked his satiny flesh downward to run her fingers over his taut stomach. Clumsily she loosened his pants, her desire overcoming her timidity. Moving as slowly as he had, she eased his pants from him. At the sight of his erect manhood she drew in her breath sharply and looked up at him for reassurance. He smiled down at her and guided her hand to him.

"Don't be afraid," he said gently.

Bending, he lifted her as easily as he had in the moonlight so many nights before and carried her to the bed. When he laid her down, he read the question in her eyes. "No," he said. "This time I have no intention of leaving you."

Darcy lifted her head to kiss him and felt her world whirl giddily as he returned her kiss. His hands caressed her breast, giving her pleasure she had never dreamed existed. Thrills of desire washed over her when he lowered his head and ran his tongue over the throbbing twin peaks. Darcy knotted her fingers in his hair and arched her back toward him as he pulled her nipple into his mouth.

He played with her, teased her body to trembling ecstasy with his lips, fingers and the deep resonance of his voice. When she felt she could bear no more, he gently urged her legs apart and knelt between them. "Don't be afraid," he said. "Just put your arms around me and hold me close."

Darcy pulled him to her as she felt his hotness against her inner thighs. Then he filled her and she cried out, more in surprise than pain, for her body had anticipated the act she had never known.

"There now," he soothed her. "This isn't so bad, is it?"

She shook her head as she felt a strange restlessness guide her. When he began to move against her, she moved with him in a desire as old as life itself. The strangeness of the sensations was forgotten as her body quickened in response to his loving.

Jesse coaxed her and taught her to follow her instincts as he caressed her to even greater passion. Then she cried out in rapture as wave after hot wave of fulfillment pounded through her. She heard Jesse moan and clutch her tighter as he joined her in the climax of their loving. Slowly the waves of delight subsided, leaving a rosy glow of deep satisfaction and contentment.

Jesse rolled from her but kept her cradled securely in his strong arms. "Are you happy?" he asked. He had never been with a virgin before, and he was suddenly afraid that he might have hurt her in his passion.

She nodded, her eyes searching deep into his soul. "I'm happy. I love you, Jesse Keenan."

He gazed into her eyes and tried to quiet the pain that those words still evoked. Would Darcy prove to be false, too? He pulled her head into the hollow of his shoulder and laid his cheek against her hair. "Go to sleep," he said gruffly.

Darcy lay still in his arms, wondering what she had said or done to displease him. At length she slipped into sleep, lulled by the steady rise and fall of her husband's powerful chest.

Chapter Nine

DARCY YAWNED IN THE PEARLY MORNING LIGHT AND stretched languorously as she recalled the events of the night. She reached out her arm, felt only the coolness of the sheets, and opened her eyes. Although the sun was scarcely high enough to fade away the night, Jesse was nowhere to be seen. She rolled over and pulled back the wall formed by the hanging blanket, but his cot was empty also. With a puzzled frown Darcy swung her legs out of bed and sat up, ignoring the cool air on her bare flesh.

After they had made love she remembered telling him that she loved him—and his reaction had been brusque. Although she had no experience to rely on, Darcy knew this was an odd response for a man in love. And now he had already left the cabin. Surely, she thought, this is not ordinary behavior.

Still frowning, Darcy dressed and brushed the snarls from her hair before coiling it on top of her head. As she pushed the day's kettle of water over the fire, she puzzled over Jesse's odd reaction to her. Was there something she should have done that she had omitted? Had she not known to do something he considered elemental? She picked up Jesse's fur-lined cap and stroked it as she gazed out the window toward the stream.

Jesse bent over the sluice box and rocked it viciously back and forth, sloshing water onto his legs. His mind was wrestling with problems of such proportion that he didn't even notice. The night before he had felt emotions awaken he had thought long dead. Emotions that only Marlene, in far off St. Louis, had ever touched. He resentfully recalled Marlene's froth of red-blond hair, her china-blue eyes, her milky skin. She had been a lady born and bred and to have seen her in her mother's drawing room, one would have believed she had never had an improper thought in her entire life. But in the moonlight, away from her parents' watchful eyes, Marlene had become an insatiable nymph whose lusts reached even greater depths than his own. Too late Jesse had discovered she had not begun nor ended her trysts with him alone. By the time he learned she had bedded most of his friends, he had fallen in love with her. Like a moon-sick calf he had assumed his love would satisfy her limitless cravings and that she would settle happily into wifehood. He believed this, despite the warnings of his friends, until the night of their betrothal party. Two hours after the announcement was made, he had caught her in the back parlor with two of his father's friends. It was, perhaps, the shortest betrothal in the history of St. Louis.

And now, after five years of congratulating himself on his escape from Marlene's unfaithfulness, he was once again in love. Of course, he had no worries that Darcy was unfaithful to him—there was no other soul within a day's ride. But eventually they would come off the mountain, and then what would happen? Darcy was even more beautiful than Marlene, and no man would pass her by without noticing. Jesse had heard enough talk of his friends and their roving girlfriends to know that not everyone was as monogamous as he was. Marlene had convinced him that no woman could be trusted. If Marlene, with her fervent proclamations of love for him, and him alone, was not to be believed, then how could he trust anyone? Jesse recalled her innocent, round eyes and her childishly pouting lips and made an angry sound.

He had come to not only love Darcy but to like her as well. Unfaithfulness on her part would deal him a blow worse than death. There was only one way to go. He must put their relationship back the way it had been before that cursed storm. As her friend he could be happy. As her lover he felt the risk of being hurt was simply too great, at least for now. Jesse straightened up and threw the shovel down on the bank. He set his jaw with grim determination and strode toward the cabin to get his decision out in the open.

When he marched into the room, Darcy looked up at him in welcome, but before she could speak, he announced, "Last night I made a big mistake. From now on I want our relationship to be just as it was before—partners." He nodded his head once firmly and turned to leave. "That's all I wanted to say."

"Well, it's not all *I* want to say," Darcy sputtered as his words sunk in. "I enjoyed last night and I want to be more than just your partner."

"No." He glared at her over his shoulder.

"Just like that? I can't turn off my feelings for you just because you want me to! Surely you can't mean that you feel nothing for me at all! I may not know a great deal about what happens between a husband and a wife, but I know what I saw in your eyes!"

"Leave it alone, Darcy," he growled.

"No! I won't be pushed away! You can't expect me to act as if last night never happened! I love you!"

Jesse felt the familiar pain twist inside him. If only he could believe her! "I told you how it has to be," he said through clenched teeth. "If you don't agree to it, you can leave."

Darcy caught her breath and drew her hand across the flat of her stomach where pain knotted. "You want that?" she said hoarsely. "You want me to go?"

Jesse gripped the door and glared at the woods beyond. "No," he said at last. "I don't want you to go."

Silence strung tautly between them. At last Darcy spoke in a barely audible voice. "All right. I'll stay."

Jesse didn't trust himself to look back at her, but he nodded and went back to the stream.

* * *

For the next week Darcy and Jesse lived in strained companionship. Darcy was silent and angry because Jesse insisted upon behaving so strangely. Jesse was equally quiet as he struggled to tamp down his growing love. At times as he lay in aching solitude in the darkness beyond the blanket wall, he felt an almost uncontrollable urge to rip down the barrier and go to her. Once he was almost certain he heard her sob and he trembled with the need to comfort her. But Marlene's tears had also flowed freely and had been effective in helping her to get her own way, so Jesse had forced himself to stay on his side of the blanket.

Darcy had no idea what was wrong, and at first had assumed she was somehow at fault. But as the days passed she decided that the blame was not hers but his, and her tears no longer flowed in the night. She had never been rebellious by nature, but she was tired of being shuffled from place to place. Whether he wanted her as his wife or not, she resolved to stay on the mountain. Besides, she knew that if she left she would never see him again.

With neither wanting to be the first to speak, a pattern of nonverbal communication developed. When Darcy planned to do the wash, she left the basket in the middle of the floor. If Jesse wanted his clothes cleaned, he tossed them in. When she needed a bucket of water and was too busy to fetch it herself, Darcy would leave the empty bucket in the middle of the door where Jesse would have to step over it. The strain of not speaking began to have a strength of its own, and soon it became a point of honor not to talk. Both ached, but were too stubborn to give in.

The first evening of the second week of the silent feud, Darcy prepared their supper as she had every night and sat across from Jesse as she ate. The crackle of the fire seemed overly loud in the silence, and outside in the growing dusk, the wind was moaning through the pine trees. The log broke, sending a shower of sparks up the chimney, and the exposed sap popped loudly. Only the click of flatware against tin plates and the occasional creak of one of the hide-bottomed chairs told of the man and woman sheltered in the cabin.

Jesse got up and bent over the black pot to get more of the red beans and salt pork that simmered there. As he raised the ladle a shout sounded just outside the door.

"Hello! Get yourself out here, Jesse! You've got company!"

Jesse froze, then dropped the ladle with a splash. "Damn!" he exclaimed.

Darcy was so startled to hear a voice that she jumped and stared at the door.

"Damn!" Jesse muttered again. Quickly he crossed to the other side of the cabin and kicked his bedroll under the bed. Before he could pull down the dividing blanket the door slammed open and the biggest man Darcy had ever seen filled the opening.

"What way is that to greet an old buddy?" the

man roared. "Get over here and give me a hand with these blamed traps!" The man lifted a burlap bag as large as Darcy and tossed it easily into the center of the room. When it landed with a clatter, Darcy jumped again, and the blond giant swung around and stared at her

Darcy's heart was pounding, but she forced herself to rise as if his entrance into her home was as natural as the sunset. She met his eyes squarely and saw with relief that he looked at her with human intelligence.

"Well, I'll be . . ." the man stammered as he looked her up and down. "Jesse!" he said, wheeling to his friend. "You've got a woman up here!"

Jesse belatedly found his tongue and grinned as he crossed over to Darcy. "Watch what you say, Nathan, this is my wife." He put a possessive arm around Darcy's shoulder and said, "Partner, I want you to meet my friend, Nathan Stoddard. He's the man I told you about right after you came here. Nathan, this is Darcy Keenan."

Slowly Nathan raised his ham of a hand and pulled off his cap. His face was a study in amazement. "Well, I'll be . . ." he repeated. He jabbed one finger in Darcy's direction. "You're that mail-order bride!"

"Hah!" Jesse exploded. "So you *are* the one that did it! You're the one that ordered me a wife!"

"Well, yeah," Nathan said slowly, "but I never really thought one would show up."

"Why did you do that, Nathan?" Jesse demanded.

Nathan glanced at his friend, then back to Darcy. "You recall last winter when we were talking about how lonesome it gets on the mountain. Well, after I left here, I went on into Bancroft and ran into some of the boys. We got to drinking, just like always, and one of them pulled out a circular advertising mail-order brides. I thought about how lonely you said you were and about how slow the time passes here, and I just said to myself, 'Nathan, you've got to do it for him. You've got to help old Jesse out.' So I went over there to the assayer's office and signed you up for a wife. Paid gold on the spot and told the man I was you." He stared down at Darcy. "I plumb forgot all about it until now."

After Darcy decided the bear of a man wasn't dangerous, she shrugged off Jesse's possessive hand. "Have a seat, Mr. Stoddard," she said tersely. "I'll serve you some beans and cornbread."

Jesse watched her warily. She saw to their guest's needs but pointedly ignored Jesse's empty plate, letting him see to his own. He spooned up his own beans and sat back down.

"Just sit here, Mr. Stoddard," Darcy said, giving him her chair.

"No, ma'am. I couldn't take your seat."

"Nonsense. I'm finished." Darcy cut him a wedge of yellow bread and pushed the crock of pickled peppers nearer to his reach. She was watching Jesse from the corner of her eye and wondering why he looked so uneasy. "I'll step out to the barn and get the stool while you eat," she said.

Nathan stared at her until she went outside, then

turned back to Jesse. "Damn! Do you reckon all the brides look like her?"

"I doubt it," Jesse replied, pushing his beans around with his fork.

"Maybe I ought to get me one."

"Nathan, you really shouldn't have done that to me!" Jesse said in a low voice.

Nathan chewed slowly and studied his friend with his penetrating blue eyes. "You mean to tell me you don't like her? Why not?"

"I'm not saying that," Jesse said hastily. "No, a man would be a fool not to like Darcy. But to just go and order a bride for a man. It's just not right!"

"Huh." Nathan stared at Jesse and Jesse shifted uncomfortably. "Not right, you say? Looks like it's turned out pretty well to me."

"But damn it, that's a decision a man ought to make for himself!"

Again Nathan watched Jesse as he chewed. "She can cook, too," he said at last. "Can't every husband say that of a new wife. I knew a man once that nearly died before his wife learned to cook. She fed him half-done peas and buttermilk every night. It's a pure wonder he didn't founder."

"Will you be serious? Marriage is more than just cooking." Jesse frowned at his benefactor.

"Yep. A lot more. How come you had your bedroll lying out on the floor and why is that blanket hanging over there dividing the room up like that?" Nathan ate steadily, his eyes on his plate. "Hand me some more of that bread."

"Since when do you peep in windows?" Jesse

countered, shoving the pan at Nathan and striding across the room to pull down the blanket.

"When a window's right in front of your face and you happen to be looking at it, it's hard not to see in."

"I was airing it out, that's all. You know how stuffy a bedroll can get." He returned to the table.

"Yep." Nathan put a spoonful of peppers on his beans. "I reckon you were airing out that blanket, too?"

"That's right!"

Nathan fastened his eyes on Jesse. "You ought to tell Miss Darcy that a blanket airs better out in the sunlight. Bedrolls, too." He chewed thoughtfully. "Everything's all right between you two, isn't it?"

"Sure!" Jesse said quickly. "Sure. Why, we couldn't be happier." He saw for the first time that Nathan wasn't a bad-looking man. Most women might call him handsome in a rough sort of way. Would Darcy think so? The thought ignited a flame of jealousy in Jesse. "We get along fine. Just fine."

"That well, do you? I'm glad to hear it." Nathan grinned. "I was worried for a minute there."

"No, don't talk foolishness. Why, you didn't hear any argument when you walked up, did you?"

"No, I can't say I heard a sound."

"See? Married life with Darcy is tranquillity itself."

"That's good to hear. I'm looking forward to observing that."

Jesse leaned forward. "What was that? Observing it how?"

"Why, just by watching you two for a day or so. I'm in no hurry to leave."

"You mean you're planning on staying here?" Jesse asked as Darcy came in carrying the stool. "Here?"

"Sure. I always spend some time with you, don't I? I was going to push on up the mountain, seeing as how you're a newlywed and all, but I would like to get a look at all that tranquillity." He smiled at Darcy.

"But I wouldn't want to hold you up," Jesse protested. "And Darcy's shy!"

"Nonsense, Jesse," Darcy spoke up. "You can't send a man out into the night. He's welcome to stay here as long as he wants."

"Thank you, ma'am. I'm much obliged," Nathan boomed jovially.

"He's used to sleeping outside," Jesse informed his wife as if Nathan hadn't spoken. "He'd prefer it."

"Hell, no, I wouldn't. Begging your pardon, ma'am. What man wants to sleep under a tree like a possum when he can stay inside? I'll bet if we hang that blanket there back up it would make a dandy wall. I'll sleep on the other side of it and Miss Darcy will never know I'm there."

Darcy had forgotten about the lack of privacy in the cabin. How could she ignore Jesse if he were sleeping in her bed? And there was nowhere else to sleep. Her startled eyes met Jesse's and she saw him grimace wryly at her sudden understanding. "Maybe you would be happier in the barn, Mr. Stoddard," she said quickly.

"No, no. I never cared for the smell of horses. I knew a man once that went crazy from sleeping around horses. Kept pawing at the ground and neighing. Tried to kick anybody that got near him." Nathan's earnest expression was belied by the sparkle in his eyes.

In spite of her discomfort, Darcy found herself suppressing a smile. "I see. Well, I wouldn't want to expose you to such a danger." She and Jesse would just have to put up with the inconvenience. The bed was large enough for two people and it was, after all, only for the one night.

While Darcy washed and dried the dishes, Jesse and Nathan sat in front of the fire and caught up on all that had happened in the months since they had last seen each other.

"I haven't heard of a good vein of gold being found around here in months," Nathan said gloomily. "I guess it's not as rich a mountain as we all thought."

"I don't know. I'm still finding nuggets washing in the river, so there must be a vein around here somewhere. I'm just afraid it's under the middle of the river where I can't get at it."

"Last week I ran into Charley Three Toes and he said the mine at Bancroft is starting to play out."

Jesse studied the dancing flames for a while before he asked, "Does Charley still have that squaw living with him?"

"Pale Moon? He sure does. I just can't understand

it. Every time I see her I swear she's gotten uglier. And you know she started off with a face that would scare an owl out of his tree."

Jesse grinned. "Must be love."

Nathan only snorted. "Convenience, you mean. I don't think she can say more than two or three English words, and old Charley doesn't talk Ute at all. He only knows Arapaho." Nathan crossed his arms across his chest. "I just can't understand anybody taking up with a woman like Pale Moon. You know what they call Charley? Squaw man! And he doesn't even fight about it. Why, I'd break a man's face if he ever called me that. I offered to do it for Charley but he wouldn't let me. He said why bother fighting over a name. Can you imagine?" Nathan shook his head morosely.

"Some of those Indian girls are mighty pretty," Jesse teased his friend. "Maybe you ought to give it another thought."

"You must have seen some I haven't," Nathan said staunchly.

Darcy laughed as she put away the last dish and came to join them. "I thought all prospectors were supposed to be taciturn. You haven't stopped talking all evening."

Nathan cocked his head slightly. "Supposed to be what?"

"She means silent," Jesse added, quickly turning to Darcy with a superior glance.

"Oh. I'm quiet enough up on the mountain. Nobody up there to talk to but my horse and mule. Lord knows they aren't much at conversation. Besides, they go everywhere I do and see all I see. After a while I don't tell them much of anything."

Jesse grinned. "Do you still have that old walleyed mare?"

"Nope, I finally found somebody new enough to the territory that he hadn't heard yet how crazy she was. I traded her for a green-broke gelding and got a rifle to boot."

"I don't know how you can sleep nights knowing you did that to some poor soul." Jesse turned to Darcy. "That mare was a May colt and, true to form, she couldn't cross water without lying down and rolling in it. Not only that, she used her lips to open the gate latch. She'd pick anything short of a padlock. He couldn't keep her penned or out of the feed bin." It was the first time he had spoken congenially to her in days and she looked up, startled.

As if he had noticed nothing unusual in the interchange, Nathan said, "She's gotten into trouble so many times it's a sheer wonder that she lived long enough for me to trade her. That new gelding may buck like Satan every time I get on him, but I haven't had to swim out of a river a single time or chase him all over the mountain even once."

Jesse chuckled. "I'm surprised you've come down to town this early, speaking of the mountain. You didn't just happen to stumble across that mother lode and are keeping it a secret, are you?"

"No, I sure didn't," Nathan replied. "In fact, I've decided to get out of the prospecting business." He nodded toward the large sack he had brought in with him. "That bag's full of traps. I traded my claim and equipment for them in town yesterday. You're now looking at a trapper."

"A trapper! You? I meant to ask you what was in that sack when you came in, but it skipped my mind. Why, I can remember when you had the gold fever as bad as any man I ever saw."

"Yeah, well, fever's one thing, but finding it is another. I couldn't locate me an obliging river to toss me a nugget or two like you did. But now animals— that's something else. This mountain is full of bear, beaver, elk and I don't know what all. You know as well as I do what a market there is for pelts. So I did it. And, of course I've got me that little cabin to winter in."

"But what do you know about trapping? You've never done that before."

"I know as much about trapping as I did about prospecting when I started that."

"When we were getting started, I had to explain to you the difference between a rocker and a long tom," Jesse argued.

"A lot of good that did me. I still never found anything worth talking about. But I have run across lots of bear and beaver."

Jesse nodded. "You might have a good idea there. Gold sure is scarce around here. Partner and I were talking a while back about the possibility of moving on."

"Partner?" Nathan asked.

"He means me," Darcy answered. "He's always talking about moving on to another place."

Nathan glanced from her to Jesse and back again.

Since he had come in he had been aware of the strain between them and now he felt it again. "That's a funny thing for a man to call his wife."

"I help out with the sluice box," Darcy explained. "It's just his nickname for me."

Nathan nodded slowly. "I see. How do you like prospecting?"

"It's fun, really. I like knowing I might find gold in the bottom of each tray. That's exciting. And the water is so pretty the way it rushes by."

Jesse snorted. "You make it sound like a Sunday picnic. It's damn hard work."

Darcy jerked as if she had been slapped and her expression became guarded. "I never said I didn't find it hard. Only pretty."

"Uh huh," Nathan said as if he now saw something clearly. "Well, it's a long way here from Bancroft, fighting a bucking bronc and dragging a mule behind you. I think I'll turn in for the night, if that's okay with you two." He stood and stretched, his bulk seeming to fill the small cabin. "See you in the morning, Miss Darcy, Jesse." He nodded to them each and went over to prepare his bedroll in Jesse's sleeping area.

"I'll go check on the horses," Darcy said as she lit the kerosene lantern.

"I'll help you," Jesse added in a clipped tone. He forced a smile to his lips as if this were a nightly practice.

As soon as they were out of earshot of the cabin, Jesse pulled her around to face him. "What do you mean by asking him to stay the night!"

"I forgot there was no other room!" she snapped. "I'm not used to living in a house the size of a hatbox!"

"So now the house is too small! Does anything suit you?"

"Not much anymore!" she said, wheeling on him. "And I was under the impression that *you* were the one that was hard to please!"

"Me! When have I ever been anything but agreeable! You're the unreasonable one!"

Darcy glared at him in the yellow lamplight. "Jesse Keenan, that's just plain stupid!" She doubled her fist and hit him on his shoulder. "I'm as reasonable a person as you can ever hope to find!" She stalked away from him toward the barn.

The structure was a low shed built into a shallow cave in the side of the mountain. On her entrance the animals looked up in mild curiosity, then lowered their heads to the hay they were methodically consuming. Darcy set the lantern on the shelf just inside the door, then stepped on in and patted her horse's shoulder and rubbed the mule's head as she frowned at her husband.

"I don't know why you followed me out here," she said, "but if it's just to argue, you can turn around and go back."

Jesse frowned at her. The top of her head barely reached above her horse's back, but she was regarding him as fiercely as a wildcat. "Look, Nathan won't be here long. I want us to try to be civil to each other while he's here."

"I gathered that by the way you introduced me. All lovey and sweet. You'd think we never passed a cross word in our lives."

"I don't want him to think we can't get along. It's not proper."

"And you think I don't know how to act in front of company?" Her face was pale with anger; the mare moved away from her uneasily.

Jesse sighed and ran his fingers through his dark hair. "I didn't mean that. My words are getting all twisted up. I'm not as smooth-talking as Nathan."

"I noticed," she remarked scathingly.

Jealousy flared in his eyes, but Jesse fought it back. "I guess my actions do seem rather odd . . ."

"No, they seem downright peculiar!"

"I have my reasons!"

"Oh? What are they? You tell me, Jesse Keenan, how it makes sense for a married couple not to live together! I can't wait to hear it."

He glared at her, then after a time said, "I can't explain it to you."

"Can't or won't!"

Again he measured his words before answering, "I won't."

Silence ominously filled the barn, and Darcy fought the lump in her throat. Why, she wondered, was he so exasperating? Drawing a deep breath to steady her voice, she said, "Will you at least tell me if I have . . . displeased you in some way?"

"You have not displeased me. In any way."

Darcy took a step closer and asked, "Do you mean all this has nothing to do with me at all?"

"That's right."

"And you won't tell me what it is?"

"That's right, too."

Darcy clamped her lips together and glared at him. "Then that is indeed the most ridiculous thing I ever heard of!"

"I have my reasons for not wanting a wife."

"They are beside the point since you already have one!" She brushed by him and was out of the door before he could see the tears spring to her eyes. "Maybe *you* should be the one to sleep with the horses!"

Jesse followed her into the darkness recalling their house guest and growled, "No way, Partner! I'm not about to let Nathan think there's anything wrong between us."

"But there is!" she answered, facing him in the silver moonlight. "There's something very wrong indeed and I can't fix it because I don't know what it is."

"Darcy," he said in a pained voice, "if I could tell you, I would. But there are some things a man has to work out for himself." He could see the wetness in her eyes and he wanted to comfort her but knew he could not allow himself to touch her. If he held her in his arms he knew he would be unable to refrain from carrying her back into the barn and loving her.

"Then maybe *I* should sleep in the barn and give you the whole bed to think in!"

"Don't you suppose Nathan might find that a bit odd?" he retorted.

"What do I care what he thinks? He's your friend,

remember?" She glared at the lighted window of the cabin and brushed her wet cheek with the palm of her hand.

"Please, Partner. Do just this one thing for me," Jesse appealed to her. "I'm asking this as one friend to another. Don't let Nathan know we aren't, well, living together."

She sighed and looked back at him. "It's that important to you?"

"Yes."

"Then I'll do it. Besides, I'd be mortified if he thought it was any different. Friend to friend, I can tell you it makes me look pretty bad as a woman."

"No, Darcy," he said softly. "Not a thing on this green earth could ever make you look bad. You're as fine a woman as ever was made. I can tell you that honestly."

Darcy studied him in the darkness. "As a wife I can say that doesn't help much. I'm still mad at you."

"It's the best I can do."

"No, the best thing you could do is to tell me what's bothering you," she said in exasperation. Then her voice softened and she said, "You're a hard man to love, Jesse Keenan."

"I know," he said sadly as he walked with her back to retrieve the lantern before returning to the cabin. "I've been told that before."

Jesse and Darcy stood on the bedroom side of the blanket wall. From the other side came muffled sounds of Nathan preparing to go to sleep. Both

Jesse and Darcy were still fully dressed and neither made a move to disrobe.

"We can't stand here all night," Darcy mouthed silently to Jesse.

"When he goes to sleep I'll slip out and sleep in the barn. In the morning he will just think I got up early," he replied almost inaudibly.

Darcy sighed and shrugged resignedly. "Turn around," she signaled with her lips and a twirling motion of her fingers. When he turned his broad back to her, she modestly turned hers to him and began unbuttoning her dress. She drew it off over her head and hung it on the wooden peg beside the bed, removed her chemise and undergarments and hastily pulled on her nightgown. She was buttoning the front placket, her full breasts barely concealed, when Nathan's gruff voice called out not two feet away.

"Good night," he said in his customary bellow.

Darcy jumped and whirled nervously toward the quilt and Jesse did the same. Their eyes met and Jesse's involuntary gaze took in the beauty of her bare flesh exposed by the gaping gown. He swallowed dryly and mumbled "Good night" to his friend. A dull flush stained his tanned cheeks and he felt a tremor of desire shake him. Quickly Darcy covered her breasts and turned her back toward him, but he was still tormented by the memory of what he had seen.

After Darcy climbed into bed and pulled the covers over her, Jesse sat shakily on the foot of the bed running his fingers through his hair. Thank goodness, he thought, there will be only one night of this! A puff of his breath extinguished the light.

For long minutes he sat in the dark, waiting for Nathan's steady breathing to indicate a deep sleep. At last he stood and looked back at Darcy. She lay sleeping as innocently as any child, one hand stretched back over her head and her lips slightly parted. He gazed down at her, wondering if he was indeed foolish not to trust her, then shook his head tiredly. She was a woman, and the equally innocent-looking Marlene had taught him well. He turned and crept silently past the curtain.

"What's wrong?" Nathan asked sleepily as Jesse passed his bedroll. "Did you hear something outside?" He sat up, suddenly awake as only a man closely attuned to nature could be.

Jesse sighed. "No. I just thought I did. Go back to sleep." He went back to Darcy's side of the blanket and looked down at her as he again nervously ran his fingers through his hair. Slowly he began to remove his clothing for the night.

Chapter Ten

NATHAN DRAPED THE BRACE OF RABBITS, TIED together by a piece of twine, over one shoulder and easily tossed the dressed-out deer over his other. After smoking and curing, the meat would last Jesse and Darcy several weeks. It was the least he could do, he felt, for having ordered a mail-order bride for Jesse, the most confirmed bachelor Nathan had ever known. He eased his way through the woods with surprising silence for a man of his size.

With the few warmer days of late summer, the aspen leaves had turned a darker, more brilliant green as if in defiance of the certainty of approaching fall. But Nathan knew they soon would wash the mountainsides with their warm golden hues, signaling the definite end to his favorite season. He liked summer—it was a straightforward season with no pretense of being anything else. Nathan breathed deeply of the fresh air and brushed past the last branches of the saplings that bordered the Keenans' cabin clearing.

Down at the river Jesse and Darcy were working the sluice and panning. Nathan narrowed his piercing blue eyes and studied them thoughtfully. Though they worked shoulder to shoulder, neither of them spoke, nor did their eyes meet. He frowned. When they had gone out the night before to tend to the horses he had assumed they were seeking a few moments of privacy. They were, after all, newlyweds, and there was no need to see about healthy horses at that time of night. He had placed Darcy's bright eyes to moments of stolen rapture in the barn and her quietness to shyness. Now he wasn't so sure. There had also been the fact of Jesse tiptoeing out of the house in the middle of the night. Nathan had listened carefully, but he had heard nothing outside after Jesse returned to bed. And he had been fully dressed. What man, hearing a varmint after his livestock, would take the time on a summer night to get fully dressed before going to check on the animals? It didn't make sense.

Nathan lowered the deer and the string of rabbits to the ground beside the door. His natural curiosity was sparked as he looked back at the couple by the water.

Striding down to join them, he nodded to Jesse and said, "Miss Darcy, I brought some meat up to the house for you. A fine bit of venison and the makings of a rabbit stew."

Darcy looked up from her work and smiled. Her

umber hair gleamed in the sunlight and her teeth were white against her lightly tanned skin. "Thank you, Mr. Stoddard. That was very kind of you."

"Surely you can call me Nathan, ma'am. Jesse and I have been friends so long we're almost family."

"Very well, Nathan," she said with another of her dazzling smiles. "I'll go up and see to it right away."

Jesse scowled at the interchange and sloshed the water across the pebbles in the trough.

Nathan smiled at Darcy and gave her his hand to help her over the rocks at the river's edge. When she was out of hearing, he turned back to his friend. "That's quite a woman you have there. I sure never knew mail-order brides looked like that."

"You already told me that—last night."

"What's ailing you, Jesse? You act like a sore-footed mule every time I mention her."

"Well, damn it, Nathan, a man just shouldn't go around ordering brides for his friends!"

Nathan sat on a boulder and studied Jesse. "It looks to me like it turned out all right. I admit it was wrong not to tell you I did it, but it's not all that bad. You know yourself how lonesome you said you were. And she's not squint-eyed or mean-tongued."

Jesse frowned as if he would like to contradict the last statement but refrained.

Nathan glanced at the cabin where Darcy was already skinning the rabbits. "She looks like a fine wife to me. You know," he said thoughtfully, "if I had signed my own name to that paper, she would be *my* wife now. It makes a man think."

Jesse straightened and scowled darkly. "A man better be careful just what and how he thinks about her since he *didn't* sign his name to the paper."

Nathan looked back at his friend in surprise. "Why, Jesse, you don't think . . ."

Jesse turned his back and sloshed out farther into the water to hide his jealousy. "I don't think anything. Not anything at all."

"Hey, you act like I said something out of line. I didn't mean to get you stirred up." Nathan looked with consternation at his friend. "I just meant that if I hadn't put your name on the marriage contract, she would be married to me. Like a twist of fate or something."

"I heard you the first time. You've got no need to keep on repeating it." Jesse studied the rushing water. He had awakened this morning to find Darcy curled in the crook of his arm, her cheek pillowed against his shoulder. He had gotten out of bed without waking her, but the memory of her warm curves and the clean scent of her hair had tormented him all day.

Forcing a smile to his lips, Jesse looked back at Nathan. "Don't pay me any mind. I guess I just got up on the wrong side of the bed this morning. I do appreciate the meat."

"Think nothing of it," Nathan said in a puzzled voice at the abrupt switch in Jesse's mood.

Jesse waded to the riverbank and tossed his shovel onto the gravel. "I guess we ought to go on up to the house. Darcy put on a mess of beans for dinner, and they ought to be ready about now. It's a shame you can't taste her rabbit stew for supper tonight, but I know you need to be moving on."

"A good hand with rabbit, is she?" Nathan asked.

"None better. She cooks it so tender you can't even tell when you chew it." Jesse decided he could afford to be magnanimous since Nathan was about to leave.

"She doesn't flavor it with wild onions, does she? Those little green ones like you find in the meadows?"

"She sure does. I'm one lucky man."

"Well, I believe you are for a fact. You know, Jesse, you talked me into it. I'll stay a bit longer."

"What?" Jesse said, stopping as if he had run into a wall.

"Yeah, those pelts can wait another few days. Shoot, it's a long time before the winter snows, and I don't get to see you all that often." Nathan slapped Jesse on the back so hard he almost knocked him down. Nathan grinned at his friend.

"Now, I didn't mean to change your plans. You know how rabbit stew is; these might turn out to be as tough as saddle leather."

"No, I found a pair of young ones. They'll be tender for sure."

"And I don't know if Darcy found any of those little green onions or not. She might use some of that store-bought garlic from Bancroft."

"That might be even better. I don't get much variety in my meals. I'm really looking forward to it."

"Sometimes she lets it boil down too low and it all

tastes scorched," Jesse said lamely as they reached the cabin door.

"What are you telling him?" Darcy said, looking up at his words. "I never served you a burnt meal and you know it."

"He was just telling me that you're a fine cook, Miss Darcy. He was bound to be teasing about the part you heard. I know I'm looking forward to tasting that rabbit stew at supper tonight."

"Supper?" she asked, looking up at him. "Did you say supper?"

"Nathan has decided to stay on a few days," Jesse said carefully.

"Here? I mean, how nice. We surely don't get many visitors. So far you're the only one," she stammered, "and I want you to feel welcome."

"Why, thank you, ma'am. I do indeed." He grinned down at her. "Maybe tomorrow I can scare up some elk. I might as well stock your smokehouse while I'm collecting pelts."

"Thank you, Mr. Stoddard," she said weakly. "I'm much obliged."

"'Nathan,' ma'am," he boomed jovially. "Trappers don't stand on formalities any more than prospectors do."

"Nathan," she repeated dutifully, her eyes searching Jesse's face for help in getting rid of their guest.

Jesse gave a slight shrug and said, "I guess I'll go start a fire in the smokehouse."

"There you go, Jesse," Nathan agreed as he again shouldered the deer. "I'll have this buck ready to hang in no time."

Darcy slowly quartered the rabbit into the stew pan and wondered how she would get through the nights to come.

The next few days were strange ones for Darcy. She found Jesse's company becoming more and more strained, while Nathan became friendlier each day. He had a thousand tall tales, each one more intriguing and unbelievable than the one before, and she found herself thinking of him as she would a brother. As Jesse grew quieter and more sullen, Nathan grew even more verbose until the cabin rang with Nathan and Darcy's laughter.

Each night grew steadily more difficult. It was all Darcy could do to lie in the same bed with Jesse yet not touch him. She had developed the painful habit of waking to watch him sleep. He looked so vulnerable then, so gentle. She wanted to reach out and smooth his tumbled hair, but her stubbornness and pride prevented her. If he didn't want her, she had no intention of forcing herself upon him. Yet the nights were long and were becoming harder to bear.

Still, after six days Nathan showed no signs of leaving. Most of his pelts were rolled in bundles of salt to green-dry, but the skin of the black bear he had killed less than a mile from their cabin was nailed to the barn, fur side down. Each day he spent several hours scraping away the bits and pieces of meat to reveal the white hide beneath. On two occasions she helped him rub salt into the hide after his day's work. Darcy could tell that Jesse didn't approve, but she saw no reason to let his unreasonable moods interfere with her courtesy toward their friend.

Darcy had continued the habit of her daily swim. She found it soothing to float lazily in the cold, clear water, and it helped her order her thoughts for the strain of keeping up pretenses in front of Nathan. One bright and sunny morning, as she paddled with growing expertise around the pond, she pondered Jesse's strange behavior. Although he seldom spoke more than a few words to her, he frequently praised the bedrock of their marriage to Nathan. He praised it so often, in fact, that Darcy had seen Nathan looking at Jesse as if he had lost his wits. Yet Jesse showed no more inclination than ever toward putting their marriage on a normal footing. In fact, she often noticed him staring at her with an odd, haunted look on his face. He was acting strangely toward Nathan, too—almost as if he were watching him as well.

Darcy took a deep breath and dipped under the water. The cold liquid washed over her head, making her ears feel curiously muffled and her hair float in masses above her. She opened her eyes and peered through the clear water to the sandy bottom. Small fish skimmed below her feet and fantastic miniature forests of water grasses and mosses dotted the floor. But nowhere did she see any gold. She stayed down as long as she could, then kicked her way to the surface. She had no fear of the water at all, but she longed for company in her swims. If only Jesse would bend just a little.

She swam to the shallows and waded up onto the bank. Taking her time, she dried her slender body and toweled her hair. Then she dressed and sat on the grass to coax the tangles from it. By the time all the knots were combed free and her arms ached from the effort, the wind had all but dried her hair. She wound it into a coil and pinned it in place before she stood and picked up her soap and towel.

Instead of going back the way she usually went to the cabin, she wandered downstream. Not ten yards into the woods she saw Jesse, his back to her, leaning against a tree.

"Jesse! What are you doing here?"

He jumped and turned to face her. "Nothing. I was just passing the time of day."

"All by yourself? Where's Nathan?"

"Down there a ways, toward the sluice."

Darcy looked back at the swimming hole, now hidden from sight by the trees. "Were you watching me?" she asked suspiciously.

"Of course not. Would I do a thing like that?"

"I don't know. Would you?"

"No, I wouldn't. A lady has a right to her privacy. I was making sure Nathan didn't come this way by accident and see you."

Darcy looked up at him in puzzlement. "Why not just tell Nathan where I am and that I'm bathing? He would stay away."

Jesse's expression darkened. "How do you know? It seems to me you understand a lot about him for the short time you've known him."

"Oh, for goodness sake, Jesse," she said with a

laugh. "Nathan's easy to get to know. He'll talk your arm off if you let him."

"I've noticed."

Darcy tipped her head to one side and her mouth flew open, aghast. "You're jealous!" she exclaimed. "That's it, isn't it! You're actually jealous!"

"Don't be ridiculous!" he snapped. "I don't have anything to be jealous of, do I?"

She laughed delightedly, her fingers to her lips. At last she understood his sullen silences and the odd way he watched Nathan and her. Jealous! That meant he must care for her at least a little. "Jesse, I never dreamed you felt that way!"

He scowled at her and restrained himself with difficulty. He had not intended for Darcy to know he often followed her to the pool in case she met with a bear or one of the few Indians that still roamed here. Since Nathan's arrival, he had followed her every day. So far Nathan had kept his distance from the pool—he was not overly fond of bathing—and Jesse had slipped away unseen as soon as Darcy started back to the cabin. Only her unexpected change of route had revealed his presence. But now she knew he was jealous and she had even laughed at him! At least Marlene had had the decency to pretend innocence when he saw her making eyes at his friends! As for that matter, why *had* Darcy chosen to come this way? He knew Nathan was fishing not far downstream, but did she? A cold knot gripped his middle as he glared down at her laughing face.

"I don't see anything funny about it!" he ground

out between clenched teeth. "Go on back to the cabin and let me get on with my work."

His angry tone swept the amusement from her and she stared at him. "There's no need for you to talk to me like that," she said flatly.

"Isn't there? Then get going!"

Darcy's anger flared and she threw down her soap and towel and put her fists on her hips. "You have no right to order me around, Jesse Keenan! I can walk anywhere I please. I can stay right here all day if I want to!"

"No, you can't!"

Glaring at him, Darcy picked up her towel, shook the leaves off it with an emphatic pop and spread it on the ground. Abruptly she sat down on it cross-legged and knotted her arms across her chest. "I'm not budging until you do!"

Jesse only hesitated a minute before he sat down opposite her in the middle of the trail. "I can outwait you any day of the year!" he proclaimed.

Darcy clamped her lips shut and refused to answer. Already she was wondering how she had placed herself in this predicament and was hoping Jesse would tire soon and leave. He looked as implacable as the trees around him and just as likely to move. This made her even angrier and affirmed her resolve to sit there until snowfall if necessary.

"Well, now what—" Nathan said as he came up behind them. "Jesse, what on earth are you doing? Miss Darcy, are you all right?" He moved toward them, looking from one to the other.

Darcy glanced up and felt a deep blush rush across her cheeks. Of all the ridiculous things for company to see them doing! She started to scramble to her feet but looked at Jesse just as she was about to rise. The triumphant gleam in his eyes sent her back down to the ground.

"Here, let me give you a hand," Nathan said, reaching for Darcy. His gesture sparked Jesse and he got to his feet just as Darcy was aided by Nathan. "What on earth were you two doing? I never in my life saw anybody but Indians sit down on the ground like that!"

"We were just talking," Jesse said tersely.

"Yes," Darcy said with equally clipped tones. "We were talking."

Nathan looked from one to the other. "I didn't interrupt anything, did I? I sure didn't mean to burst in on an argument."

"Nonsense," Darcy snapped. "We never argue. All happily married couples do this." She grabbed her towel and slapped it over her arm. "Good morning, Nathan, Jesse." With her head held high, she strode toward the cabin.

"You know, Jesse," Nathan said slowly, "sometimes I don't think I understand women at all."

"I don't know where you ever got that idea," Jesse snorted. "That seems to imply they can *be* understood!" He cast a glare at Darcy's rigid back, then struck out downstream toward his sluice.

Chapter Eleven

DARCY WALKED QUIETLY THROUGH THE WOODS, PICK-ing the hard rosehips from the wild rose brambles that tangled upon themselves by the stream. The gurgling of the nearby water blended harmoniously with the whispering of the shiny leaves above her. Most of the wild roses had burst into bloom and the pink blossoms had fallen to the ground, leaving behind a good crop of rosehips for tea. She had already harvested a large sackful and soon would have enough to see them through the winter. When added to water, the rosehips made a tea as good as any she had ever tasted, and it was a delicacy Jesse particularly liked.

Since their argument the day before by the swimming hole, she had more or less ignored Jesse. She was still angry that he felt he had the right to talk to her the way he had, and she was also deeply embarrassed that he had been the means of an outsider seeing her temper. She suspected she was being unreasonable, but she didn't care.

She was almost upon Nathan before she saw him. The burly man was sitting on a fallen log, his rifle resting across his lap. Darcy jumped at his slight movement, then, recognizing him, let out a deep breath.

"You scared me," she said. "I had no idea anyone was around."

"Sorry, ma'am. I was waiting for a deer to come down to water and I thought you saw me. I didn't mean to startle you."

"I'm fine now. I had my mind on something and wasn't paying any attention to my surroundings." She came over to the log and sat down beside him. "Summer won't last much longer, will it? I saw a tree already turning red up on the far slope."

"No, fall's on its way." Nathan glanced at her profile and said with studied casualness, "If you don't mind my asking, how are things between you and Jesse?"

Darcy shot him a quick look. "You don't mince words, do you!"

"No, ma'am. I found it's too hard to figure out who means what. It's like a man once told me: If you want to know which is a skunk and which is a kitty cat, just pick one of them up. You'll find out which it is a whole lot faster than if you stand around trying to guess."

She suppressed a smile. "Sounds to me like that's a dangerous way to learn."

"Yes, ma'am. It surely is. Now what seems to be the trouble?"

Darcy gazed off into the woods and sighed. Back

in Plymouth a question so blunt would not likely have been asked; and if it had been, she would have put him firmly in his place. Here on the mountain it was all different. "I don't know," she answered. "At first I thought he just didn't like women. Now I think it's me he objects to. I've tried every way I know to be a good wife,"—she blushed and her speech faltered—"but he keeps me at arm's length. He likes me as a partner, but not as a . . . a wife." She ran her fingers through the rosehips and fought against her embarrassment.

"You mean he won't—" Nathan began.

"Please, Mr. Stoddard! Don't elaborate!" she exclaimed, lapsing into formality as a defense against Nathan's lack of shyness.

Nathan pursed his lips and narrowed his eyes at the same trees she was observing so closely. "That sure doesn't sound like Jesse. Why, before you came we were the wildest—" He choked off his words as he recalled Darcy was Jesse's wife as well as his partner. "What I mean is—"

"I know what you mean," Darcy said quickly. "What I don't know is what to do about it."

Nathan thought carefully, then said, "Well, now, I may be talking out of school, but he did tell me something once that you might ought to know." He dropped his voice as if someone might overhear him. "He told me this in confidence and I never let it out to another living soul. I wouldn't now, except that it's causing more grief than it's worth. You see, Miss Darcy, Jesse was engaged once several years ago. She was a lady born, but she did him dirt. Had no more morals than a possum. Not near as much, in fact."

"Jesse was engaged to be married? He never told me that!"

"No, ma'am, he wouldn't. He only told me because old Charley Three Toes slipped us some bad moonshine. It's a small wonder we lived through it. Anyway, it seems he caught this Marlene—that was her name, Marlene—with some of his papa's friends the very night they announced their engagement."

"So that's why he acts as if I'm not to be trusted!" she gasped.

"That's right. See, it hurt him real deep."

Darcy stood and gripped the handle of her basket. "Now I understand! What a terrible thing that must have been to him!"

Nathan propped his gun against the log, slapped his big hands on his knees and pushed himself up. "I don't know why he's so closemouthed about it. A woman like that would do the same to any man, not just him." He reached out and patted her shoulder awkwardly. "Now maybe it will all—"

Jesse's hand grabbed Nathan's arm and spun him away from Darcy. With an agonized cry Jesse swung at Nathan's jaw and felled him in one blow. Darcy screamed as Jesse lunged at the trapper, his fists flying.

As soon as the astonishment fell away, Nathan gave a roar and grabbed Jesse in a crushing bear hug that squeezed the air from his lungs with a whoosh. When Jesse's struggles weakened, Nathan shoved him away. "Get back to the cabin, Miss Darcy,"

Nathan yelled. "We have a difference of opinion we need to work through."

Darcy backed away a few steps, then turned and ran for home. By the time she reached the small cabin, her breath was coming in ragged gasps and she had a painful stitch in her side. She flew in the door and grabbed the table for support as she gulped air into her burning lungs. Over and over again she saw the fury of Jesse's face that gave lie to the raw pain in his eyes as he had gone after Nathan. Again and again she heard the resounding chorus of Nathan's words. Words that explained Jesse's jealousy in terms all too clear. No wonder he never trusted her! Darcy pressed her hands to her lips and shut her eyes tightly. Bending from the waist as if she were in physical pain, Darcy remembered the battle rage in Jesse's face as he attacked Nathan—a man nearly twice his size—in order to keep him from touching her. Trembling all over, Darcy prayed, but for whose safety she wasn't sure.

After what seemed hours but must have been only minutes, Darcy saw a movement at the edge of the woods. Her bloodless lips moved silently and she took a step forward. Recognizing the man, she ran to meet him.

"Jesse!" she cried out. "Are you hurt? Where's Nathan!"

He ignored her and brushed her aside. Going to Nathan's bedroll, he scooped it up along with the pack of traps and went back out the door. Darcy stared after him, her heart pounding painfully in her chest. "Jesse!"

At the edge of the woods he stopped and tossed the trapper's gear as far down the trail as he could. Turning, he went back to the cabin past Darcy and grabbed the two bales of pelts. Again he went to the woods line and threw them after the other gear. He turned on his heel and strode purposefully back toward the cabin.

Darcy ran to meet him. "Jesse! Jesse! Answer me! Where is Nathan! You didn't . . . you didn't kill him, did you?"

Jesse didn't pause in his stride but bent and threw Darcy onto his shoulder and continued silently back to the cabin. He kicked the door shut behind them and drove home the heavy bolt that locked it. Still carrying Darcy, he jerked down the blanket wall and dropped her unceremoniously onto the bed.

"Jesse!" she cried in fright as he threw himself down beside her. "Jesse, where's Nathan!"

Jesse roughly held her chin in his hand and in a clipped voice said, "He's back there in the woods. Don't worry—I didn't kill him."

Darcy relaxed somewhat, but the anger written on Jesse's face made her tremble. "It wasn't at all what you thought, Jesse," she tried to explain.

"Don't tell me what I thought," he snapped. "Did you two think I was so blind you could put something so obvious over on me?" His deep voice was hard and biting, but agony lay like a veil over his eyes. "I trusted you!" he managed to grind out. "I trusted you both!"

Suddenly Darcy saw his pain and her fear left her. "Jesse," she said softly, "I would never do you wrong. What you thought there was between Nathan and me never happened!"

"You can't expect me to believe that! I saw him touch you. I've been watching the way you two are always talking. Laughing together. Did he ask you to go away with him?"

"No! Of course not! And if he had I would have said no!"

Darcy felt her own anger rise and she tried to roll away from him.

He jerked her back. "You're my wife, Darcy! I won't let you go!"

"You mule-headed ox! I wouldn't go if you threw me out!" Darcy's temper flared to meet his and she struggled in his strong arms. "I only talked to Nathan because you wouldn't talk to me. All you do is roam around with a sullen look on your face. How can I laugh with you when you're acting like that?" She shoved against his shoulder with all her might, but he didn't move.

"I don't believe you."

"What?" she exploded. "Ask Nathan if you don't believe me! Go on—ask him!"

"I did. He said the same thing."

"And you still don't believe me? Of all the stupid, ridiculous . . ." she sputtered in frustrated fury, unable to find a name bad enough to call him. "Turn me loose!"

"So you can go to him? Not likely! If it's attention you want, it's attention you're going to get!" He pulled her face around to his and kissed her forcefully.

Darcy fought against him as she felt her body becoming eager for what had so long been denied her. Even as she felt her pulse quicken eagerly, she recalled the long, empty nights when she had ached for his touch, even for a soft word. As a tremor ran through her she tried to cling to her righteous anger, but her body and then her mind betrayed her.

Jesse kissed her thoroughly, deeply, drinking in the sweetness of her breath and lips. When her mouth parted involuntarily he took the advantage and drew her more securely into his embrace. He let his tongue explore the softness of her mouth as he ran his hand down the curves of her body. Under his skillful touch she began to yield and her struggles grew less forceful. He left her lips and kissed the smooth column of her neck, feeling her pulse race against his lips. When he nibbled at the hollow of her throat, she gave a scarcely audible moan and he again claimed her lips.

Knowing she fought a battle she no longer wished to win, Darcy again pushed against him, but her shove became a caress as his kisses turned her skin to flame. Her stubbornness melted before his assault, and as she began to return his kisses, he became gentler. Slowly she let her arms slip around his neck and then ran her fingers through the darkness of his hair.

His hands glided along her slender back and pulled her against him as he stroked her narrow waist. When he felt her move toward him of her own will, he raised his hand to cup the swell of her breast. As he teased her nipple to tautness she moved eagerly against him. Slowly, slowly, Jesse unbuttoned her dress and drew it off her shoulders. Lifting her hips from the bed, he eased the garment from her and in one lithe movement pulled off his own shirt.

Gazing down at her, he ran his fingers along the swell of her breasts as they strained against the thin cotton of her chemise. With maddening slowness he removed the rest of her clothing and let his eyes feast on the wonders of her body.

Darcy's breath came quickly as she felt his eyes rake over her nakedness, and when he reached out to take her breast in his hand, she trembled. Still he made no move to lie beside her or to hurry in his scrutiny of her. Darcy forced herself to lie still beneath his gaze.

After several long minutes, Jesse removed his boots, socks and pants, then lay beside her on the bed. Still his eyes searched hers as if he would find an answer in their brown depths. When she could stand it no longer, Darcy lifted her hand and pulled his head down for her kiss. As thoroughly as he had claimed her lips, she now took his. Waves of desire rushed through her as he teased her nipple to aching ecstasy. When he lifted his lips from hers, he traced a trail of kisses down to her breast and began to send rivers of fire coursing through her as his tongue urged her nipples to even greater tautness. Darcy arched her back to bring herself even closer to him as he drove her to heights of delight she had never felt before.

A soft moan of pleasure escaped her and he lifted

his head to smile down at her. Darcy knotted her
fingers in his thick hair and raised her head to kiss
him deeply, lingeringly.

Jesse rolled over, carrying her with him so that she
lay across his deep chest. Carefully, he pulled the
pins from her heavy hair and let it cascade in dark
waves over his hands. Loosened, it framed her
heart-shaped face and made her look even smaller,
younger somehow and more vulnerable. It lay
against his tanned skin like sheaves of dark silk, and
the softness of it sent flames of desire through his
body. Jesse wrapped the long strands around his
hand and gazed deeply into her eyes. Gently he
rubbed her hair against the velvet skin of her cheek.

"Jesse," she said so softly he scarcely heard her
words. "I will never leave you. You couldn't drive
me away because you see, I really do love you."

A dark shadow passed behind his eyes and she
reached up to place her hand on his cheek. "Don't,"
she whispered. "Don't mistrust me. I will never be
untrue to you."

He turned, pulling her beneath him so that his
long body covered hers and her soft breasts pressed
tantalizingly against his chest. Once more he silenced her with his lips. As his large hand stroked
the smooth roundness of her hip, he lifted his head
to look at her. She lay silhouetted in the dark pool of
her hair, her pale skin in creamy contrast to it. If
only he could believe her, he thought. But such a
thing was impossible. Only an hour before she had
been alone with Nathan in the woods.

"I love you," she said longingly.

Jesse put his fingers to her lips to gently quiet her. When he took them away she sighed and her brown eyes held a deep sadness. Slowly he bent and kissed her until he again felt her passion quicken. As he brought her to a need as great as his own, Jesse felt a burning lack he had not experienced since the first days after he had broken his engagement with Marlene. He yearned to believe her, to convince himself that her love could really be believed. That she would want him and no one else but him.

Jesse kissed her with an urgent passion and drew her higher and higher into the whirlpool of desire. When at last he entered her, Darcy cried out in her need and moved against him instinctively, melding her flesh with his. When she reached the peak of her desire he felt his own body respond with a shattering burst of pleasure that made his own moans blend with hers. He held her tightly as he felt the need drain from him, only to be replaced by a warm depth of love he had never experienced before.

He rolled to his side, still cradling her in his arms, and kissed her forehead, her temple, her closed eyelids. "Darcy," he murmured into her hair. "My Darcy."

"Oh, Jesse," she whispered as she rubbed her cheek against the corded muscles of his shoulder. "Please let me love you, even if you can't love me."

He lay still, his cheek against her hair, his thumb lightly stroking her chin. "I want to love you," he said at last. "But I can't let myself. You see, I've been in love before. Engaged, as a matter of fact. But she made a fool of me. I pledged myself to her

141

and her alone, only to find out later that she was in and out of bed with a half dozen men during our courtship. I didn't give my love or my trust to her easily, and I was *sure* she loved me. But she made me a laughingstock."

Darcy nodded and said carefully, "You must have been hurt terribly. I'm sorry. But, Jesse, I'm not like that."

Jesse kissed her forehead and laid his cheek back against the soft pillow of her hair. "If I could believe that I would be the happiest man alive."

"But you can!"

He was silent for a while. Then, "I believed her, too."

Darcy felt a desolation pass over her. Would she always have to fight a ghost? Dully, she asked, "You didn't hurt Nathan too badly, did you?"

With a sigh, he moved his hand to rest on her hip. "Are you all that worried about him?"

"Don't start that again. He's our friend. I don't want him to be badly hurt."

"He's not. I just knocked him out."

She raised up on one elbow. "You did what?"

"I hit him with a tree limb."

"You may have killed him!"

"No, I didn't. Do you think I'd do that to a friend?" He frowned up at her. "I've hit him harder than that before."

Darcy stared at him. "You're sure he's all right?" She had never before known two men who treated each other so roughly.

"Sure he is. Hell, as big as Nathan is, you couldn't

fell him with anything less than a tree limb. He's as hard-headed as that red mule of yours." He looked at her closely. Her eyes were guileless, her face innocent, but she seemed to be protesting far too much. He had already told her Nathan was not hurt. Jesse's eyes narrowed suspiciously.

"I don't want you hitting my mule, either," she said stiffly.

"Your mule doesn't give me as much cause as Nathan," he pointed out.

"Just the same, you ought to go look after him."

Jesse sighed and moved away from her to sit up. Tiredly, he ran his fingers through his hair. "You want me to do that for you?"

"I want you to do it for yourself!"

With resignation, Jesse stood up and pulled on his clothes. Without a word he left the cabin. Darcy lay on the bed, looking up at the rafters and wondering how to convince Jesse that she could be trusted. After a while he returned and looked at her from across the room.

"He's gone," he said. "So is his gear. I guess he went on up the mountain to his own place."

Darcy moved over and gestured to him. "Come here, Jesse. Please."

He looked long at her, then did as she asked. When he sat beside her on the bed, she stroked his arm and said simply, "Thank you."

"Like you said, he's my friend. I'd have gone anyway."

"I still thank you." She took his hand in both of hers and kissed his palm.

Chapter Twelve

Jesse looked down at Darcy, who was still curled against his side. In the dawn light her skin was pearly white and looked as smooth as fine satin. The masses of her dark hair tumbled unrestrained about her face and shoulders, forming a cape of silk to frame her. Her fully rounded breast was brushing his arm and Jesse felt an almost overwhelming desire to wake her once again with kisses. But in the morning's light she was not only the sensuous vixen who urged him to greater and greater passion, she was also his friend and partner. And this recalled the reason for their tumultuous lovemaking the evening before.

Nathan. Jesse was certain his friend was unhurt. Angry, perhaps, at being felled by a tree limb, but not injured. Jesse knew Nathan's cabin was up Wolf Creek about three miles in a grove of pine trees. Not hard to find at all. If he and Darcy planned to be together, she need only travel upstream until she saw his house. Jesse frowned. He wasn't at all sure she hadn't proclaimed her love and fidelity in order to save her own skin. Certainly his anger must have frightened her—it had even frightened him. And she had insisted that he check on Nathan. Why hadn't his word been enough?

His conclusion must be right, but then what could he do? Jesse lifted a dark tendril of her hair and let it curl about his fingers as he thought. He couldn't watch her every minute, and if she wanted to go to Nathan she would find a way to get out of his sight. The mere thought of losing her sent a sharp stab of pain through him. Not now. Not when he had come to love her more than anyone else in his life.

Darcy moved in her sleep and her lips lifted in a smile as she dreamed. She snuggled closer to him and slid her bare arm across his lean stomach.

Jesse's teeth clenched as he resolved he would not lose her! He could not!

Quietly he eased out of bed and pulled on his clothing.

Darcy was dreaming of Jesse. They were running like children through a field of red clover, hand-in-hand and laughing. He pulled her to him and kissed her as a warm summer breeze blew about them. Then he whistled and a great white horse galloped up and they leaped onto his bare back to race across the field. The dream horse's large hooves beat a rhythm in the clover as his snowy mane whipped against her. Yet somehow his hooves sounded louder and louder—steady, but not in the pattern of a horse's gait.

Groggily Darcy opened her eyes. The pounding continued. She saw at a glance that Jesse was not in the cabin and she sat bolt upright. The hammering noise was coming from the direction of the door.

"Jesse?" she called out doubtfully.

"Out here," he responded.

Darcy smiled quizzically. What could he possibly be doing out there? She drew the sheet off the bed to use as a wrapper and went to pull open the door. It seemed to be stuck. She yanked harder.

"Jesse, the door won't open," she called out. "Push from that side."

He quit hammering and answered, "I want you to stay put today, Partner," he called out. "I need to get some panning done. Nathan's visit put us way behind on our work. I took enough venison for my noon meal, and I'll come home about sunset."

"What are you talking about?" She shrugged off the sheet and used both hands on the latch. When it remained shut tight, she hurried to the window. By standing on her tiptoes she could get her chin above the windowsill. "Jesse Keenan, what are you doing out there!"

He smiled at her guilelessly. "Morning, Partner. You sure are looking good today. Did you sleep well?"

"Don't you make small talk with me," she said crossly. "Just open the door and let me out."

Jesse tossed his hammer down beside his small keg of nails. "I can't do that, Partner. I need to work and

I can't spend all my time worrying whether or not you're heading up the mountain."

"Up the— Are you standing there telling me you think I'd . . . Jesse Keenan, you open this door right this minute!" She ran back to the door and jerked repeatedly at the latch.

"Can't do it, Partner. Tell you what I'll do: I'll go downstream and work that shallows where the elderberries grow and bring you back enough to make a pie. See you tonight." Whistling, he strode off toward the river.

"Jesse!" she yelled, aiming a kick at the door. "You let me out!" She raced back to the window and jumped up to stretch her vision enough to see him leaving. "Oh!" she exploded. *"Oh!"* She grabbed the first thing her hand fell upon—his shaving mug— and hurled it at the door. It cracked neatly in two and the cake of soap and brush rolled under the table.

Unable to sit still in her fury, Darcy pulled on her clothes and began pacing back and forth in the confines of the small cabin. So he dared nail her in, did he, she fumed. She would get him for that! A chair got in her way and she kicked it across the room. Caged like an animal! She came as close to actually seeing a red haze of anger as she ever had in all her life. Again she went to the window and hopped up and down to see the river. He was out of sight.

Frustrated with anger, Darcy slammed her chair up to the table and made herself a cup of beechnut coffee. Propping her arms on the table, she glared at the door. Locked in! She took a sip of the hot liquid and grimaced as it burned her tongue. He had no trust in her at all! To even think for a minute after last night that she would follow Nathan up the mountain!

Darcy glared at the tiny window, then looked again with greater interest. It was built high under the eave of the roof so that the interior of the cabin was protected from rain, yet it still allowed a good bit of light. No glass stood between her and the outside, and a teasing breeze wafted through it. Slowly Darcy stood and walked over to it. It was small, but still . . .

She measured the opening with the span of her hands, then tried to compare it with the width of her hips. It would be close, but it might be wide enough. She pulled the table over to it and carefully climbed on top. Up close she could see that there was no way she could sit on the sill and swing her body through, but she might make it if she went out head first and trusted her luck.

Quickly Darcy pulled off her dress and kicked her petticoat to the floor. In only her chemise and bloomers she was much thinner. Hoping the table would continue to hold her weight, Darcy eased her head and shoulders out the window. A quick glance told her Jesse was still out of sight. She turned to face the house and sat on the windowsill while she tried to find a secure handhold on the roof. It was made of corrugated tin hauled up from Bancroft, and she had at one time been glad of its solid construction. Now she wished for something on which her fingers could get a better grip.

Cautiously she wiggled farther out until only her legs from the knee down remained inside. She brought up one leg and managed to pull her foot over the sill. But the ground was several feet farther than her toes could reach.

Darcy looked around for a better way out, but there was none. Her glance fell on the door and the newly bright nails that secured it and her eyes hardened. Not caring what harm she might do herself, Darcy pulled her other leg as far out as she could and turned loose.

Getting down was easy, but the landing knocked the breath from her lungs. For a moment she lay still trying to catch her breath and wondering if she had broken anything important in her fall. Gingerly she moved her arms and legs and sat up. The wind was cold through her nearly transparent chemise and the ground felt damp beneath her bloomers, but she was none the worse for her escape. She stood triumphantly and dusted off the grass and dirt from her as well as she could.

Taking up the jimmy that protruded from the keg, she began pulling out the nails. Jesse had only driven two and it didn't take her long to remove them. The door then swung open easily. Darcy went in and put back on her dress and petticoat, then began to gather up all of Jesse's belongings. She wadded up his extra clothes, along with his coat, hat, and old boots, and threw the bundle into the yard. His plate and coffee mug followed to clatter on the ground. She kicked out his bedroll and found satisfaction when it unrolled and sprawled crookedly in the grass. His chair she tossed out in an arc that landed it upside down by the path. His razor, shaving brush, soap and hairbrush followed. She even threw out his towel and the woolen blanket that had once walled his bed from hers.

With a decisive nod, Darcy took up the hammer and nails and went back inside, slamming the door behind her.

Jesse filled his hat with elderberries, shouldered his sluice box with the shovel inside and headed for the cabin. He had had plenty of time to think and he was somewhat afraid he might have been too hard on Darcy. After all, she had never tried to leave him before and she had not attempted to run to Nathan after the fight. Certainly she had loved him in the night as if she had no one else on her mind. Surely no woman could be so convincing as she had been in his bed in the intimacy of the darkness unless she meant it. For this reason Jesse had decided to go home early and forgive her.

As he neared the cabin, his eyes narrowed. Was that a chair lying over there? Why were clothes strewn all over the yard—*his* clothes? Jesse quickened his step. When he came to the chair he stopped and stared down at it. It was his chair, all right. But why was it out here? He bent and lifted the corner of his bedroll and stared at it in perplexity. How had Darcy managed to shove all this through a window so high she could hardly see out of it? Especially the chair. It was much too large to fit through such a small opening.

Frowning, Jesse went to the door and lay down the sluice box. His nails and hammer were nowhere to be seen, and there were two raw holes in the door where nails had been. For the first time it occurred to Jesse that something might have happened to Darcy in his absence.

"Darcy?" he called out, pushing against the door. It didn't open. "Darcy!"

"Yes, Jesse?" she called out in honeyed tones.

His frown deepened and he said, "Open the door. Why are all these things out here?"

"I put them there," she replied with syrupy sweetness.

He rested his hands on his lean hips and looked from the door to his belongings and back to the door. "Well?" he said finally. "Unlock the door."

"Oh, it's not locked, Jesse," Darcy sang out. "It's nailed shut. It seemed like such a good idea to you that I thought I'd do it, too."

"Enough is enough, Partner. You've had your laugh. Now let me in."

"Can't do it, Jesse. I put that whole keg of nails in the door. It would take me until dark tomorrow to pull them all out again."

"*All* of them? Why in the hell did you do that, Partner?" He was trying hard to control his anger until he could get in.

"Seemed like a good idea to me." She was quiet for a while, then said, "It's a real shame you can't taste this quail I baked. I used those little green onions like you like for the sauce and I made a pot of red beans and a big pan of cornbread. Wasn't much else to do in here all day but cook."

"This has gone on long enough, Darcy. Let me in."

"Didn't you hear me, Jesse? I told you I can't open the door."

"What about my half of the cabin, Darcy? It's not right to leave me out here!"

"Right, did you say?" her voice called out sweetly. "It seems right to me. If you look around you will see all your things are out there where you can use any or all of them."

He growled ominously deep in his throat and shoved hard against the unyielding door.

"It won't work, Jesse," she said helpfully. "I know. I tried that this morning."

"How in the hell *did* you get out?" he demanded.

"Through the window, but you won't fit. You're much too big."

"So are you!"

"Not without my clothes on I'm not."

Jesse's mouth gaped open. "You mean to tell me you . . . Darcy! Did you crawl out that window buck naked!" Jesse was as shocked as if this had occurred in downtown St. Louis.

"Close enough," she confirmed in clear tones. "This cornbread really is the best I ever made. Steaming hot, too. Say, Jesse, do you suppose we might be able to get us a cow? I do miss butter and milk. Maybe some chickens, too."

"Stop talking like some fool farmer's wife and let me in!" he roared.

"You have a short memory, Jesse. I never noticed that about you before. You're probably right about the chickens. Some possum would probably make off with the eggs and a bobcat would likely have a chicken supper the first night we turned them loose. It would take a real big possum to carry off a cow, though. You might want to ask about one next time you go down to Bancroft."

"All right! I've had enough, Darcy. I'm going to break this door down!"

"I sure wouldn't try that if I were you, Jesse," she sang out. "But you go ahead if you think you ought to."

Jesse backed off several feet and flexed his shoulder muscles. The tantalizing smell of food gave him even greater determination. Lowering his head like a charging bull, Jesse ran at the door and threw all his weight against it.

Darcy looked up from her plate at his yelp of pain and the expletive that followed. She smiled smugly. "See, Jesse?" she called through the solid door. "I told you that wasn't a good idea."

Only silence met her and she cast her eyes toward the door. After a while she called out, "Jesse? Are you still out there?" Still there was no answer. Darcy got up from the table and went to the door to listen. She could hear no sound at all. "Jesse?"

When he didn't answer she put one hand tentatively on the door and held her ear closer. Surely he couldn't have hurt himself too badly by running into a door. She went to the window and tiptoed to peer out, but she could see nothing.

Then she heard the first whack of steel on wood. He was chopping his way in! Feeling fear for the first time, Darcy put her fingers to her lips. Had she gone too far? Again the heavy ax thudded against the door and she heard the wood splinter. The next blow let the tip of the ax gleam through and she stifled a cry of fright.

Quickly she went to the table and sat back down. Her only chance was to bluff her way through and hope he wasn't as angry as she had been earlier. As the door gave in and shredded before Jesse's onslaught, she watched in fearful fascination. Jesse ripped the remaining lengths of shattered wood from the door and stepped into the cabin.

"Cornbread?" she asked in tones far calmer than she felt.

He stared at her, then looked back at the door. She had indeed used all the nails, and he ran his hand down their shiny heads embedded in the wood. Slowly he shook his head and looked back at her.

Darcy swallowed nervously. "The beans are still hot if you care for any." She was determined not to show her fear.

Jesse leaned the ax against the ruined door and nudged the empty keg with the toe of his boot. He shook his head slowly as if he were perplexed, then crossed the room to the table. As he sat down, he glanced back at the door and flexed his bruised shoulder.

Darcy got a serving platter down from the shelf and spooned beans onto it along with one of the golden-brown quails from the spit. The food looked small on the large platter, but his plate lay outside in the grass. She put it in front of him and said, "Coffee?"

He looked long at her, his dark eyes probing into hers. Then he sighed and nodded. After she had poured some into her cup for him, she sank down across from him on the stool. He said casually, "Looks like we're going to need a new door before winter. That one has a hole in it."

She nodded and answered with studied casualness, "You're right, Jesse. It does for a fact. Cornbread?"

He nodded. While he ate he looked at the door and the gathering dusk beyond. "You're right about the cornbread. I believe it is the best I ever tasted." After a while he said, "You know, Partner, there must be an easier way for you to tell me things." He was still looking at the door.

Darcy moved uneasily. "If there is, I haven't found it yet."

"Maybe you're right. I never was fond of that door anyhow. It always did stick when it rained." He turned back to his platter and Darcy saw the light of amusement in his eyes.

A wave of relief washed over her.

"A cow, huh," he said conversationally. "Maybe we could manage that." He lifted his head and grinned at her. "But you have to milk her."

"I don't know, Jesse," she smiled. "Who ever heard of a prospector with a cow? We could pull up stakes any day, you know."

He shrugged. "If we do, we can use her for a pack animal. She's bound to be better than that old red mule of yours." Their eyes met and he grinned at her.

"We'll see, Jesse," she said. "We'll see."

Chapter Thirteen

DARCY PLUCKED THE GLEAMING PEA-SIZED NUGGET from the shallow pan and dropped it into the small pouch she wore at her waist. It was the third one she had found that day. She straightened her back and stretched to relieve her aching muscles and looked over at Jesse. The last two days had been wonderful ones in which he had often smiled at her or found some excuse to come talk to her as she did her chores. The nights had been filled with passion that tapered to tenderness, and she had slept the remainder of the hours in the protective circle of his arms.

A magpie flew over their heads making a raucous cawing sound. In the distance Darcy heard another answer him in faint, discordant notes. A quail in the valley below whistled hopefully, but his call went unanswered.

"Jesse, what do you suppose birds say to each other," she said, sitting on a boulder and staring dreamily into the distance.

He glanced at her but kept working at the sluice. "I don't know the answer to that, Partner."

She unbuttoned the neck of her dress to let the breeze cool her throat. "I think they probably pass the time of day pretty much like people do. You know, where's the best place to hunt grubs or whether the weather's in for a change."

Jesse grinned. "You sure heard a lot in such a short bird call. I never knew you spoke the language so well."

Darcy leaned back on her elbows and squinted up at the sky. Above her, the oddly twisted pine was silhouetted darkly against the blue and its stubby needles made deep green tufts along its gnarled fingers. "How do you suppose that old tree grew so bent?" she asked idly.

"I imagine some mean-hearted bear came along when it was just a sapling and chewed it into that shape." He glanced at her sideways.

"I never heard of a bear eating trees," she said before she caught the twinkle in his eyes. "Oh, you're teasing me!" She tossed a pebble at him. "That sounds like one of Nathan's tall tales."

Nathan. Jesse frowned and bent to his work. "Most likely a winter storm twisted it," he said at length.

Darcy looked at the panorama of horizon that lay along the end of their valley. "Are the winter storms very bad here?" she asked with studied casualness.

"No worse than anywhere else in the Rockies," he answered. "They can get pretty rough, though. Are you as afraid of snowstorms as you are thunderstorms?"

"I don't like any storm at all," she told him uneasily as she sat up and hugged her knees to her chest.

"Well, don't start worrying about it now. It was so bad last year we are probably due for a mild winter this time, Besides, our cabin is warm and sturdy."

Darcy sighed and tossed another pebble at him experimentally. It bounced off his arm and landed in the sluice. "I wish there were a place, somewhere, that didn't have storms. There's nothing in the world that I'm more afraid of."

"Not even of having to go back to your Aunt Petra?" he teased.

"Pooh! I've gotten so mean from living around you that she couldn't even get my attention." Darcy grinned at him. "I sure would like to see the two of you together, though." She lobbed a dry twig at him.

"I'd have her cooing over me in ten minutes. You know what a way I have with women, Partner. Ouch!" he exclaimed as a larger rock hit his arm. "Watch it!"

"Your wife threw that one," she informed him primly. "Not your partner."

He playfully splashed a stream of water at her. "Better watch it, woman." he pretended to growl.

Darcy tossed another stick at him. "I'm not scared of you, Jesse Keenan," she announced.

"Oh, no?" He came plunging across the shallows, sending sprays of water in all directions.

With a delighted shriek, Darcy threw one last pebble and slid off the rock to run for the woods with Jesse in fast pursuit. He caught up with her in the aspen grove and trapped her in his arms. Laughing, he spun her around for his kiss.

Darcy met his lips with an eagerness that matched his own. When Jesse pulled the pins from her hair she laughed in sheer delight and shook her head until her hair tumbled in rich, deep brown waves to her waist. Jesse knotted his hands in the thick tresses and tilted her face upward to meet his lips.

"I never will find that lode at this rate," he murmured into her neck.

"I don't care," she answered with a smile.

"Wanton hussy," he commented as he nibbled at her earlobe.

Darcy laughed and tickled his ribs until he burst out laughing. As she wheeled to run away, he grabbed her around the waist from behind and pulled her back. "Oh, no, you don't!" he said, tickling her in return. "You started this and you're going to stay to finish it." He bent and lifted her easily in spite of her playful struggles. As he carried her to a patch of emerald moss that encrusted the aspen roots, she entwined her arms around his neck and teased his ear with the tip of her tongue.

"Stop that or I'll drop you!" he exclaimed with a chuckling grimace.

Gently he lay her on the bed of moss and began to slowly unbutton her dress. She was a miracle of loveliness, her cheeks flushed from their play, her eyes sparkling with happiness. All around her the velvety moss rolled over root and rock and was studded with minute white violets. Jesse brushed aside her clothing and lifted her shoulders, then her hips, to pull it away from her.

Darcy's fingers loosened the buttons of his shirt and then his trousers as he shrugged the shirt from his broad torso. As he removed his pants and boots, she ran her fingers caressingly down the hard muscles of his back. Above his head the bright aspen leaves whirled and shimmered in a breeze, many of them already shading to gold and tinged with russet.

"Soon it will be too cold to do this," she murmured.

"I'm hurrying as fast as I can," he replied, tossing his pants into a heap beside her dress.

"You goose," she laughed. "Whatever would Aunt Petra say if she saw me now?"

He grinned down at her. "From all you've told me about her, she would probably have apoplexy."

Darcy traced his taut chest muscles with one finger and drew her fingernail across his deeply tanned nipple. "I probably have no sense of shame nor decency," she said in mock seriousness.

"Probably not," he agreed as he lowered his head to kiss her deeply.

The world swam around Darcy as she felt her body respond to the warm probing of his tongue. Her own tongue met his and she in turn explored the smoothness of his inner lips. Jesse left a trail of fiery kisses down her throat and nuzzled the softness of her breasts. His hands were caressing the rounded swell of her breasts and his fingers insistently teased her nipples to urgent hardness. When he lowered his head to flick the peaks with his tongue, she moaned in ecstasy. Jesse chuckled at her obvious delight and took one throbbing nipple into the warm recesses of his mouth.

Darcy threaded her fingers through his hair and held him to her, feeling a searing desire that grew more and more a need with each movement of his lips. The sweet torment raged in her and she arched her back to bring herself even closer to him.

"Please, Jesse," she whispered as his hand stole lower to further awaken her womanhood. "Please love me now."

He nudged her legs apart and knelt between her thighs, drinking in the sight of her swollen breasts crowned by the rosy buds of her erect nipples, the hunger for him that was mirrored in her fathomless eyes. She reached out and stroked his fully awakened manhood and Jesse could wait no longer.

He claimed her body and she gasped in delight as she felt him fill her and begin to move inside her. "Jesse, Jesse," she murmured in his ear as she clung to him. In perfect rhythm their bodies moved together in the ageless ritual of love. When she felt she could not bear another moment of bliss, she was hurtled into the timeless explosion of passion that rocked her in throbbing waves of sheer pleasure.

Spent, she held him close and gloried in the warmth that still seemed to be coursing through her. She could hear his breath coming quickly against her hair and she moved slightly so he could roll to his side, still holding her in a tender embrace. Darcy stroked his long arms, reveling in the muscles that, though relaxed, were firm beneath her hand. She rubbed her cheek contentedly against his shoulder and felt his lips brush her forehead. With all her heart she felt her love for him blossom inside her, but she prevented herself from speaking the words. She couldn't ruin this moment of closeness by speaking of her love. Experience had told her that he would only grow distant if she did. Only this marred her newfound contentment. Resolutely she put aside the unpleasant thought. She turned her head and kissed his chest as she ran her hand over his flat stomach. Jesse smiled and stroked her hair from her face before he pulled her back to the pillow of his shoulder.

"You know, Partner," he said softly, "I sure am glad you came up that mountain."

"So am I, Jesse. I am for a fact."

"You know, Jesse, a large porch would be nice," Darcy said as she gazed across the valley. They had quit panning for the day and were enjoying the final moments before sunset. She was peeling and slicing potatoes for supper as she spoke.

"You want a bigger porch?" he asked as if he had never heard of such a liberal idea.

"Yes, I would. And maybe a rocker, too. So when we sit out here in the evenings and watch the sunset, I could rock."

"I should have known that any woman that would buy a red mule would want a big porch and rocker." He grinned at her.

"Don't you start in on my mule," she warned. "Flower can hold her own against any mule you ever saw."

"Flower?"

"That's her name."

"Since when?"

"Since now. I named her that because she's pretty."

Jesse shook his head and his grin deepened.

From the woods nearby came a lone bird's call that seemed to emphasize the quiet rather than break it. Darcy sighed happily and reached for another potato. The sunset had filled the valley below with a rose light that softened the greens of the pines and mellowed the vast distance beyond the mountain peaks. Clouds of blue-gray had gathered along the horizon and pillared upward like castle turrets against the vivid sky.

"Look, Jesse," Darcy said, holding up a long curl of potato skin. "I peeled it without breaking it. That means we'll have good luck."

"I thought that was a saying about apples."

"If you get a whole apple skin it means you'll marry your true love," she scoffed good-naturedly. "I thought everybody knew that."

"That's not the way I heard it." He gazed dreamily off into the hazy distance.

Darcy thought a minute. "Maybe you're right. Anyway, it's lucky either way." She sliced the potato into the bowl of cold water in her lap. "Do you think this is enough?"

He glanced at the bowl. "Maybe one more small one. I'm hungry tonight."

A distant rumble, more felt than heard, caused Darcy to look up. The clouds were even taller now, though the sky above was clear.

"Looks like they're getting some rain over toward Wilmont," Jesse commented.

"I hope it stays there."

He snorted. "Some farmer's wife you'd make."

"I don't mind rain," she defended herself. "Just storms."

Far away lightning illumined the clouds from within, but no sound reached the cabin. "I guess this is plenty of potatoes," Darcy said. "I'll go in and put them on to boil."

"Wait a minute." Jesse caught her skirt as she hurried by him. "You can't go all your life being afraid of a little lightning." He pulled her into his lap, took the bowl from her and set it on the doorstep beside them. "Look," he said as the clouds again seemed to explode silently from within. "Can't you see the beauty in that? They are like thunder ships sailing in the sky."

Darcy reluctantly looked where he pointed and leaned back in the circle of his arms. "I guess they do look a little pretty. From way over there."

He hugged her and said, "Let's watch the clouds some more now. We can eat later. Maybe it will help you to stop being afraid of storms."

A jagged finger of lightning gouged a far distant mountain. "I doubt it," she affirmed.

A pale gray veil of rain began to fall from the clouds and slant downward to the lower valley. A hawk, out hunting for his supper, was briefly silhouetted against the storm cloud, then dipped lower and vanished against the darkening trees. In a clearing Darcy watched as three elk emerged cautiously from the pines to scent the air. She pointed silently at them, though they were much too far away to hear even a shout. Jesse nodded and smiled at her.

"I love it here on the mountain," she said as she leaned her head against his shoulder. "I could never go back to living in a city."

"You don't miss being able to shop and visit with friends?" he asked as he placed a kiss near her ear.

"No. I never did much of that anyway. Whenever I had some spare time I usually walked by the sea."

"Do you miss that?"

"I was afraid that I might, but I don't. At times I remember how peaceful the waves sounded hitting against the beach or how the gulls sounded, but I don't regret leaving it."

He drew a deep breath of the crisp, pine-scented air. "I hear you can smell salt in the air near the sea."

"After you live there awhile you don't notice it anymore. It's not like it is here where the smells change with the seasons. Does that mean you've never seen the ocean?"

"In St. Louis? And someday you'll stop noticing the scent of the seasons here, too."

"Not me. I'll never stop that. And one of these days I'm going to show you an ocean."

"I'd like that." He tightened his arms about her. "I like knowing you," he said softly. "You're the best friend I ever had."

Darcy turned her head to smile at him. "You're my best friend, too." But in her heart she longed for more than his friendship. She wanted his love.

As if he read her thoughts, a veil of sadness deepened his eyes and he looked thoughtfully back toward the valley.

Only the upper slopes of the craggy mountains were still bathed in the pink-gold light. The valley lay swathed in deep purple shadows and the sky behind the clouds was darkening to navy. An occasional flicker of light showed the boundaries of the nearly invisible clouds, but even that was quietening under the hand of night.

Darcy patted his hand that lay on her waist. "I guess the performance is over," she said as she stood up. "Let's go start supper."

Jesse got up and rested his arm across her shoulders as they went into their house.

Chapter Fourteen

THE FIRST SNOWS FELL, LIGHTLY FROSTING THE HIGHER reaches of the mountains and leaving them with a grizzled countenance not unlike that of an old man who needed a shave. A few flakes drifted down the slopes to the cabin but they were fleeting things and soon gone. Jesse had set the glass-paned window into the opening in the wall several weeks before when it appeared that winter had come to stay, and now the pane was frosted over against the cold wind.

Darcy sat across the table from Jesse with her chin propped on her clasped hands, intently watching as Jesse lathered the shaving soap over his face. "Do you do that for me?" she asked as he carefully scraped away a swath of lather, holding the straight-edged razor deftly in his left hand.

"Nope," he said, contorting his face into a smooth plane for the razor. "I do it for me." He grinned at her. "And for you."

She watched the familiar ritual in silence for a while. "Doesn't that hurt?" she asked as he shaved under his chin.

"Only when I draw blood. By the way, Partner, do you know what time it is?"

After a glance at the window, Darcy shrugged. "I guess it's getting close to seven o'clock. Why?"

"I mean what time of the year. It's time to go down to Bancroft for our winter supplies. Do you want to come with me?"

"Do I! You just try to stop me," she said in answer to his teasing tone. "I'm not about to let one of Prairie Belle's beauties get her hands on you."

He sloshed the razor clean in the pan of hot water. "Take my word for it, they're no beauties."

"I don't want to hear about it," she said firmly. "When can we go?"

"How about today?"

"Today? Do you mean it?"

"Sure. Get your bedroll together and a change of clothes while I saddle the horses and harness that fine red mule of yours."

"Just like that?"

"Why not? Do you have something else planned? A tea party or a sewing bee, perhaps?"

"I'll hurry!" Darcy drew the water pot from the fire and pulled the logs apart with the poker. A shower of red sparks danced up the chimney and the smell of wood smoke filled the room. It took her very little time to bundle her clothes into her bedroll and tie it into a long roll that would fit behind her saddle. She then prepared Jesse's and looked around to see what else needed attention before their return.

She wrapped her fur-lined cape around her and fastened the front of it snugly to block the wind. Silently she thanked her friend Nathan for leaving her the tanned bear skin as a wedding gift. Her gloves were also fur-lined, made from rabbit skin, and reached halfway up her forearms and well under the edge of her cape. She pulled on a heavy wool knitted cap and snugged it down over her ears.

The wind outside was whipping wintery gusts that felt as cold as the snow it promised, but the sky was a clear, robin's-egg blue. Darcy lowered her head against the wind and went to meet Jesse at the barn.

Jesse took one final tug on the cinch of his horse's saddle and tied the end securely as he nodded to Darcy. Her horse nickered softly to her and Flower flapped her long red ears in welcome before nuzzling her with her velvety nose. Darcy patted them both before getting into the saddle. "Why are we going today?" she asked as Jesse mounted his bay horse and took up the lead rope that tethered Flower to the other mule.

"We'll have snow soon. I should have gone down last week, but the river was too obliging with its gold."

"You did remember to pack it, didn't you?"

"Yes. At least, I have all we're going to show in Bancroft. It's enough to buy anything we may want, but not enough to start word of a strike. We don't want a pack of prospectors moving up to work the river all around us. I tied the packet of nuggets on my mule's harness. I didn't want to weight Flower down, since my mule will have to pull her down the mountain, more than likely."

"Flower isn't the stubborn one around here," she retorted with a meaningful look.

"I know, but you're riding on the horse," he teased.

"Don't push your luck, Jesse Keenan." She nudged her horse from the barn and firmly turned the mare's reluctant steps down the path. "How long will we be gone?"

"At least one night, maybe more if you want."

"I can hardly wait to see Clara again. She married the man who owns the general store. Goodness knows what has happened to the other women I knew on the wagon train. I wonder if they are still in Bancroft or if they've moved on."

"If they're still in town Clara will know it," Jesse remarked philosophically. "There's no place else for them to buy supplies."

He led the way down the mountain with Wolf Creek racing them on their right side and large trees hovering overhead. The bare limbs made a silvery lace against the sky and brittle leaves long since fallen eddied beneath the horses' hooves. Darcy lifted the collar of her cape against the wind and tucked the lower edges securely around her legs.

"It's cold today," she called out.

"Not as cold as it will be," he assured her cheerfully.

In the months that had passed since she first

climbed the mountain, Darcy had nearly forgotten the tortuous steepness of the trail. Even without ice or rain to contend with, the horses often slipped on the declines where slick rocks jutted out beneath sheets of dead grasses. By the time Darcy saw, over the treetops, the thin threads of smoke that marked the location of Bancroft, she ached from the exertion of staying in the saddle. Clouds of pale steam puffed from her mare's flaring nostrils and her pace was no longer eager.

Soon they rode out of the encircling woods, and directly below and in front of them lay the boom town of Bancroft. The small meadow that flanked the town and through which all roads passed was rutted and gouged from the constant travel of the work animals hauling heavy mining equipment and wagon loads of ore. Numerous deep scars of raw earth lay gaping toward the sky, abandoned by the miners in search of more likely claims. The path Darcy had traveled in the wagon train was wider now and rutted so deeply that, as they crossed it, their horses had trouble keeping their footing. And everywhere she looked, Darcy saw people. The cacophony of their bustling activity pounded against her ears after the peace of the mountain and she felt an unreasonable tremor of fear.

Jesse's face was grim as he surveyed the ruin the town had sown on the mountain. Buildings weathered gray from exposure to the harsh elements staggered down both sides of the narrow street with no thought or planning toward appearance or even permanence. The names of the various establishments were painted in crude letters on their fronts, occasionally with a descriptive picture for those miners who were illiterate. All sizes and shapes of men crowded onto the street and elbowed for room among the crowd and the horses and oxen. Here and there he saw an occasional Chinese with a bag of laundry slung over his back, or tired-looking women who navigated the crowd as well as they could. But for the most part, he saw only miners, their faces streaked with the grime and soot of their profession.

He motioned needlessly for Darcy to stay close to him and guided his horse toward the assayer's office. When he dismounted and tied his horse at the rail, Darcy quickly did the same. She was all too aware of the stares from several men within the building and she had no intention of letting Jesse out of her sight in such a threatening crowd. He went to his dark brown pack mule and unstrapped the bag of gold. As he did so a gust of wind lifted the corner of his wool poncho and Darcy saw to her surprise that he was wearing a pistol.

Although Jesse hadn't been obvious about it, Darcy realized he was fully aware of all the activity about them. When two scruffy miners seemed to be sidling too close to the horses, Jesse's hand moved toward the lower edge of the poncho and his expression became threatening. The men ambled back toward the building and continued on their way.

Darcy followed close behind Jesse, stepping cautiously over the rock-hard ridges of the reddish clay ruts. It had not rained recently and the dirt was as unyielding as stone. She followed Jesse inside and immediately felt uncomfortably hot after the frigid air outside. A pot-bellied stove glowed almost orange on its bed of rocks and a handful of grimy men were gathered around it.

Jesse went to the man who sat behind the scarred desk in the corner and lay his bag of gold in front of him. "How are you doing, Quince?" he said amiably but with an air of coolness.

"Fine, Mr. Keenan. Just fine," Quince said, glancing up through the wire frames of his glasses. "Is your claim still holding up pretty well?"

"Fair to middling is all," Jesse said conservatively. "Seems about to peter out, if you ask me."

"Yeah, they all are around here." Quince opened the pouch and spilled the contents onto the desk top. "Wouldn't surprise me none if we all had to move on soon."

Darcy stood silently while Jesse exchanged his raw gold for currency and kept the concealing cloak wrapped tightly around her. She was still uncomfortably aware of the men's scrutiny. When Jesse had completed his business he took her arm possessively and escorted her out.

In only moments they were indoors again as the general store occupied the other end of the same long building. Darcy felt much more at home here. It, too, was warm, but not stifling like the assayer's office; and although there were quite a few men here as well, there were also several women. As Darcy loosened her cloak and removed her gloves, she looked about her. Along one side was a polished pine counter, its surface laden with bolts of gingham in yellow, blue and red, and there were spools of cotton thread hanging at the end. A metal ball with string dangling from its opening and another one containing a heavy twine sat by the long roll of brown wrapping paper. Behind the counter were smaller items arranged on narrow shelves. A large barrel of crackers and another one of pickles stood at the end of the counter that housed the various dried or canned foods. The larger sacks of beans, rice and flour were stacked along the back row as were the bags of livestock feed. Plows, washtubs and washboards hung on the whitewashed walls and merged with the smaller items such as colanders, baskets, mixing bowls and pots. Pans for washing gold and several sluice boxes vied for space with bags of cornmeal and slabs of salt. It was all an orderly jumble and one that only its proprietor could hope to decipher.

"Darcy?" a woman's familiar voice called out from behind the counter. "Is that you?"

"Clara!" Darcy hurried across the store to embrace the large, rawboned woman. "It's so good to see you again. This is my husband, Jesse Keenan," she said proudly as Jesse came up.

He nodded to Clara and tipped his hat as he gave her a slow smile. "I've heard a lot about you, ma'am. All good."

"Go on with you," Clara beamed and blushed. To

Darcy she said, "I was beginning to think something might have happened to you. When you didn't come back down the mountain I was fearing the worst."

"We live in a cabin up there on Wolf Creek, and it's as pretty a spot as I've ever seen. You can see all the way down the valley from there." She smiled up at Clara and asked, "Is all well with you?"

Clara laughed heartily. "All that worrying I did was for nothing. My Hiram is as good to me as the day is long." She leaned close to Darcy's ear and whispered, "I'm going to be a mama come spring!"

"Really? Oh, Clara, that's wonderful!" Darcy hugged her again.

Jesse had moved away to let the women talk, and as he browsed he cast glances at Darcy. She was a beautiful woman, he thought uneasily. Far more beautiful than any woman he had ever seen. How long could he expect her to be content on the mountain? He had been all too aware of the men's attention toward her in the assayer's office and he felt jealousy pierce him. Not that Darcy would ever look twice at one of them, but how long would it take before she began to long for the niceties of the eastern cities, for a social life and the ease of having servants to do her chores? She was a woman, and experience had told him that women required fancy clothes and doodads and above all the company of other women. Sadness lay heavily around his heart at the very thought of her leaving him. Almost angrily, he began throwing their supplies into the gunnysacks he had brought.

As Clara tallied up their purchases she and Darcy

kept up a steady stream of conversation. Jesse tried to look interested as he learned that Elsie was also pregnant and had moved on to Central City with her husband, and that no one had seen or heard from Crystal since she was claimed by the trapper. Jesse wondered who these people were. Darcy had seldom mentioned anyone but Clara, or if she had, he didn't remember it. Yet they had evidently been a significant part of her life for at least the months spent on the wagon train. Jesse tried not to feel left out of her confidences. It was his own fault, he supposed. He had never asked her many questions about her former life for fear of learning the lecherous "Cousin Marcus" had been only one of a series. When she had proved to be untouched, he had ignored her past for fear of learning she had married him on the rebound from some unrequited love. Perhaps, he thought, he should get to know her better.

When the account was settled, Jesse hesitated. To sleep in the wild town with all their winter's provisions would be foolhardy. Had Darcy not been with him, Jesse would have started back up the mountain and slept on the slopes when it became too dark to see, but it didn't seem right to tear Darcy away from the only woman friend she had seen in months.

"Could we leave these here while we are in town?" he asked Clara. "I'd be glad to pay for storage."

"Why, I wouldn't hear of charging you a cent! You put it all in that back storeroom there and just pick it up before you leave town."

When Jesse shouldered one of the large sacks and

went back down the hall, Clara nudged Darcy. "You sure got a fine one. Did you have any idea what he looked like before you came out here?"

"No. I was just lucky," Darcy said with a proud glance at Jesse's broad back.

"Lucky's not a strong enough word," Clara assured her. Then on a more solemn note she asked, "Are you happy?"

"Oh, yes. I'm very much in love with him." She laughed. "He calls me Partner."

Clara nodded. "It's clear to see he loves you, too. I never saw a man look at a woman like he looks at you."

Darcy blushed. It wouldn't do to tell Clara she must be mistaken. She had learned that people always saw what they wanted to see, and above all Clara wanted her to be as happy as she was herself.

"Look at you!" Clara boomed. "As rosy cheeked as any bride and all because someone noticed your man loves you. You and my Hiram would make a pair—as sentimental as the day is long, both of you." Jesse was coming back down the hall and Clara made a shooing motion with her hands. "Go along now, you two, and see some of the nightlife. Store up some memories for the long winter."

Darcy hugged her again and placed a kiss on her cheek. "It's so good to see you again. We'll be back tomorrow."

Jesse again tipped his hat and said, "It's been a pleasure, ma'am."

"You call me Clara, beings you're Darcy's husband. Don't stand on formalities around here."

"All right, Clara. We'll see you and your husband tomorrow."

When they stepped out onto the street, the evening mine shift had changed and even more men clogged the darkening road. Lights poured from the many saloons and from the windows above, and the tinny sound of a badly played piano mingled with the drunken shouts. Jostling against Jesse and Darcy, the begrimed men, many still sweat-stained from the heat of the deeper mines, hailed friends with gusto. Darcy wrapped her cloak tighter about her and leaned against Jesse for protection.

"I've seen all the nightlife I care to see," she called up to Jesse against the noise. "Do you mind?"

"I'm glad to hear that. Let's see about a place to sleep." He steered her across the street to a row of tents, collecting their horses and mules on the way.

After wrangling at the makeshift hotel, Jesse procured them a tent belonging to a miner who worked the night shift. It had cost him extra, but he made sure they would have the shelter to themselves during the night and that their livestock would be cared for in the nearby stable. At the owner's directions, they counted back twelve tents from the street and Jesse cautiously pushed back the flap to look inside. When he was sure the tent was empty he called to Darcy, "Come on in out of the wind."

Darcy ducked inside and pulled the flap shut behind her. It was a small enclosure with barely enough room to either stand erect or to lie stretched out. Rumpled quilts were strewn across the crude bed frame and the lamp's chimney was black with soot. Darcy eyed the bed warily and picked up a quilt by one corner, using her thumb and forefinger.

"I'm not sleeping on that," she announced firmly.

"Neither am I. Toss the bedding into a corner and we'll spread our bedrolls on the rope frame. It won't be very comfortable, but we won't take away any fleas or lice."

Shuddering, Darcy prodded the quilts and thin mattress into the far corner as Jesse brought in their bedrolls. She untied them and spread them on the bed, draping their extra clothes on the rough bedposts.

She waited nervously inside the tent while Jesse hurriedly led the horses and mules to the stable to see that they were fed and watered. He cautioned her that she should be as quiet as possible while he was gone so as not to attract attention to herself, but his warning was unnecessary with her recollection of the leering stares she had already gotten. When he returned, she jumped, then smiled wryly. Town life was frightening after the solitude of the mountain.

Without even bothering to light the ill-used lamp against the gathering night, she took off her brown wool dress and hastily pulled on her warm nightgown. Exhaustion was fast overtaking her as she stretched out on the bed. Jesse secured the tent flap and pulled off his poncho. With a casual movement he removed the gun belt and lay it on the floor beneath the outside of the bed.

"You take the side next to the tent," he said.

Darcy didn't argue and slid over to make room for him. When he lay down fully clothed she raised up on one elbow to look at him. "Are you going to sleep like that?"

"I will feel more comfortable if I can jump up at any minute. Bancroft always makes me nervous." He grinned at her worried expression and brushed her hair from her face. "Go to sleep. I'll worry for both of us."

"How can I sleep with you talking like that?" she scoffed. "I doubt my eyes will close all night!"

He pulled her head down to his shoulder and said, "Whatever you say, Partner."

Within minutes she slept and soon he dozed, too. But his rest was fitful, and even the slightest sound jerked him to readiness. At one point two miners seemed likely to shoot each other just beyond the beige canvas of the tent. Jesse tensed, wondering what would be the best way to protect Darcy against their stray bullets, but soon their quarrelsome voices faded into the cacophony of Bancroft's night and he let out a long sigh.

Dawn found Jesse no more rested then when he lay down, and the dark circles under Darcy's eyes told she had not slept much better. Wordlessly they dressed and rolled up their bedrolls in order to be gone before the miner completed his shift. Darcy shivered in the cold morning air and wondered how long Jesse would want to stay in this bedlam.

Darcy followed Jesse back to the main street. In spite of the early hour, the nasal piano music still leaked from the saloons, and here and there a gaudily dressed woman lounged in the opening of a tent. One gave Jesse an appraising stare, then turned away when Darcy glared at her. As they passed the Yellow Dog Saloon, Darcy did a double take at the sight of one of the street women.

"I know her," she exclaimed aloud. "She was on our wagon train!"

Jesse pulled her back around as one of the miners looked at her appreciatively. "Well, now's not the time to strike up an acquaintance. Keep walking."

Darcy stumbled along by him. At the assayer's office two bearded men were arguing loudly over the location of a claim. She quickened her pace lest they be caught in the gunfire which might be used to solve the dispute.

"Jesse, can I ask you something?" Darcy said as she dodged a team of mules.

"Of course you can."

"How much longer do you plan for us to stay in Bancroft?"

"That's up to you," he said with grim determination. "We will stay as long as you're enjoying yourself."

"Enjoying myself? Me?" She stopped in her tracks and stared at him. "I'm just staying because you want to!"

Jesse studied her face. "You mean you don't like it here?"

"Jesse Keenan, I hate it here! Let's go home."

"What about Clara? We haven't even found whatever her name was—Elsie. Don't you want to visit some more?"

"Good heavens, no! You heard Clara say that

Elsie moved on, and there's no telling where Crystal may be. I've already seen Clara and there's nobody else I made close friends with. Please, Jesse, could we leave now?"

He looked down at her beseeching face and then smiled. "Sure, Partner. I'm more than ready to leave."

Within the hour Jesse had packed the mules with the provisions and Darcy was telling Clara good-bye. "You take care of yourself now, you hear?" she told the older woman. "Next time I see you I want to be able to play with that baby and spoil him rotten."

"Surely you'll be back down the mountain before that," Clara protested. "I have until next spring."

Darcy hugged her friend as Jesse came out of the store. In spite of her dislike of Bancroft, Darcy found it hard to part from the only woman she had spoken with in so long. "I'll be back down before you know it," she told her. "Good-bye, now."

Clara's pale eyes were wet with unshed tears as she stepped back from Darcy. She patted Jesse's arm and directed, "You take good care of her. There's not another one like her."

"You're right," he beamed. "I'll see to it that she stays safe and sound."

They mounted their horses and both waved to Clara as they negotiated a trail across the street. Darcy seemed unusually quiet as they passed the gutted meadow and started up the path by Wolf Creek. Jesse rode in worried silence, glancing back from time to time to see if Darcy's expression might be more revealing. At the clearing above town, Darcy abruptly reined in and turned to look back down at the mining village.

Jesse hesitated a moment, half afraid to ask, but did so anyway because he had to know. "Are you regretting coming with me?" he asked gruffly. "If you are, I'm sure Clara can put you up until the next wagon train heads east."

She cast him an exasperated look. "Jesse Keenan, for a smart man you sure say dumb things. I was just thinking that if I had wavered half an inch either way my finger would have landed on a different name and I would be the wife of one of those miners."

"You might have loved him, too," Jesse said testily.

"No, I would have had to live in Bancroft," she said as if that proved it. "From here it doesn't look quite as unattractive. Maybe if we go high enough up the mountain it will even look pretty."

"This mountain isn't that tall," Jesse answered grimly. "By the way, I bought you something." He dug deep in his pocket and held out his closed hand to her.

Darcy let him drop the object into her palm and drew in her breath in amazement. It was a small gold locket engraved with twining leaves and flowers, and it opened at her touch of the tiny clasp. Inside there was room for two miniatures or space for a lock of hair.

"Oh, Jesse! It's beautiful! Give me your knife."

"What for?"

"Just give it to me."

When she had it, she caught a lock of his thick, dark hair in her fingers and neatly cut if off.

"Ouch! That hurt," he said, rubbing his scalp.

"Don't be such a baby," she admonished as she tucked his hair into her locket. "There now. Doesn't that look nice?"

"If I had known you planned to scalp me, I would have thought twice about getting it for you."

She handed him back his knife and slipped the chain around her neck. "Thank you, Jesse. It's the most beautiful gift I ever had." When she looked up at him, tears glistened in her brown eyes.

"Well, I guess it didn't hurt all that bad," he conceded. "And the locket does look nice on you. When I saw it on the shelf in Clara's store, I just knew it belonged to you."

Darcy stroked the locket that was already taking on her body heat and dropped it into her bodice for safety. "Let's go home. I want to thank you properly."

He grinned and pulled his horse's head around. "I'm all in favor of that!"

Chapter Fifteen

THE FIRST REAL SNOWFALL WAS A LIGHT ONE WITH BIG, puffy flakes that drifted silently from the silver clouds. By afternoon the ground was covered with a pristine powder, and small drifts banked against the cabin and filled the crevasses between the rocks.

As soon as the last flakes settled to the ground, Jesse had gone hunting for deer to restock the smokehouse. Darcy worked for a while at some knitting she had brought back from Bancroft. It was heavy wool yarn the color of a cardinal's wing, and she was trying to surprise Jesse with a new sweater for Christmas. She had already drilled holes in some halved walnut shells for the buttons. But her mind wouldn't stay with the simple knit-and-purl stitch, and again and again she found her eyes wandering to the frosty pane in the window. Finally she put her knitting back in the box and pushed it far beneath the bed where Jesse would be least likely to look.

Bundling up snugly against the cold, she went out into the snow. Her breath made a cloud of smoke whenever she breathed, and the cold air made her face tingle and her eyes feel moist. Since Jesse had said he would be hunting toward the pine woods out front, she circled around behind the cabin and followed the path to the pond.

The tall trees made a canopy of lace above her, the silvery limbs of the aspens intertwining with the deep greens of the pines and firs. An occasional breeze ruffled the fluffy needles, sending an aromatic scent in its wake. Now and then a more persistent gust stirred the bare limbs of the other trees and they moved reluctantly, their branches stiff with the cold.

Darcy walked down the familiar path, now grown so altered with snow. Her boots made very little sound in the fresh snow and left a pattern of dark tracks behind her. She saw several trails made by rabbits, squirrels, or the numerous chipmunks, and once she found a paw print where a lone wolf had loped across the path.

At the edge of the swimming hole's clearing, Darcy hesitated, unwilling to mar the unbroken blanket of snow. Slowly she skirted the tree line until she came to the water and stood gazing down at it. The rapids tumbled as vigorously as ever, but the water was now a froth of white on black. The pond where she had learned to swim was a still, ebony mirror with seemingly endless depth. Crusts of ice clutched at the roots and the dried hairlike grass that lined the bank, and even the plummeting waterfall did little to stir the surface. The rocks above the falls and along the far bank were wetly dark, and only the red and orange lichen encrusted on their rough surfaces gave a hint of color to the scene. No rainbow hung between the falls and the leaden sky, and the only sign of movement beyond the water was a solitary buzzard that circled in wide arcs, riding the high currents of the wind.

Darcy wandered through the woods, gradually working her way back to the cabin but being careful not to stray into the area where Jesse was hunting. Idly she picked a spray of red berries from a bush and a few short twigs of spruce to brighten the cabin. The serenity of the woods was unbroken except for the faraway tapping of a woodpecker.

Back at the cabin she arranged the berries and spruce in an old bottle and placed it on the table. She thought it was as nice an arrangement as any she had ever seen.

The sound of Jesse's shout brought her head up and she hurried to the door. He waved at her from across the clearing, a small deer, already dressed out, slung across his back. He went into the smokehouse to hang the meat to be cured, and a puff of gray smoke followed him out again.

Darcy watched him fasten the door to the shed; then, acting on impulse, she scooped up a handful of snow, packed it firm and threw it at him.

Jesse ducked instinctively, but the snowball hit him squarely in the back. Another followed and he gave a surprised gasp. Darcy's laugh brought a grin to his lips and, leaning his rifle carefully against the shed, he suddenly wheeled and ran at her like a charging bear.

He grabbed her around the waist, sending her over his shoulder, and dashed across the yard to dump her in a snowbank. Panting, he pinned her beneath him and grinned down at her. "Had enough?"

She lay still a minute to gather her senses from his unexpected attack. "Not quite," she retorted, rolling away from under his arms.

Jesse grabbed at her and missed, falling into the snow she had just left. Darcy laughed and threw another snowball that powdered the back of his hat. Jesse scrambled to his feet in a flurry of snow and ran after her. Intent on staying out of his reach, Darcy ran around the woodshed and behind the smokehouse, throwing another snowball at him as he nearly caught up with her.

Dodging back the way he had come, Jesse circled the smokehouse and caught her backing toward him. Triumphantly he swooped her up and ran, with her squealing in pretended fear, to the barn, which was the nearest building. He shouldered open the door and went in to kick it shut behind him. Unceremoniously, he dumped her in the loose hay and threw himself on top of her. Unmercifully he nuzzled the ticklish hollow of her neck until she gasped for breath.

"Give up!" he demanded, breathing as hard as she was.

"Never!" She tried to run her hands under his coat to tickle him back, but he grabbed them and pinned them over her head.

"Give up or I'll kiss you until you do!" he growled playfully.

"Never!" she repeated with a laugh. "I'm no fool!"

He effectively silenced her with his lips and held her firmly until she struggled to hold him closer rather than get away. She met his kisses with eagerness, the warmth of his breath tantalizing against her cool cheek.

"I'll never give up," she whispered melodramatically when he raised his head. "Never, never, never. You'd better kiss me some more."

With a chuckle he complied, exploring the warm softness of her mouth with his tongue. She returned his ardor and wrapped her arms around his neck. The pungent hay was billowy beneath them and the heat from the animals in the nearby stalls warmed the air until the barn was nearly as warm as the cabin.

Jesse removed her cloak and spread it out, fur side up, as a blanket for them to lie on. "You aren't too cold, are you?" he asked as he shrugged out of his coat.

"No. I seem to be getting warmer by the minute." She laughed as she kicked off her shoes and snuggled down on the cloak.

She lay there, looking up at him, a half-smile on her face. Jesse leaned on one arm and gently ran his fingers across her lips, marking her happiness with his touch. In her eyes he saw the love she felt for him, and, in spite of himself, the old knot of wariness seeped through him. Had she ever looked at another man in that way? Marlene had. And often, if he could believe the words of his friends who had tried to warn him. He had been so sure he loved her and that she had loved him. Now he was even more in love with Darcy. Did that mean she would hurt him even more than the false Marlene? His troubled emotions warred within him, making his face lined and his eyes pools of pain.

"Jesse," she whispered as he gazed down at her. "Don't look at me like that. You can trust me." She could see all the doubts and fears as clearly as if she could read his innermost thoughts. It hurt her to know he still didn't trust her, and she felt a stab of anger at the flighty girl who had thus scarred him toward love. "I'm going to make you forget," she vowed. "I'm going to love you until you can't even remember her name, Jesse Keenan. And one of these days you're going to realize you love me more than you ever dreamed you loved her!"

Closing his eyes, Jesse kissed her hungrily and pulled her pliant body closer to mold it against his own. He hugged her desperately as if he feared she would slip away and rubbed his face against her hair. When she reached behind him and pulled out his shirttail to run her hands over his bare back, Jesse moaned. A passion seized him and he began almost feverishly to unfasten her buttons.

Darcy matched his eagerness and pulled off his shirt and pitched it onto the hay. Unable to wait, she helped him remove her clothing, and, as he undressed, she ran her fingers across his shoulders, his arms, his ribs. As he tossed his clothes into a heap beside hers, she nuzzled his neck eagerly, her tongue darting out to taste his skin. She knelt behind him, her nipples tracing twin trails of fire across his sensitive shoulders as she kissed the back of his neck, his ears. Her hands caressed the breadth of his chest and his lean belly, sliding lower to the fount of his desire.

Jesse rolled over, pulled her on top of him, his fingers fumbling to remove the pins in her hair. When it was released, he shook it down to cascade around their faces like a silken veil. Darcy sat across his stomach and rubbed her hair over his chest until he trembled with need of her.

When he tried to tumble her over, she pushed him back down and raised herself enough to let him enter her. As she felt him fill her, she gave a small cry of passion and leaned back to let him feast his eyes as well as his body. Jesse stroked her warm flesh, brushing aside her hair to see her full breasts. Her nipples were rosy and erect with her passion, and he rolled them gently between his thumbs and forefingers to bring them to even greater tightness. She sighed with pleasure and moved against him, her hands braced against his chest.

Unable to take his eyes off her, Jesse caught his breath at the vision of her abandoned lovemaking. His hands were free to touch her wherever he chose, to encircle her slender waist, smooth her sensuously moving hips and thighs, to return again to her pouting breasts. Urged on by his touch, Darcy began to quicken her love movements and lifted her hand to brush back her hair when it fell forward, obscuring her breasts. When he tried to pull her down to kiss her, she laughed teasingly and shook her dark mane in taunting refusal.

Faster and deeper she loved him, giving and receiving in turn all the pleasures they could imagine, spinning her emotions as well as his in an upward sweeping ecstasy. When neither could bear the tension another moment, she leaned forward to kiss him, her breasts tantalizing his bare flesh, his firm body meeting her own. At the sudden contact, they both seemed to explode together in a flame that was life-sustaining.

For a long time afterward, Darcy lay still, her body supported by his, her cheek nestled on his muscular chest. She was content to merely float there, feeling the steady rise and fall of his breathing. At last she said softly, "Am I too heavy?"

"Not at all," he murmured sleepily as he caressed her smooth back.

"Well, I soon will be." She rolled over, pulling him with her. The hay crackled pleasantly beneath their weight, and the barn's warm smells were pungent in her nostrils. As he kissed the warm hollow of her neck she plucked the bits of hay from his hair.

"What do you mean by that?" He put her fingertips in his mouth one at a time, nibbling them gently.

"I'm pregnant."

Jesse froze in his motions and stared at her. Then

he removed her hand from his mouth and said, "Say that again? You're pregnant? Just now?"

"No, no, silly. I thought I might be when we went down to Bancroft, but I wasn't certain then. So I asked Clara and she said I would know for sure in two weeks. It's been three now and nothing has happened, so I guess that makes you a Papa."

For another minute Jesse stared down at her with a stunned expression; then he exclaimed and hurriedly rolled off her. "My God, Darcy," he thundered. "What do you mean wrestling around like this in your condition! That's the damnedest fool thing I ever heard of."

"I knew you'd be pleased," she said smugly. Then more seriously she asked, "You *are* pleased, aren't you?"

"Yes," he said, looking at her numbly. Gathering her into his arms, he repeated, "Yes, yes, I'm pleased!" But he pulled away again and shook his finger in her face admonishingly. "No more of this wild behavior now, you hear me? We want our baby to be perfect!"

"He will be. With you for a father, how could he not be?"

"Pregnant!" he repeated in a stunned voice. "You're sure?"

She nodded.

Jesse pretended to frown at her. "He will probably turn out to be a hellion like his mother."

"*And* his father. He might even turn out to be a she."

Jesse's face relaxed into an uncertain smile. "A

girl. I'd like that. I want her to look exactly like you."

"I'll do my best."

He gazed down at her and said in exasperation, "Darcy, you could have picked a better way of telling me! I might have hurt you playing that roughly." He began hurriedly retrieving her clothes.

Darcy laughed and pulled his hands back to her. "Are you planning to do without me for the next few months?" she teased. "If so, you have another guess coming."

"Well, I don't want to do anything that might hurt you."

"You won't," she said with assurance. "I'm strong and healthy." She pulled him down to bury his face in her neck and whispered, "Hold me, Jesse. Tell me you really do want this baby."

He cradled her tenderly in his arms. "I do, Darcy. I really do. A baby! I just can't believe it! We're going to have a baby!"

"I love you," she whispered into his shoulder. She didn't know if he heard her or not because he didn't answer.

Chapter Sixteen

DARCY HAD BEEN THROUGH HARSH WINTERS BEFORE, both in Pennsylvania and Massachusetts, when the snow had been deep and had covered the ground for weeks before the sun returned to melt it away, but this had done little to help prepare her for wintertime high in the Rockies. By mid-November, ice crusted thick over the still waters of the swimming hole and the ground was hidden under ten inches of powdery snow. Six weeks and two moderate snowfalls later, Jesse estimated the accumulation to be between two and three feet. The pines and firs were heavily tufted following each storm but dumped their billowy masses as the frigid northwesterly wind resumed. The bare hardwoods creaked and moaned, their stiff, icy limbs drooping heavily downward, sometimes snapping as the burden became too great to bear.

As the forces of nature seemed bent on their destruction, with the wind stacking the drifts against their cabin higher with each snowstorm, Jesse and Darcy were ironically provided with a very good insulation against the freezing wind. To further minimize the loss of heat, the couple kept to the warmth of the cabin as much as possible and refrained from opening the door except when necessary. Sometimes at night Darcy would wake to the mournful howl of wolves or to the raucous yowling of coyotes, but Jesse assured her they would never attempt to come near the cabin with its feared man-scent.

As their supply of meat dwindled, bread and beans appeared more and more often as the only course at their meals. And, of necessity, Darcy had become proficient at baking sourdough bread and always kept a starter of yeast fermenting near the hearth. Although she didn't complain, Jesse often heard her sigh dismally at the red beans as she heaped her plate. With the passing months she had rounded with the coming baby, but her cheeks and arms were thinner than Jesse would have preferred. Finally in mid-January he could stand it no longer.

"I'm going hunting," he announced without looking at her.

"But the snow is too deep! Surely we can do without meat for a while longer. The snow will have to melt sometime."

"We can wait, but the baby can't. You have to keep your strength up."

Darcy ran her hand across her stomach in a reassuring caress, in the same way she had done so often of late. "I really don't want you to go."

"That's silly, Partner. I'll soon be able to track down an elk and I'll be home before you know I'm gone."

"All the elk have moved to the lowlands months ago." She was watching him fearfully, her dark eyes large in her pale face.

"A rabbit, then, or maybe a squirrel. I'll come across something out there, even if it's just those blamed wolves that keep us awake at night." He grinned at her. "Ever taste wolf meat?"

"No, and I'm not going to," she said making a face. "Really, Jesse, I don't want you to go. I have . . . I have a bad feeling about it."

"Now, listen, Partner, you aren't going to start having the vapors, are you?" he questioned suspiciously.

Darcy's smile became strained. "If I do, will you stay here where it's safe and warm and not go hunting?"

"Nope. You just faint over there on the bed so you don't hurt yourself." He shrugged into his coat and fastened the buttons to his chin, then pulled on his hat and gloves. "Don't look at me like that. I've been hunting in the snow before and you didn't worry then."

"I know, but today feels different somehow."

"It's just your condition," he said with his maddening grin. "Women in the family way are all nervous."

"I'm not nervous!" she snapped.

He bent and kissed her as he reached for his gun. "I'll be back soon."

She stood in the middle of the room and watched as he went out the door, a flurry of snow swirling into the room behind him. For some reason she felt apprehensive to the point of fear, yet it was foolish, she told herself. Jesse was always careful and he was an excellent shot. It was true that she had been rather nervous of late and short of temper in a way that was quite unlike herself. Although she never told Jesse, she was very much afraid of having her baby without another woman to aid or comfort her. She wasn't even entirely certain what having a baby would entail. Surely, she tried to tell herself, it was only these worries that were sending the prickles of fear up her back.

By noon she was no longer able to sit still by the fire and knit, so she paced the tiny cabin and straightened and dusted the scant furniture that was already spotless. She swept the dirt floor and made a design in the dirt with her broom to make it pretty for Jesse's return. She scoured the cooking pots until they were spotless inside and out and would need to be primed again before their next use. She even went over the square-hewn logs and plucked off the more obvious splinters.

Still time crept by and there was no sign of Jesse. Darcy went to the window, but frost was too thick inside and ice too heavy outside for her to see through it. She opened the door a crack and peered out, hoping to see him emerging from the woods. Instead, she saw a line of angry blue-black clouds that seemed to be pressing almost onto the mountain. Although Darcy had never seen a blizzard in the mountains, she instinctively knew one was imminent.

Her heart thudding, Darcy grabbed on her warm cloak, cap and gloves and shouldered open the protesting door. In the few minutes she had looked away, the sky had become even darker and a moaning wind could be heard in the pine trees.

She started off as fast as she could, following Jesse's tracks. Several times she found herself backtracking almost to where she had entered the forest, only to see his footprints lead off on another tangent.

"Jesse!" she screamed against the rising wind. "Jesse!"

There was no answer and she hurried on in the dimming light. Where was he! How much farther could he have gone? Could he have circled back and returned to the cabin by now? Icy fingers of wind began tearing at her cloak and she blinked back tears that were not entirely due to the cold. Every few feet she called his name and listened intently, but she heard only the popping of the icy trees in the growing gale.

Snow clotted the hem of her skirt and made the going even harder. She was already short of breath and her nose stung from exposure. Not daring to go back, she rubbed her face with her gloves to restore her circulation and kept doggedly after Jesse's trail.

The tracks led in a long curve that brought her back to Wolf Creek. By now the wind was whipping the snow so hard that the icy crust was wearing away, and with it were going the footprints. Darcy tried to swallow her terror and knotted her fists to keep herself going. She followed the black, churning waters of Wolf Creek and almost fell over a mound in the path. Beneath the layer of snow she found Jesse.

Half crying, Darcy brushed the snow from his face and slapped him until he moaned and twisted his head to one side. At least he was still alive! She pushed the snow from his body as well as she could and found his ankle was tightly wedged between two rocks.

"Jesse!" she cried out to him. "You've got to wake up and help me!" Suddenly she was furious that this should happen to her Jesse—a man so alive and vibrant. Angrily she beat at him with her fists until he seemed to be breathing again. Quickly she scrambled around until she found a limb large enough to use as a lever. She hurried back to him and again brushed the snow from his face.

"Breathe, damn it!" she yelled in his face. "Don't you dare die!"

She put the limb beneath the edge of the smaller rock that pinned him and put all her weight against it. Her determination to save their lives—for she never considered leaving him—gave her a strength she had never possessed before. Slowly the rock seemed to move a bare inch.

"Pull, Jesse!" she shrieked against the howling wind. "Pull your leg back!"

Either he couldn't hear her or he was beyond movement. She shoved harder against her lever. As if in slow motion the rock moved again, and she managed to grasp his pants leg and pull his leg free before the rock settled back in place.

Sobbing, Darcy knelt beside Jesse and hit him again and again on his broad chest. "Wake up!" she screamed. Slowly, as if his arms were not connected with his brain, Jesse moved. Ice glutted his eyelashes and he couldn't open his eyes, but he made a feeble gesture with his hand. It was sign enough to Darcy.

She threw his arm around her neck and heaved him to a sitting position. "Get your feet under you!" she demanded. "Do it, Jesse! I can't lift you by myself!"

He struggled to obey and rose enough so that she could help him stagger forward. To follow the river upstream was a sure path home, but it dipped into a hollow below the cabin and Darcy wasn't at all certain she could get him up the hill on the other side. Resolutely she turned and started back through the woods the way she had come.

The way was difficult through the densely spaced trees, often so close that it was impossible for them to walk side by side, but the frigid wind was slowed somewhat and that helped a great deal. She kept his legs moving woodenly with threats, cajoling and orders until she felt her throat closing with hoarseness. Above her the heavy, bruised clouds hovered, and as she staggered over the ridge that led to the cabin, the snow began to fall.

It was a snow unlike any she had ever seen. The flakes, mixed with ice, hurtled straight at her, whipped about and hit her again from the other side. Darcy was suddenly disoriented. Was the cabin there? Or there? All the familiar landmarks were gobbled up by the swirling whiteness. The anger that had kept her going was dissolved into unreasoning fear. Darcy tried to hurry forward but she lost her footing and fell.

Clutching Jesse tightly, she rolled with him in a headlong tumble down the ridge. When they came to a stop, Darcy felt frantically around until she came in contact with his shoulder. The snow was coming down so furiously she could no longer see him and wasn't even positive that her eyes were open all the time. Sobbing brokenly, she again shouldered his arm and dragged him up with threats and curses. No matter what, she wouldn't leave him! Nor would she merely lie down and die simply because that was the easiest way! Her bedrock stubbornness forced her to push forward and to her joyous amazement, she collided with a wall.

It was the cabin! She felt her way, hysterically eager now to find the door, and at last blundered against it.

She fought it open and let Jesse fall into the room. She slid down the snowdrift after him and shoved the door shut. After the freezing cold, the room felt blazing hot, and she began dragging off her wraps. When she was freed of her cloak and gloves, she knelt beside Jesse and once again started slapping his face with her hands, still clumsy from the cold. He groaned and rolled his head from side to side.

Quickly Darcy ran to the black water pot that hung by the fire and plunged a dish towel into its steamy liquid. She gasped as fiery prickles of pain returned the feeling to her hands, but she hurried back to Jesse and began wiping his face with the hot cloth.

He drew in his breath painfully and blinked as the ice melted from his eyelashes. A low moan told her he was beginning to come around, and she lay the towel across his cheeks and forehead as she ripped off his gloves and tore at the buttons of his coat to let him breathe more freely. She had no idea if this was the proper way to restore a half-frozen man, but she had no time to reason it out.

"Get closer to the fire, Jesse!" she commanded. "We've got to get you warm!"

"Darcy?" he murmured.

"Of course! Now get over there!" She stripped the coat from him as he rolled over, and grabbed the warm quilts from the bed to replace it. When Jesse managed to get to the hearth she covered him and sat on the floor with his head in her lap. "Be all right, Jesse," she whispered frantically as tears poured down her cheeks. "Don't you dare die!"

By slow degrees Jesse regained consciousness, and after a while he sipped some of the coffee she held to his lips. Color was coming back to his chalky features and his eyes followed her movements.

When she rose to get him some food, Jesse caught her wrist. "You came after me?" he said hoarsely in wonder.

She blinked back her tears and swallowed the

lump in her throat. "Of course I did. Did you think I would let you freeze?"

He licked his chapped lips and his own eyes were suspiciously bright. "But the storm. You came out in the storm."

"I'm not about to lose you, Jesse Keenan," she answered. "You're stubborn as a mule, but you're my man. Besides, I love you."

He smiled weakly. "I love you, too."

Darcy stared down at him, but he seemed to have fallen asleep. Had he even realized what he had said? She stroked his black hair from his brow and eased his head from her lap to a pillow. Whether he meant it or not, he had said it and she could treasure it all of her days.

Now that they were safe, a deep, bone-tiredness permeated her body and she sank exhaustedly onto her chair. Leaning her arms on the table, she let her head rest on them. Up until now she had not let herself think of what would have happened had she not been able to find Jesse—what a monumental effort even that had been, much less the herculean task of getting them both back to the safety of the cabin. Fear swept through her and made her shiver as if she were gripped by a chill. Never in her life had she felt as exhausted as she did at that moment.

A tiny kick, not stronger than a mere flutter, made her press her hand to her abdomen. The baby! Had she harmed it? She raised her head to gaze into the dancing flames as she tried to communicate with her unborn child. All is well now, she thought frantically over and over as if to soothe the baby. We're safe now. A good, strong kick made her wince and rub her side tiredly. Surely it was unhurt, she tried to tell herself, or it would not be so strong.

Tears gathered in her dark eyes and she bit her lower lip to hold back the sobs. She suddenly felt very young and frightened, and the storm was rattling the thick door like a vengeful monster. She longed for another woman to talk to, to ask if what she was feeling was normal and what she should do about it if it weren't. The tears overflowed and coursed down her cheeks and despite herself, she choked out a sob.

Large hands, as weak as she felt, touched her and she looked up to see Jesse's haggard face looking down at her. Even in his own need he had found the strength for her. Together they pulled the bed closer to the fire and lay down in each other's arms.

Chapter Seventeen

THE BLIZZARD LEFT A LAYER OF SNOW THAT SEALED them inside for weeks. Sounds were muffled and quickly silenced by the insulation levels. Drifts as high as the roof were piled against both the house and barn, and only the cabin's crisscrossed beams kept the small structure from sagging with the weight and the wind.

Jesse, warm in the red sweater Darcy had knitted, kept himself busy whittling birds and flowers onto the maple cradle he had made, while Darcy sewed tiny sacques and caps and crocheted socks no larger than two of her fingers. Between them spun a new happiness that had at its core a deep steadiness that enhanced, rather than supplanted, their passion. He had not, since the day she rescued him, said that he loved her, but Darcy kept the memory alive in her mind.

When Darcy thought she could stand the frozen isolation no longer, a warm Chinook wind sped across the mountains from the west, with the force of a hurricane, melting the ice and snow in its wake. As suddenly as the winter had come, it was gone. And with the early spring the trees became knobby with hard, brown, leaf buds. A stirring filled the air with excitement. Then, overnight it seemed, the forest burst into life and leaves of vibrant, glowing green topped every tree and bush and the ground became strewn with wild flowers of every shape and color imaginable.

Darcy welcomed spring as she never had before. As her bulk increased, Jesse had insisted she stay inside lest she slip on the ice. She had scoffed at him that she had safely crossed more snow and ice in that blizzard than she would ever see again but had given in to his wishes. Now she was free again to come and go as she pleased.

Supplies had run low during the hard winter, and only enough beans for a few meals remained in the burlap bag. All the dried corn was gone, and she had to be sparing with what flour was left.

"I've got to go down to Bancroft soon," Jesse fretted as he scored the last of the salt pork to put in the bean pot.

"Then go on and get it over with. But I don't think I'll ride with you this time." She grinned at him and patted her swollen stomach. "When are you leaving?"

"Now don't be in such a hurry, Partner. I haven't said that I'm going. After all, I think we have enough food to last us another week or so." He glanced at her with studied casualness. "When do you suppose the baby will come?"

"Oh, Jesse, how can I know for sure? I guess it will be another couple of weeks. Maybe a little longer. I think if you are going down the mountain you should do it now." She lay her hand lovingly against his face and said seriously, "I don't want you to wait too long and have to be away when it's time."

"You know how far it is," he said as if she were being stubbornly unreasonable. "I can't get back before late tomorrow, even if I hurry."

"Now you're just being silly. I'm fine here. What if you wait around here another two weeks and we really *do* run out of food? It's much better for you to go now while I'm feeling so much livelier."

He sighed and appraised her thoughtfully. "I don't know."

"You know you have to go sometime. Why not now?" She rested her hand on his shoulder. "I promise I feel just fine, Jesse. If I thought there was any chance of the baby coming this soon, I'd tell you. Goodness knows I don't want to be alone on the mountain at a time like that! That's why I want you to make the trip now."

Jesse drew in a deep breath and let it out slowly as he watched the fire. "I guess you're right. Maybe it does make sense to get it over with as soon as possible."

"Of course it does. We're going to get up before daylight tomorrow and you're going on your way. I'll be just fine for one night alone, and you'll be home before dark the next day."

"Are you sure?" he asked, catching her skirt as she moved away.

Darcy laughed at him and said, "Of course. Why, I have more energy today than I've had in a month or more."

Her logic was unimpeachable; it would be less risky now than later. So Jesse agreed. But he was uneasy with the idea of leaving her alone at all. Later that night, he awoke from restless sleep and pulled her into the protection of his arms. Reassured by Darcy's easy, rhythmic breathing, Jesse slept.

Dawn was fading the sky behind the mountain peak above them by the time he had saddled the horse and harnessed the two mules. He didn't want to go and was stalling his inevitable departure.

"Are you sure now?" he asked for the dozenth time.

"Yes, Jesse! I'm sure! Now get on your way or you'll not get there in time to shop. You know Clara isn't going to stay open all night and her with a new baby." Darcy handed him a sack of biscuits to eat on the way and led him firmly to his horse. "Not another word now! And stay away from Prairie Belle's!"

Resignedly, Jesse mounted and grinned down at her. "I wouldn't think of going anywhere near Belle or her ladies. You're more woman than any of them ever could be."

"Even like this." She made an exaggerated circle beyond her extended abdomen.

"Yeah, 'even like this.'" His grin broadened into a full smile. Reaching down, he cupped her face in his palm. His touch and the expression on his face moved Darcy more deeply than any words of love could have. As often happened, a current seemed to leap between them, and she smiled up at him.

"I love you," she said.

Jesse patted her cheek gently, his eyes full of his unspoken feelings. "You're a beautiful woman," he said softly. "I'll be home as soon as I can, Darcy. Don't you do anything you shouldn't while I'm gone."

"I won't."

Unable to put off leaving any longer, Jesse pulled his horse around and headed down the trail. Darcy stood in the yard and watched until he was out of sight. A vague unease had been troubling her, but she was determined not to let Jesse see it. She had never before spent a whole night alone and, as soon as Jesse rode around the bend, the silence of the mountain pressed against her. She shivered and pulled her lightweight shawl closer to her body. This was foolishness. Often he had left her alone for the entire day while he went hunting. Yet the day ahead seemed to stretch endlessly before her. She looked up the mountain to the east where the sky had lightened to a faint blue. They had never seen the sun rise because of the peak; the sun just burst over the trees into an already blue sky. Today it had not yet appeared.

She couldn't bear to go back into the solitude of the cabin, so she wandered downhill to the river. She spread her shawl for warmth on a large, flat boulder and sat down on it to gaze out over the river and the valley through which it flowed. The recent thaw had gorged the river to almost overflowing, and the water plunged by in brown masses frothed with white. The roar of the swollen water drowned out all the other sounds and made the valley seem even more peaceful by comparison. The sun had now reached her cabin, but the vista below still lay in semidarkness. Before her eyes she saw first the tips of the trees, then the branches, become greener with the approach of sunlight. Night's gray shades melted into verdant hues, and she felt awed to witness the daily miracle and to think how this same sun had awakened this same valley for more years than anyone could know. All this made her feel so small and insignificant, yet, at the same time, very important. It was much the same sensation she felt when she looked up into the nighttime sky and realized each star was a sun and many had whirling planets of their own.

Darcy waited patiently until all the valley was bathed in light, then got up slowly from the rock. All morning she had felt odd. Not excited, exactly, but . . . waiting. She was tired from her pregnancy, and she had done more housework the day before than she had been accustomed to, but this was a different feeling. Wearily she rubbed the persistent pain in her back and regarded the hill to the cabin. Only a few months ago she would have run up it. Now it seemed steep and a long way to go.

The pain in her back increased and a dull throb began to course down her thighs. Darcy leaned back against the boulder and watched the river rush by.

There seemed to be no reason to hurry. She had all day and not much to do.

Bits of bark, a few of the previous fall's leaves and an occasional small twig rushed by in the rapids. A fallen log, several yards upstream, created a whirlpool and a small harbor within its roots before letting the water out to pummel the rocks in its hurtling race down the mountain. Darcy broke off a stick from a small branch that lay at her feet and tossed the twig into the water. It was instantly swept away, bobbing above and below the surface as the current proved its mastery. Absentmindedly, Darcy threw another, larger stick and watched the course it took.

The sun was well up in the sky now and she looked longingly at the trail Jesse had taken. She tried to picture in her mind's eye where he was by now. Had he reached the outcropping of rocks that looked like giant turtles? Surely he wasn't as far as the cliff with the Indian ruins clinging to its side.

Darcy stood up, rubbed her aching back and sighed. She couldn't stay by the river all day; the moisture seemed to be settling into her bones. She took a step and bent double as the pain hit her. Grabbing a nearby rock to keep from falling, Darcy gasped in surprise. Surely it couldn't be, she told herself! Not now! Not on the only two days she would be alone for months! But the pain persisted, a band of red-hot flame that left her weak.

As suddenly as it had started, the pain dissolved. Darcy looked anxiously at the cabin on the hill. It seemed so far away! How long would it be before the pain returned? Did that mean her baby would be born right away? Whatever it signified, she couldn't stay here!

She pushed away from the rock and started up the gentle incline. With her growing fear, her breathing became shallower and more rapid. In her distraction, she stumbled on a half-buried stone, but caught her balance clumsily and pressed on. Soon she had reached the cabin doorway and the familiar feel of the latch reassured her. The pain had been gone for several minutes. Perhaps it was a false alarm. Then the second pain swept through her, driving her to clutch at the door frame for support.

Frantically, Darcy tried to recall all she had ever heard about the birthing process, which was pitifully little. In Plymouth, pregnant women were retired to their chambers when it was time. Their husbands and children were sent elsewhere for the day, and when they returned a baby lay in the crib. Of what happened in the meantime, Darcy hadn't the slightest idea.

She waited until the pain allowed her to stagger to a chair. If only she had let Jesse stay even one more day! This was all her own fault! Self-recrimination swamped her, blotting out reason. Jesse would know what to do. He had told her that he and Nathan had delivered colts several times and that it probably wasn't much more complicated to deliver a human baby. But Jesse was not even halfway down the mountain by now and wouldn't return until the next night.

Sweat popped out on Darcy's forehead as the next contraction began.

When Jesse rode into Bancroft, he was astonished by the changes he saw. Where there had been clusters of tents, only muddy flats remained. Nearly vacant streets made the storefronts look even more tawdry than ever. More than half the stores had a deserted look that proclaimed their owners were no longer in residence. A rain had fallen the night before and the ruts he remembered as rock hard had become mounds and hollows of slime.

Unable to believe his eyes, Jesse rode to the assayer's office. A plank nailed across the door told him there was no need to dismount. He nudged his horse on to the general store.

"Jesse Keenan!" Clara called out in glad recognition. "I was hoping you were still around. Where's Darcy? Isn't she with you?"

"No, ma'am." He grinned. "She's in the family way and couldn't make it down this time."

"Glory be!" Clara whooped, slapping him on the back. "I told her so last fall! Wait until I show you that son of mine. He's quite a fellow."

Jesse murmured a suitable reply, then asked, "Where is everybody?"

"I guess you haven't heard," she said, instantly solicitous. "The mines have closed down. They got a bad seepage problem in the Number Three and there was a cave-in in the Silver Betty. Lost two men in it. With the winter being so hard like it was and all

215

the other things happening, it seemed like there were more problems than gold, so the mines started to fold. There are a few diehards left, but at this rate Bancroft will be a ghost town soon."

"That's bad news, Miss Clara," Jesse said in deep concern. "Supplies will be hard to come by if Bancroft shuts down."

She shook her head dismally. "You could go over to Fire Bluff. There's a trading store there run by a couple of Indian brothers. It's another day's ride, though. We've heard of a large wagon train of settlers heading this way. The story is they plan to stay here in Bancroft, but what they intend to do for a living wasn't mentioned. With the mines played out here, I suppose they'll either try some farming or move on after the gold. Anyway, me and Hiram are staying put until we find out. If most of those two hundred settle here, we'll have as good a business as before and civilization as well." She grinned at him as she glanced over his list of supplies. "I always did want to be a 'founding family.' What's this second word here? I can't make it out."

"Cornmeal," he said vaguely. "And put in some of that blue hair ribbon there. Darcy may need some cheering up when I tell her this news."

Darcy lay on her bed, the sheets as damp as her nightgown. Dusk had fallen and the pains were so constant now that her mind had begun to wander. She couldn't recall if Jesse had left that morning or the day before. Her eyes searched out the window and found the violet sky of sunset. Surely Jesse should be home by now! Something must have happened to him! No, she reminded herself, he had only left that morning. He wouldn't be back for another day.

She groaned in abject distress. Somehow she knew she couldn't stand another day of this torment. As the too familiar pain gripped her, she knotted her hands in the sheet and tried not to cry out.

All of sudden she was aware of two large hands touching her, and she opened her eyes to see a face swimming above her. "Jesse?" she whispered.

"Good Lord, Miss Darcy! How long have you been like this!" Nathan's big voice boomed out at her.

"Nathan?" she asked in weak confusion. "You're not dead?" In her present state she saw no incongruity in thinking Jesse had killed his friend after all and his spirit had now come for her.

"No, ma'am, I'm not any such thing. Where did you get an idea like that? Where's Jesse?"

"Gone to . . ." she searched for the right word. "Gone to Bancroft. Supplies."

"That damn fool went off and left you like this?" Nathan was already rebuilding a fire in the ashes of the hearth.

"He didn't know. *I* didn't know . . ."

"Has he been gone long? When is he due back?" Nathan swung the pot of water over the flames.

"He'll be back tomorrow, I think." She brushed her hand across her wet forehead. "I've lost track of time."

A cool cloth was wiping her face. Darcy opened her eyes to see Nathan bending over her. He was smiling with his lips, but his eyes were solemn.

"Listen, Miss Darcy, we've got to get some dry bedding and another nightgown on you and I've got to have your help. Now, I've seen many a young thing come into this world and I know what to do, so you leave the worrying to me."

He left her and rummaged through the chest by the wall until he found an old blanket. "This will do for bedding until I can wash and dry the sheets. Now you just roll over on your side so I can get the sheets off and the blanket under you. Do you have another nightgown?"

As if this were all a dream, Darcy waved vaguely toward a peg on the wall. He found her other gown hanging beneath her blue dress and jerked it down.

"All right, Miss Darcy, we're going to get this dry gown on you before you take a chill. You help me out all you can."

When the soiled linens had been taken away, Nathan knotted two towels and tied one end of each to the posts at the head of the bed. Darcy watched him with her enormous, brown eyes as if he were a messenger from Heaven.

"Hold on here, Miss Darcy," he instructed, putting the end of a towel in each of her hands. "And bite down on this leather." He hurriedly unstrapped his knife and put the scabbard between her teeth. "Now you just push when I tell you to and trust me."

Darcy watched him move to the end of the bed

and closed her eyes tightly as the pain swept over her in pounding waves.

Jesse nudged his horse forward past the huge, misshapen pine that marked the lower boundary of his five-acre homestead. He was later than he had expected, but he knew Darcy would forgive him when she saw the gift he had for her. Tied behind the red mule was a tan cow, her eyes rolling miserably at her enforced march.

As the oddly assorted train rode into the clearing by the river, the tired horse and mules caught sight of the barn and quickened to a trot. Thin curls of smoke rose in silver threads toward the half moon, and the window glowed with the gold of firelight.

Jesse rode past the cabin and bedded down the livestock. As soon as the cow saw the oats he threw into the trough, she settled down as stoically as if she had been born there. Jesse patted his horse's rounded hindquarters and frowned slightly as he looked back at the house. He had expected Darcy to at least come to the door to see who rode into her yard.

He shouldered a large sack of supplies and crossed the sloping ground to the cabin. As he pushed open the door and strode in, her name on his lips, he came to a sudden stop.

Nathan stood by the bed where Darcy lay, her eyes closed. When Nathan saw Jesse, he put a finger to his lips to signal him to silence.

A cold dread gripped Jesse as he slowly lowered the bag to the floor. "What are you doing here with my wife?" he demanded in a low voice.

"Saving her life. It's lucky for everybody that I came along when I did." Nathan pulled the covers up around Darcy's chin.

"What do you mean?" The dread knotted into fear. "Why is she lying there like that! So quiet and still!" His voice rose and he took a step forward, only to be waved to silence by Nathan.

"She's asleep, damn it! Don't go waking her up. She had a hard time, but she's through it now."

Jesse swallowed dryly. "You mean . . . she had the baby?"

Nathan's bearded face broke into a grin. "Yep. She sure did. Come here and look."

On benumbed feet Jesse approached the crib. In its depths lay a tiny baby, its head sleek with soft, dark hair. Its eyes were closed in sleep and one tiny fist was flung out over its head. Even with the blotchy redness of a newborn, its beauty was evident.

Jesse knelt, his mouth open in amazement. "It's so little!" he whispered to Nathan. "Do you suppose it's healthy?"

His friend chuckled. "This is a human baby, not a colt. They're supposed to be little."

Experimentally Jesse touched the baby's cheek and grinned up at Nathan. "Did you say Darcy's all right? She is for sure?"

"Go see for yourself."

Jesse went to his wife and gazed down at her. Darcy lay with her hair in tumbled disarray, a slight smile on her lips. As if she felt his attention, she stirred and opened her eyes. "Jesse?"

"I'm right here, Partner. Are you all right?"

She nodded tiredly. "Thanks to Nathan, I am. Have you seen the baby? Isn't she beautiful?"

"It's a she?" he asked happily. "We have a little girl?"

"A beautiful little girl," Darcy corrected him softly.

"A daughter," he said with wonder. He sat beside her and stroked her hair until she slept.

"Come outside where we can talk," Jesse said to Nathan as he reluctantly left Darcy's side. When the door was closed behind them, he remarked smugly, "It's a girl, Nathan. I have a daughter."

"I know it. Who do you think delivered her?"

Jesse's head jerked toward him. "What do you mean by that? How long have you been here?"

Nathan sat tiredly down on the doorstep and sighed. "I got here about dark yesterday. And it's a good thing I did," he added fiercely, "or you wouldn't have either one of those womenfolks."

Slowly Jesse sat down by him. "You mean that?"

Nathan shook his head in an exhausted gesture. "Miss Darcy was in a bad way. The baby was turned crooked like that foal my dun mare dropped year before last. Remember? It couldn't get born and we had quite a struggle before it slid around the right way. Miss Darcy alone couldn't have managed it. As it was, she was at it all night. The baby was born about daybreak."

Jesse felt the cold knot return to his middle. What if he had lost Darcy! The possibility had never really occurred to him—women had babies all the time.

Even the thought of what he might have arrived to find made him weak. "You're sure she came through it without a problem? She's not . . . harmed?"

"She's just fine. Only tired. That woman's too scrappy to give up easily. That's probably what saved her."

"That and you. I want to thank you, Nathan." Jesse faced his friend on the dimly lit step. "I don't think I could live without Darcy. She's become a part of me."

Nathan looked away in embarrassment at Jesse's open expression. "What I don't understand," he said gruffly, "is why you hauled off down the mountain when you knew her time was near! That's the biggest fool thing you ever did!"

"Well, how was I to know she'd have the baby now? It might have been weeks for all we knew. Darcy told me herself that I ought to go."

"Shoot." Nathan dusted at his leather pants. "She's got no more sense than you do. Next time you stay put until it's all done. Don't go traipsing off to Bancroft at a time like this!"

Jesse looked away and frowned. "That reminds me. Have you been down the mountain lately?"

"Nope. I was on my way when I looked in here. Why?"

"Bancroft's not there anymore. All the mines closed down and there's not more than half a dozen people still there."

"You don't mean it!"

"Yep. You'd better go on over to Fire Bluff to trade your hides. Bancroft's a ghost town."

Nathan looked into the night in a dazed fashion. "Well, I'll be!"

"I heard there's a wagon train of settlers headed this way and they may stay in Bancroft. If so, it'll build back up, but in the meantime, I thought I'd save you a useless trip."

"For such a blight, I sure hate to see Bancroft go. It sure was handy to be able to trade so close to home."

"Well, you never know," Jesse said. "Those settlers might be fur crazy and buy all you can catch. For sure you can send pelts back east by wagon if Bancroft becomes a real town. Besides, there might be a pretty girl in the bunch that could settle you down." He grinned at his friend.

"Ha! No woman's been born that could bring me to heel," Nathan scoffed. "No, I'm happy as I am. I'll leave the family life to you and Miss Darcy."

Jesse looked out at the dark ruffles of pines that edged the clearing. Offhandedly he remarked, "You know, Nathan, I probably shouldn't have hit you with that tree limb last time you were here. After all, you did me a good turn by fixing me up with Darcy, and I might have been a mite hasty in the conclusions I jumped to."

Nathan nodded sagely. "It's a woman's influence. Makes you a little crazy at times. I've seen it happen with goats. Everything is going fine and wham! Two rams will try to butt each other's brains out over some little ewe. Half the time they both lose and she goes trotting off on her own while they're still fighting." He shook his head in perplexity. "Nine times out of ten that ewe doesn't look any better than a dozen others right beside her."

"I'll bet she does to one of the rams or he wouldn't be fighting in the first place," Jesse growled.

"I reckon you're right," Nathan mused. "I never did understand goats."

"Neither did I until lately."

Chapter Eighteen

THEY NAMED THE BABY KATHLEEN, AND THOUGH Jesse complained that it wasn't a very prepossessing name, he had to admit that it fit her personality. She gurgled and cooed happily most of the time and slept a great deal of the other hours. During the day Darcy put her in her crib by the river and sang to her as she and Jesse panned for gold.

Darcy straightened her aching back and glared at the tumbling river. "How about it, Jesse? Have you found any gold yet?"

He took his time about answering, glancing first at the water that had promised him a fortune. "Not too much," he admitted reluctantly. "How about you?"

"Not a thing. This is the third day we haven't found so much as a trace of color. What do you suppose has happened to it?"

"I don't know." He shook his head and ran his fingers through his hair as he often did when he was troubled. "You don't suppose all the gold has played out entirely, do you?"

She shrugged. "We seemed to be finding more than usual last fall. Has this ever happened before?"

"Not to my knowledge. It never happened to me, anyway." He leaned his shovel against the nearest rock and climbed to the top of the boulder Darcy had gone to sit on. Standing above her, his hair ruffling in the wind, Jesse stared upstream.

Below the curve in the river he could see the end of the rough white water that spilled out of the swimming hole. Beyond that his mind's eye pictured the calm water, surrounded now by grasses and wild flowers. Then the falls with their waters roaring with the last of the melted snow. Above the falls, he knew the river broadened and was deceptively calm to entrap the unwary into the funnel of boulders that formed the falls. Past that it didn't matter, because his claim to the land ended at the far end of the placid water.

If there was a mother lode and if it was going to profit him, it had to be located in this stretch of water. Jesse shook his head and frowned at his liquid opponent.

"You know what I'm beginning to think?" He looked over his shoulder and watched Darcy lift Kathleen to nurse. "I'm beginning to think there isn't any mother lode here. Just some stray nuggets washed down from who knows where."

"Surely not," she said hopefully as she unbuttoned her dress and lifted Kathleen to her breast. "It all seemed to be going so well."

Jesse sat down beside her and let Kathleen curl her minute hand around one of his fingers. For a few minutes he watched their baby and stroked her velvety skin. "If we don't find it soon, we'll have to move on."

Now Darcy was quiet. "I know," she said at last.

"Well, we always knew we would someday. It's not like we planned to stay here all along."

"That's right."

Neither of them wanted to meet the other's eyes. Finally Jesse looked at her and his expression softened. Her profile was presented to him, her face bent toward the baby. Her creamy skin glowed healthily and her dark hair held ruddy highlights. Long, dark eyelashes fringed her chocolate-brown eyes, and her nose was straight and delicately shaped. Even in her distress her rosy lips curved slightly upward. The clean line of her chin flowed gracefully into the column of her neck. Her exposed breast was pale and full, with a faint tracery of small blue veins. Nestled in the curve of her arms, the baby fed hungrily in greedy abandon, her eyes already closed contentedly.

Jesse touched the baby's fine hair and smiled. "She's so beautiful. How can anybody look at a baby and not believe in miracles?"

Darcy smiled at him tenderly. "You're a good father, Jesse. Our Kathleen doesn't know yet how lucky she is."

His eyes met hers and he felt the profound emotion that he could no longer deny was love. "I'm lucky, too."

Without disturbing the baby, Darcy leaned over and kissed him. "Thank you for not being a miner," she whispered.

Jesse looked past her at the valley, now clad in the brilliance of spring. It would be hard to leave here, he realized. For years this had been his home.

"Maybe it won't stay this bad. Could be just some fluke of the river that no gold has washed down."

"Could be." Darcy lifted the sleeping infant to her shoulder and patted her back as she, too, gazed down at the valley and the mountains beyond.

"We shouldn't do anything too drastic. Not until we're sure. Let's give the river a little longer." He reached over and helped Darcy fasten her dress, then took the baby and lay her in the crib and covered her with a blanket. Smiling down at her, he said almost reverently, "She's nearly as pretty as you are."

Darcy felt an almost overwhelming joy at his simple compliment and the tone of love in his voice. Tears of happiness rose to her eyes and she blinked them away with a laugh. "You're a good man, Jesse Keenan."

Several weeks later as the rosy glow of late evening rapidly deepened through violet toward the inevitable sooty blackness, the trio headed back to the cabin.

"What do you think, Jesse?" Darcy said as she poured her sparse day's find of gold onto the kitchen table. "Should we move on? The yield from the river doesn't seem to be getting any better, and without Bancroft to go to for supplies it's going to be a lot more inconvenient."

"I don't know, Partner. Maybe it's just the time of year. Let's give it a little longer before we move on," Jesse said stubbornly. "Just a little longer."

Darcy sighed and scooped the gold back into the worn leather pouch. "I used to think it would be so easy," she mused. "I thought gold lay on the ground out here in nuggets as big as chicken eggs and all you had to do was lean over and pick them up." She tightened the puckered neck of the pouch and tossed it to Jesse.

He studied her face thoughtfully before asking, "Are you sorry you came?"

"No. Not for one minute. It's every bit as hard as you said it would be, but if I hadn't come up this mountain I would never have found you." Her dark eyes melted softly into his and she smiled. "I just need to complain once in a while."

"You don't complain much," he said quietly. "I'd say you're just about perfect."

The unexpected compliment touched her and she blushed prettily. With a glance at the sleeping baby, she said, "Let's walk down to the river and back. I noticed the moon coming up as we started in, and I haven't been out under a full moon in months."

He grinned at her as he stood up and handed her a shawl to warm her against the cool night. "We never did get this mountain named."

"No-Name Mountain," she teased. "Maybe some-day that will go on a map."

"I hope not. That's as dumb a name as calling a red mule Flower."

She swatted at him with her shawl before wrapping it around her shoulders. Going to the cradle, she looked down at Kathleen and smiled across at Jesse. "We will have beautiful children."

He came to her and put his arm possessively across her shoulders as he gazed at his daughter. "I'm not sure I want to put you through that again."

"Nonsense, Jesse Keenan. Nathan says the first one's always the hardest. Besides, I don't know that you have a lot to say about it. Not unless you go back to sleeping on your bedroll."

"No chance of that," he said firmly as they went out the door. "But I'm also not so sure I want Nathan talking to my wife about such a personal matter."

"It was a pretty personal situation, Jesse. Kathleen was born right after that." She took his hand as they walked in the moonlight. "And if you decided to move back to that bedroll, I'd move right into it with you."

"You probably would," he said in mock exaggeration. "You have a real shameless streak in you."

She smiled and leaned her head back against his shoulder as they walked and looked up at the stars. "So much has happened since I came up this mountain."

He hugged her as their steps matched in perfect unison. The trees were inky blobs and the valley a smear of darkness below the deep blue sky. A lemon-yellow moon hung over the notched mountain to the left, and the silence seemed eerie after the familiar sounds in the cozy cabin. Far away on the mountain slope, Darcy saw a pinpoint of light from a campfire.

"Who do you suppose that is?" she asked dreamily.

"Maybe a trapper, maybe Indians settling in for the night. There's a tribe that hunts over that way."

"Funny how we never see any Indians."

"They see us. But the tribe on the other side of this mountain has never given settlers any trouble. They trade over at Fire Bluff and go their own way."

"Have you ever seen them?"

"Sure, a time or two. After I staked my cabin claim in the government office I went to Chief Many Rivers and paid him for the land as well. Every spring I send a bundle of hides to him by way of Charley Three Toes as a good-will gesture. They won't bother us."

"I never knew that," Darcy said in surprise.

"That's because Charley came by early last year before you got here and this year he's late. Old Charley never was very punctual. I look for him within the month. His wife, Pale Moon, will be with him. She always is."

"What a pretty name! It will be nice to have a woman to talk to."

Jesse chuckled. "I'm afraid you'll be disappointed there. Pale Moon doesn't speak any English beyond a word or two. For that matter, she rarely says anything at all."

"Oh. Well, at any rate, she *is* a woman and it will be a nice change."

They neared the river and listened to its night song as the water coursed over rocks and logs. "It's so nice out here," Darcy said as she sat down on a patch of thick grass. "I could never go back to the city."

"Neither could I." He lowered his long frame to the ground beside her and leaned back on one elbow. "I've heard people say the night woods are spooky, but I never felt that. I'm glad you're at ease here, too."

Darcy lay back on the cushion of grass and studied the night sky. Absentmindedly she plucked a long blade and twirled it between her fingers. As the moon rose, it slowly brightened the clearing until she could see easily. Soon it would be high enough in the sky to blot out the thousands of stars that arched the velvet blackness.

"For you I would leave all this," Jesse admitted softly. "I'd go back to the city if you really wanted to."

Touched by the scope of his confession, Darcy put her hand on his shoulder and rubbed her thumb across the pulse that beat in his throat. "I'd never, never ask that of you," she whispered. "I love you too much."

He bent to kiss her lingeringly and gathered her into his arms. They lay in silent communion on the thick grass, each savoring the feel of the other. Jesse ran his hand down her slender back and around her ribs to her flat stomach.

"You've gotten too thin," he complained lovingly. "I'll have to fatten you up on that cow's cream."

"You make it sound as if I could have rolled up and down the mountain easier than I walked," she protested with a playful shove. "I don't recall being all that plump to begin with."

He nuzzled the warm curve of her breast. "You're plump in all the right places."

She laughed and hugged him tightly as a shooting star left a trail of light across the sky. "Look, Jesse!" she exclaimed. "Make a wish, quick!"

He lay on his back and pulled her head to his shoulder comfortably. "I wish we could find that lode vein so I could burn up that blamed sluice box."

She poked him in the ribs. "You're not supposed to tell or it won't come true."

"Well, that's one wish I sure would like to see come about. I don't like seeing you work so hard, Partner. You ought to have more leisure time for sewing or playing with Kathleen, or just sitting, if that's what you want."

"I don't think I'd be happy without something to do."

"I want you to be able to find out if you would be or not." He stared broodingly at the night sky. "Sometimes I watch you working and I can't help but think about the ladies in St. Louis. The most difficult work Mother ever did was shopping for dresses and going to fittings. You haven't had a new dress this whole year."

She put her fingertips to his lips to silence him. "I don't need a new dress, but if it will make you feel better, I'll get some material next time we go down to Bancroft."

"If there still is a Bancroft by then," he prophesied gloomily.

"What a mood you're in tonight," she fussed gently. "If there is no Bancroft, I'll go on over to Fire Bluff. If it will make you any happier I'll take every one of those nuggets we have saved and buy us all new clothes for every day of the week."

"Start flashing gold around like that and you'll have more neighbors than you can shake a stick at. We'd have to draw lots to get a yard of water to pan in and Bancroft or one just like it would be right here under our feet. That is until they realized that there's so little gold left here."

She shuddered. "I really would rather do without that dress, if you don't mind, Jesse."

They lay quietly, stroking each other affectionately with the steady assurance of knowing just how the other felt, how he thought, what he dreamed.

"You know, Jesse," Darcy said after a while, "I've been thinking."

"Oh?" he asked warily.

"That acre of land behind the cabin is good, fertile earth. And not too many rocks, either. Why don't we get some seeds and make us a garden?"

"Now there you go again sounding like a blamed farmer! You never will make much of a prospector, Partner."

"No, really. We could grow most of our produce and not need to rely on Bancroft except for the things we couldn't grow." She smiled at him beguilingly. "You said once we could plant some pole beans, remember? It wouldn't take much more work to put in corn and potatoes as well."

"First you want butter, now it's potatoes. Is there no limit to your list?" He pretended to frown at her.

Her lips tilted in a wider smile. "We could harness Flower to a plow. I'll bet she would be just fine."

"What plow is that, Partner?"

"And a nice row of apple trees along the woods over there."

"That should fatten up the deer around here. They'll be so full of apples and corn they won't even bother to run."

"Do you suppose squash will grow here?"

Their eyes met in the darkness and Jesse sighed in resignation. "All right, Partner. We'll put in a row of beans and maybe some corn, but that's it. I have to have some time left for prospecting if we're going to make ends meet."

"Yes, Jesse." Thinking aloud, she said, "A row of cucumbers would be nice, too. I could make pickles and relish."

He groaned and got to his feet. Extending his hand to her, he pulled her up. "Let's go wake up Kathleen and tell her she's going to be the daughter of a farmer rather than a gold heiress."

Darcy slid her arm around his waist and again matched her steps contentedly with his.

Chapter Nineteen

CHARLEY THREE TOES ARRIVED WITHIN THE WEEK ON his pinto pony. Pale Moon followed docilely on foot, leading a roan gelding that pulled a travois laden with furs and their folded wigwam. At first Darcy thought both were Indians, so dark was Charley's skin, but as they drew closer, she was surprised to find his eyes were blue.

"Come in," she said in welcome. "I'm Darcy Keenan."

Charley slid off his bareback horse and dusted the brown and white hairs from his grimy leather trousers. He wore a fringed shirt made of buckskin that looked scratchy and very weatherworn. Over this was draped a wool poncho with broad bands of red and green. His brown hair was braided into two pigtails, which were bound with beaded rawhide thongs. A shapeless felt hat of no particular color was pulled down over his deeply lined forehead. He was obviously dirty, and even from the doorway Darcy could detect his rather pungent odor.

"I'm Charley Three Toes," he said at last in a high, nasal voice that belied his rough exterior.

"How nice of you to stop by," Darcy said uncertainly. Turning to the woman, she added, "You must be Pale Moon."

The woman gave no sign of having understood, but Charley nodded to show the Indian woman did indeed own that name.

Darcy surmised the woman had been well named, for not only was she as aloof as her namesake, she was almost as round. Like her husband she was dressed in fringed leggings and high-topped moccasins. Over this she wore a tunic that stopped below her knees and was decorated with bright beads such as merchants traded to Indians for furs. Her hair was also plaited in two thin braids, the greasy ends of which were tied with strips of rabbit hide with the fur still attached. A lone turkey feather dangled from one of them. Her felt hat could have been a replica of Charley's or perhaps one he had cast off in favor of his present adornment. Certainly she was every bit as aromatic.

"Jesse?" Darcy called over her shoulder. "We have company." She felt uneasy under the unblinking stares of her guests.

"Charley!" Jesse exclaimed as he joined Darcy. "It's good to see you. Welcome, Pale Moon."

The swarthy woman blinked her acknowledgment

and Charley solemnly shook Jesse's hand. Nodding his head toward Darcy, he said, "You have taken a woman?"

"Yes, this is my wife, Darcy."

"She's from Bancroft?"

"No, I'm from Plymouth," Darcy began, but Charley's eyes remained fixed on Jesse's face and she faltered and grew silent.

"She came by wagon train," Jesse said.

Charley took in Darcy from head to toe, lingering for a moment on her full breasts. "A mail-order bride," he confirmed. "Is she stronger than she looks?"

"Now, see here, Mr. Three Toes," Darcy snapped angrily. She wondered if Jesse had noticed the way Charley Three Toes had looked at her.

"She is very strong," Jesse interrupted as he put a restraining arm around his wife. "And she has already given me a child. Come see our daughter."

Darcy glared at Jesse and hurried into the house to stand protectively by Kathleen's crib. She was prepared to slap Charley's dirty hand if he so much as tried to touch her baby.

Charley peered down at the infant. "A girl. Well, maybe next time you'll get a boy. A man needs sons."

Pale Moon remained by the door and merely gazed stoically at the child. After a time her black eyes returned once more to Charley.

"We will have a son next," Jesse said with confidence.

"Maybe," his wife interjected sharply.

Charley nodded. "She is also fiery tempered. You had better beat her when she needs it or she may just give you daughters out of spite. I've heard Chief Many Rivers say that more than once, and he has several sons."

Darcy fought to control her anger. This was the Indian's emissary of sorts and it would be a mistake to make an enemy of him, but it took all her strength to refrain from ordering him out of her house. Already the small room reeked of the bear grease he had rubbed on his skin to ward off the insects. "Partner, why don't you push the beans nearer the fire and start supper?" Jesse suggested hurriedly. "Pale Moon will help you."

"And where will you be?"

"I'll take Charley to the shed and get the packet of furs for Chief Many Rivers." He smiled encouragingly at her and got Charley out of her sight as quickly as possible.

Darcy sighed and turned to face the woman. "Make yourself at home, Pale Moon. Just sit down and rest while I make the corn bread." When the Indian remained standing, Darcy asked, "You do speak English, don't you?"

The large woman merely looked at her with a blank expression.

"That's wonderful," Darcy said, her hands on her hips. "You're the first woman ever to come visit me and you can't speak my language." With improvised sign language, Darcy indicated that the woman was to sit down. After a pause, Pale Moon complied.

Darcy got down the bowl she used to mix the corn

bread and poured in two coffee cups of coarse yellow meal. "Well, that needn't stop us from visiting," she said determinedly. "How have you been doing this past year? Have you seen any of the new styles from back east? When I left Plymouth the trend was toward more narrow cuffs and wider skirts. Tell me, Pale Moon, have you found a way to get berry stains out of clothing?" Darcy chattered on in her one-sided conversation, determined not to give way to the frustrations she felt.

Kathleen awoke and Darcy broke off a piece of sugar, tied it in the end of a dish towel and gave it to the baby to suck on. Waving her pudgy arms, Kathleen succeeded in bringing the sugar to her mouth and gummed it gleefully.

Pouring some milk in the cornmeal, Darcy added a pinch of salt and began to beat it with determined strokes. "This is better with eggs, but hens are more dear than gold out here." She added a spoonful of lard to the heavy black skillet and put it over the fire to melt. "You'd never guess how I broke this handle," Darcy said glibly. "I threw it at a bobcat. Next I may throw it at your husband." She tossed her guest a smile, but Pale Moon only sat there. Then slowly a broad grin split her face, showing yellowed stubs of teeth. Darcy caught her breath for fear Pale Moon had really understood her all the time, but the Indian woman only grinned and nodded in a slow-witted manner.

"Are you sure you don't speak English?" Darcy asked doubtfully.

Pale Moon beamed and rubbed her belly as she pointed toward the pot of beans.

"They'll be ready soon." Darcy tossed a handful of flour into the mixture and continued beating it. She looked up just as Pale Moon got to her feet and was about to go to the baby, who had dropped the sweet cloth and was starting to fret. Darcy quickly moved between Kathleen and the Indian. "No," she said firmly. "I'll take care of the baby."

Pale Moon shrugged and waddled closer to the fire, picking at her teeth with one fingernail. Darcy suppressed a shudder and closed Kathleen's small hand around the sugar cube. With another swift motion she intercepted Pale Moon's gesture toward the corn bread.

"Here," Darcy said, handing Pale Moon a long wooden spoon. "If you want to help, stir the beans."

Pale Moon obligingly took the spoon and did as Darcy pantomimed.

Darcy wondered how a hostess went about suggesting that a guest wash her hands but decided not to push her luck too far. The dirt couldn't travel down the spoon handle to the beans and that would have to be good enough. Pale Moon looked across the room at Darcy, her head cocked slightly to one side, so Darcy smiled back encouragingly, making circular motions with her hand. The Indian again shrugged and turned back to her chore.

By the time Jesse and Charley returned to the cabin, Darcy had supper finished and the table set. Because there were not enough plates for all four, she had put the two platters at the places where she and Jesse sat, leaving the plates for their company. She set the stool at her place and had shoved the flat-topped trunk over for Jesse.

"Wash up," she said with forced cheerfulness. "I'm putting the food on the table."

Jesse obligingly went to the washbowl; Charley merely sat down at the table. Pale Moon continued to stir the pot of beans. Darcy looked doubtfully at her guests. Charley showed no sign of intending to wash, and she had no idea what to do about it. With a repressed sigh she handed a towel to Jesse to dry his face and hands and began serving.

Because she knew Charley was Jesse's friend, she was determined to be courteous to him. She took her seat beside Jesse and motioned for Pale Moon to sit opposite. The Indian woman remained immobile beside the fire.

"Have some corn bread?" Darcy asked Charley as she offered him the pan.

Charley stared at her as if she had committed the gravest of offenses. Looking across at Jesse, he said, "Your woman is sitting at the table!"

Jesse and Darcy exchanged a surprised glance, then Jesse answered, "Of course. It's supper time."

"I don't eat with women. It's disrespectful for them to sit at the table with us. Like they were our equals."

"Mr. Three Toes," Darcy said angrily, "in our home, we eat together. If you plan to eat here, you will sit with me or go cook your own meal!"

"You see?" Charley told Jesse. "Already it starts."

Jesse looked from his friend to his wife, and back again. "That's the way it is, Charley. Partner eats with us."

"A woman should serve her man's food and eat after he has his fill," Charley maintained stubbornly.

Darcy's eyes flashed black fire and she had opened her mouth to retort when Jesse said, "That may be your way, and that's fine for you and Pale Moon, but it's not my way. Darcy eats with us and that's the way it is, Charley. Take it or leave it." Jesse never raised his voice, but there was steel in his tone and his eyes told Charley that there was more at stake here than a meal.

Charley was quiet for a moment as he weighed Jesse's displeasure against his own principles. "I will have some bread now."

Although she wanted to throw it in his face, Darcy merely stabbed the pan toward him and jerked it away as soon as he took a piece. She offered it to Jesse, then took one for herself. Soon she almost wished she had agreed to eat later, for Charley's table manners were deplorable. She refused to look at him and tried to ignore the sounds he made, but she had no enjoyment in the meal. Pale Moon hovered near his chair and served him without even once being asked.

When Jesse rose to get some more beans, Charley glared at Darcy and said to his friend, "My woman will serve you."

"No, thank you," Jesse replied. "I would rather get my own. Just keep your seat, Darcy."

She frowned at him and made no move to rise.

After another round of beans and corn bread, Charley belched one more time and wiped his greasy fingers on his stained shirt. "Your food was good," he said to Jesse.

"Thank you," Darcy replied frostily.

Totally ignoring the women, Charley motioned for Jesse to walk outside with him for man talk. When the door closed behind them, Pale Moon sat down in Charley's place and began to finish his food.

Darcy stared at her. "Here, Pale Moon," she protested, "this clean plate is yours. Let me get you some food."

The Indian glanced up at her, then continued to eat.

With a sigh, Darcy put the clean plate back down and grimaced. Charley was insufferable, but Pale Moon had allowed him to be that way. While the men were gone and Pale Moon ate, Darcy lifted Kathleen out of her crib and fed her.

After the women washed the dishes, they sat silently looking at the fire, each locked in her own thoughts. When the men returned, Charley made a gesture and Pale Moon rose ponderously and followed him out.

"Did you two have a chance to talk about important things?" Darcy asked poisonously. "I never knew a woman's presence was so inhibiting to you."

"Now, Partner, Charley's the one you're mad at. Don't take it out on me."

Darcy ran a tired hand over her eyes. "You're right. I don't see what there is about Charley that makes you want to be his friend."

"When I first came here, I didn't know how to stock up for the winter. Charley happened along and kept me from starving to death. I feel like I owe him something for that. Besides, he's a good man to have as a friend if we start having trouble with the Indians. He's pulled me out of several scrapes in Bancroft."

"I didn't know that. Well, at least they're gone now. I'm sorry, Jesse, but I just can't be friends with them." She cast a suspicious look at her husband. "They are gone, aren't they?"

"Maybe not gone, exactly. A man doesn't want to travel the mountains after dark. Charley usually beds down here for the night."

It took a minute for his words to soak in. "Oh, no, Jesse Keenan! They aren't sleeping in my house! It will take all day to air it out as it is!" It wasn't just his smell that offended Darcy, but she was afraid Jesse wouldn't understand her other reasons. The insults, maybe, but not the look in Charley's eyes. She wasn't sure Jesse had ever actually believed her story about her Cousin Marcus.

Jesse put his arm around her. "Don't get so upset. Charley seldom sleeps inside a building. It seems he had some trouble with the law back east, and when he got out of jail, he swore never to sleep inside again. He and Pale Moon will spread their bedrolls in the yard."

"Jail! He was in jail? What for?" Darcy's eyes were large and her lips parted in astonishment.

"I don't believe he ever said," Jesse replied thoughtfully. "Anyway, that was years ago. He came west and took up with the Indians and has stayed out of trouble ever since."

"That's a matter of opinion."

"Now, Darcy," he said cajolingly, "it's just his way and he'll be gone soon. I never noticed before, but he is rather hard-nosed about women, isn't he?"

"I have another word for it," Darcy replied sourly.

Jesse smiled. At least he would have no worries about Darcy casting eyes at the likes of Charley. It gave him a feeling of security. He hugged her, and they walked toward their bed.

"I can't see why Pale Moon puts up with him," Darcy muttered as she undressed. "Why would any woman marry a man like that?"

"I don't think she did, exactly." Jesse sat on the edge of the bed to remove his boots.

"What do you mean by that?" Darcy's words were muffled as she pulled her dress over her head.

"Charley bought her from her father. I don't know if that means they're married or not."

"What!" Darcy hissed, jerking the dress off her head. "Are you trying to tell me we've got two people living in sin in our own yard!"

Jesse chuckled and pulled her to him. "This isn't Plymouth, sweetheart. Things are done differently out here." He leaned down and kissed her, then nuzzled her hair. "You smell good."

"After being around them a polecat would smell good to you." In spite of her apprehension about their guests, Darcy felt her pulse quicken at Jesse's nearness. "I feel sorry for her. Imagine being sold to a man like that."

"She doesn't seem to mind." Jesse slowly pulled loose the bow that secured her chemise and eased it off her shoulders. His strong hands glided down the silken skin of her arms. He brought each of her hands up and brushed his lips and hot breath across her slender fingers.

Darcy caressed his light growth of beard and buried her face in the curve of his neck as he cupped her bare breast in his warm hand. She reveled in the pleasurable sensations of his palm and fingers on her naked flesh and let the thoughts of her unwanted guests flee from her mind. Familiarly she unbuttoned his shirt and pulled it off his shoulders. His firm muscles gleamed dully in the firelight and his cheeks and brow were golden beneath the midnight thatch of his hair. Darcy caught her breath at his handsomeness. Even after a year she was still startled at times by his perfection. Luxuriously she ran her hands over his thick chest and his hard brown nipples to the knotted leanness of his belly. "Can a man be beautiful?" she whispered as she unbuttoned his pants. "You are."

"Darcy," he murmured, making her name a caress. "Darcy."

Almost reverently they removed each other's clothing and Darcy lay down, sliding over to make room for Jesse. He stretched out beside her, his long frame dwarfing hers. His skin was tanned to a golden bronze and contrasted against her fairness. Darcy ran her fingers along his arm and shoulder, admiring their differences and their sameness. His skin was as smooth as her own, yet firmer, with steel muscles beneath the surface. Touching him, caressing his raw masculinity, made her keenly aware of her own femininity. Her body seemed designed to fit perfectly against his.

Experimentally, she ran the tip of her pink tongue across his chest and flicked his nipple. Jesse murmured with pleasure and wrapped her thick hair around his hand to direct her lips. She teased him by licking him again and again, cooling his skin between caresses by blowing on him gently. He pulled her head up and their eyes met. For the eternity of a moment they gazed into the other's soul. Then slowly Jesse raised his head and claimed her lips.

Kissing her deeply, searchingly, he rolled her over so that she lay beneath him, her head cradled on his arm. He ran his hand over her, feeling the warm curves of her breast, the hollow of her waist, the rounding of her hip and thigh.

Darcy moved against him, urging him to deeper passion with the sensuous undulations of her body. She ran her hands down his back, marking the groove where his muscles curved into his spine, then touching the tightness of his waist and the firmness of his buttocks. With circular motions she kneaded his back with the heels of her hands, pressing him more tightly to her. His manhood was hard against her and she could hear his breath coming harsh in her ear. Running her hand down his thigh and over the muscles of his leg, she let her fingers admire his throbbing masculinity.

"Oh, God, Darcy," he gasped in her hair. "I need you so. I want you. Now."

"Jesse," she murmured. "I need you, too. Love me."

He knelt between her thighs and savored the moment before entering her with tormenting slowness.

Darcy pulled him to her and they lay locked in love's complete embrace. When he found her lips they began to move with the lingering sensuality of a couple who knows and understands the other's desires.

Almost as soon as she felt him move within her, Darcy's world exploded into a shower of fireworks. She muffled her cry of pleasure against his shoulder and let wave after shuddering wave of ecstasy pound through her. Jesse let her passion spend itself, then gently, expertly, brought her to pleasure again.

She wrapped her arms about him and clung to his strength as sensations even greater than the ones before shook her to the depths of her being. She heard his breath quicken and knew that her pleasure was stimulating him even more. Again he moved in the rhythm of love. This time he rode with her on the golden sky burst and together they floated in love's half-dream that followed.

After a long blissful silence, she whispered sleepily as she snuggled deeper into his embrace, "You can't make me believe that it could ever be like this between Charley and Pale Moon," she whispered sleepily as she snuggled deeper into his embrace.

He laughed softly and stroked her dark hair back from her face. "It may be. She has never left him."

Darcy stroked his cooling flesh and marveled at the idea that any other woman in the history of the world could ever have been as much in love as herself. It seemed unlikely. Unbidden, her thoughts found voice. "I love you," she said.

Jesse pulled her even closer and kissed her forehead. "Good night, Darcy."

She lay in the heaven of his arms and warred against the hell of her thoughts. He had never again told her he loved her. Perhaps he didn't. She could hardly count the words he had murmured when she had rescued him, half-frozen from the blizzard. Upon reflection, she couldn't be certain she had even heard him correctly. And worst of all, he might in his delirium have been speaking to someone else. To Marlene. Darcy tried to regain her serenity from moments before, but she failed.

Chapter Twenty

DARCY'S SLEEP WAS FITFUL, AND ON WAKING HER thoughts returned to her feelings of resentment from the night before. She knew if she didn't get up soon and busy herself with her morning activities, she would become even more upset. With determination for this to be a better day, she slipped out of bed and moved silently around the cabin, being careful not to awaken Jesse or the baby. It was so rare for either of them to sleep late that she hated to disturb them. She gently stacked more wood onto the fire and fanned the embers to flame, then eased the pot of water over the blaze and put the coffee pot on the black iron spider in the hot coals. By the time Jesse awoke she would have coffee ready for him.

She flicked imaginary dust from the spotless table top and straightened the chairs before she went over and opened the door to let in the morning's fresh air. At the sight that greeted her she jerked to a stop.

Pale Moon squatted by a small fire, stoically

cooking their breakfast. Behind her stood a tent made of scraped hides, painted with incomprehensible marks and emblems. Even as she watched, Charley ducked out of the wigwam and yawned as he scratched himself unashamedly.

Darcy slammed the door and stormed across the cabin. "Jesse!" she blurted out none too softly as she shook his arm. "They've pitched camp out there!"

"What?" He started up sleepily, fighting to wake up. "What's wrong? Is something wrong with the baby?"

Startled by the sudden commotion, Kathleen had awakened with a lusty bellow and began screaming at the top of her lungs.

Darcy scooped her up and patted her brusquely as the baby yowled loudly. "Of course not. She's fine." Darcy's words were clipped in her anger at finding Charley still in her yard. "But that's all that is. Your company never left."

Jesse rubbed his eyes and shook his head to clear his muddled thoughts. "Charley? In here?"

"No! Out there! In the yard! They set up their tent and it looks like they have moved in for good."

Her words were starting to make sense and Jesse peered from Darcy to Kathleen. "Here. Give her to me." He lifted the crying baby and lay her against his chest. As if by magic Kathleen stopped crying and snuffled as she loudly sucked her thumb. "She's wet," he observed.

"Jesse! Don't you even care that we have Indians living in our front yard?"

"Of course I do, Partner. But I can't do anything about it yet. Let me wake up first. Besides, only one of them is an Indian." He reached for the stack of diapers and lay Kathleen down on the bed beside him.

"They aren't going to stay here!" Darcy took the diaper from him and efficiently changed their daughter. When Kathleen's face puckered and began to redden before her next wail, Darcy hastily unbuttoned her dress and started to nurse her.

"Nobody said they would, Partner. What's the matter with you?"

"I don't like Charley. Surely you can figure out why!"

Jesse rolled to a sitting position and started to pull on his pants. "I'm sorry his attitude about women offended you so, but we can't afford to get him mad at us. Charley's the main reason Chief Many Rivers allows the white men to live here unharmed. I can't just go out there and order him to leave." He stood and flexed his arms into his shirt.

"Do you mean to say you won't do anything about it?" Darcy demanded. Kathleen started to fret and Darcy jiggled her to quiet her.

"Don't nag at me, Darcy." Jesse was holding his temper as well as he could, but he disliked being awakened so abruptly.

"Nag at you!" she sputtered. "Just because I want them to leave? How can you say that to me!"

Jesse drew a deep breath to calm himself. "Partner, Charley is my friend whether you like him or not. I won't be rude to him. Not even to please you." He frowned down at her, then strode out of the cabin.

With seething emotions Darcy watched him go. Only the baby in her arms prevented her from continuing the battle. But no sooner was he out of sight than large tears brimmed in her eyes. He didn't love her. He couldn't! Not and subject her to an animal like Charley! By the time Kathleen was full and eager for play, Darcy's cheeks were stained.

Because of their argument and her desire to avoid Charley, Darcy stayed close to the cabin. Let Jesse work the river alone, she fumed. Maybe he would appreciate her then! Kathleen was in an inquiring mood and into everything all morning. She had learned to scoot well enough to get across the room, although her movements could not yet be called a crawl. Darcy spent more time removing bits of dirt, small twigs and other things of an alien nature from her tiny hands and mouth than she did in accomplishing housework.

At last Kathleen fell asleep, exhausted from her exploring, and Darcy laid her in her crib. Taking her chance to escape for a few minutes, Darcy headed for the barn. The animals had the run of a small pasture, but their stalls always seemed to need cleaning. It was a job Darcy detested, but she knew Jesse hated it even more. Therefore it usually was her lot to do the mucking out.

No one was around, so Darcy pulled the back of her skirt between her legs and tucked the hem into her waistband to form culottes and took the old shovel from its nail on the wall. She attacked the first stall, tossing the waste out the window to the rocky ravine below.

She and Jesse seldom argued, and she felt a bereavement in their mutual anger. She wanted to go down to the river and put her arms around him and kiss away their differences, but pride prevented her. It was his fault, after all, for being friends with such a revolting character—and how that friendship had flourished, she couldn't understand. If she tried to smooth away their differences Jesse might think she didn't care if Charley stayed there or not. No, she decided, there was time enough for kisses and apologies when her unwelcome guests were gone.

Again she dug the shovel in and heaved the load out the window. So engrossed was she in her thoughts that she was not aware that she wasn't alone until Charley's shadow fell upon her. Darcy turned to see him staring at her. She blushed as his eyes took in the way her breasts strained against her bodice and her modified skirt separated her legs into trousers and left her ankles and much of her lower legs shamefully exposed. Quickly she yanked her skirt tail free and let it fall into more conventional lines.

"No need to do that for me, Miss Darcy," Charley said in his irritatingly nasal voice. "You've got mighty pretty legs."

Darcy's face reddened uncomfortably. How dare he even insinuate such a thing! "Mr. Three Toes . . ."

"Now surely you know my name is Charley. You call me that."

"I have no intention of doing any such thing. If you will be on your way now, I have work to do." Darcy lifted her chin regally. She didn't like the way he was standing in the stall door watching her.

Instead of leaving he came into the stall and stood much closer to her than she preferred. She stepped back and felt the feed box against her hips. "I can't work with you in my way. Please leave."

Charley grinned and showed his yellowed teeth. "You talk fancy for a mail-order bride. I've heard tales of girls like you." He reached out and touched the narrow lace at her collar.

Darcy jerked her head back, too astonished to cry out.

"That's the way Jesse likes his women? Frisky like a green-broke colt? Not me. When I'm around, you learn to be docile. Can you remember that?" His hand shot out and grabbed her breast.

Darcy slammed the shovel down on top of his foot and pushed past him as he let out a howl of pain. She ran down the incline toward the river where she could see Jesse at work.

"Jesse!" she cried out in fear. Was Charley about to catch her and haul her back into the barn? "Jesse!"

Jesse straightened and came to meet her, his eyes full of apprehension. "What's wrong, Darcy!" His hands fastened on her arms and helped support her.

"It's Charley!" she gasped. "He . . . he . . ."

"Now don't start that again, Partner," he interrupted. "I've already said all I'm going to about that."

"But, he touched me. Here! And . . . and he said things to me. Awful things."

"Charley did that?" His tone was one of disbelief. The man was his friend, his trusted friend.

"I just said he did, didn't I? Jesse, he has to leave here. Now!"

Jesse liked being told what to do only a little less than he liked being manipulated. Marlene had taught him well about manipulation. She had embarrassed him more than once, twisting the truth to get her way. They were all alike!

"I never thought you'd stoop to this, Partner," he said sadly. "To spreading lies about one of my friends just so I will ask him to leave."

"What?" Darcy stared up at her husband in shock. "You don't believe me!"

"How can I?" Jesse defended. "Pale Moon is never more than two feet away from him. Do you expect me to believe he would do something like this in front of his own woman? Even Pale Moon wouldn't stand for that."

"Pale Moon was nowhere around. I was mucking out the barn and Charley came in. He touched me and said rude things to me! He tried to kiss me!"

"Now you add a kiss to your list of accusations. Stop while you can, Partner. My patience is growing thin."

"You believed the worst about Nathan, who was totally innocent, yet you call me a liar when I tell you Charley tried to take advantage of me!" Tears of angry frustration welled up in her eyes and she shoved them away with her palm.

"That's enough! I'm not going to ask them to leave no matter what stories you dream up and that's final!" Jesse felt sick at heart that Darcy had tried to play on his jealousies, just like Marlene!

Darcy stepped back from him, her face ashen. She knew what he must be thinking as clearly as if he had spoken his thoughts aloud. Marlene again! For a long moment she stared at him, her dark eyes large and haunted. Then she turned and went back to the cabin. He called out to her but she ignored him.

An idea came to her as she passed the wigwam, and she walked over to Pale Moon. Charley was nowhere in sight and the Indian woman was kneeling near the low fire, grinding corn on a flat rock.

"Pale Moon, I have to talk to you," Darcy said nervously. How would she take the news of Charley's infidelity? With rage? Disbelief? "A few minutes ago in the barn, well, Charley tried to . . . to . . ."

"Come on now, Miss Darcy. Surely you can do better than that," Charley's voice drawled from behind the tent flap.

Darcy jumped as if she had been stung. Pale Moon turned back to her grinding.

Charley lifted the flap and peered out. "Pale Moon don't know any more English than my horse does. You're wasting your time."

"I want you to leave, Mr. Three Toes. Now! If you don't, Jesse may kill you when I tell him what you've done!"

"Now you and I both know you've already done told him. Didn't believe you, did he?" Charley snickered nasally. "He's a loyal man, old Jesse is. Won't believe ill of anybody unless it's proved to him."

Darcy drew herself up and looked again at Pale Moon. If the woman had understood a single word, she had shown no sign. Perhaps she really didn't speak English.

"Don't you ever try to lay a hand on me again, Mr. Three Toes," Darcy said with barely controlled anger in her voice. "If you do or if you make another unseemly remark to me, I'll kill you myself." She turned on her heels, Charley's raucous laughter ringing in her ears.

When she reached the house she closed the door behind her and drew in the latch string. So there was no one she could turn to for help! Not even Pale Moon! Darcy recalled the utter disbelief on Jesse's face and she felt a stab of pain. Would she always have to live with Marlene's ghost?

Darcy sat down at the table and lay her head on her folded arms. She would have to take care of herself. Not that she wasn't accustomed to doing just that, but she had never felt so physically threatened before. Not even with the advances of Cousin Marcus.

Her hand touched something cold and sharp, and Darcy raised her head and stared at the paring knife that lay on the table. Slowly she picked it up and looked at it. The blade was not long, but it was made of strong steel and the handle was the right size to comfortably fit her hand. Darcy took the worn whetstone and honed the blade, then slipped the knife into the pocket of her skirt. She now felt more prepared, if no more secure. Could she use the weapon if necessary? She didn't know.

Despite her anger at Jesse, she decided to stay beside him as much as possible. If she kept him by her side and if Pale Moon continued to dog Charley the way she usually did, the chances of Charley finding her alone again were greatly lessened. Perhaps that would be good enough. She only knew one thing for certain—she had changed a great deal since Cousin Marcus had caused her to run away from Plymouth. This time she had no intention of leaving.

Chapter Twenty-one

Darcy held Kathleen in her arms, bouncing her gently to quiet her, as she tried to prepare supper. For two days now the baby had been restless and fretful, awake most of the night and sleeping fitfully during the day. Darcy had never been around any other baby and she had no idea what could be wrong with her. Since that morning Kathleen had whimpered and refused to eat. Most alarming of all, her skin felt dry and hot and her shallow breath rasped loudly.

Jesse had taken his turn walking the sick baby, but still Darcy had had little rest from her worry. There was no doctor within miles—a day's ride at least—and no other mother to answer her questions. Was this a mere trifle that all babies did regularly, or was Kathleen seriously ill? Darcy had no way of knowing, nor did Jesse.

The baby's illness had eased the rift between Darcy and Jesse, but there remained a strain in the air. When necessary they spoke, but the silences were long and tense.

Darcy shifted the infant to her other arm and tried not to worry about how hot she felt even through her clothing. Kathleen's raspy breath sounded so painful that Darcy hurt along with her. A spasm of coughing shook the baby, a tight, desperate sound that left her red and crying. Darcy kissed the dark hair and tried helplessly to soothe her child.

At last Kathleen fell asleep from sheer exhaustion and Darcy laid her down to ease her aching arms. Bending over her, Darcy felt genuine fear. She was still so tiny. If she were even a few months older she would be so much stronger, so much better equipped to regain her health. Darcy covered Kathleen with a clean dish towel and straightened.

For two days she had gone without sleep and she wasn't feeling well herself. With Kathleen asleep, Darcy decided to go down to the river with Jesse and get some fresh air. She wouldn't be long and she couldn't bear to stand helplessly by and hear the terrible rasping breath that she was powerless to change.

Darcy slipped out and quietly pulled the door shut to keep out drafts. She squinted for a moment against the bright sun. The late spring day was beautiful after the gloom of the small cabin. A clear blue sky arched overhead and the trees were aching-ly green with the vibrancy of new growth. A yellow butterfly swooped and danced in the air above the wild buckwheat that grew in the clearing. The grass beneath her feet was shiny and silky with blue and crimson wild flowers in abundance, as well as the pale pink buttercups. Darcy drew the first deep breath she'd had in days. Even the wigwam across the clearing was not as offensive to her at the moment. She had worries of a far greater magnitude to occupy her mind.

She skirted the wigwam, keeping Jesse in sight, and hurried down the well-worn path to the river. Over her head the tall, graceful cottonwoods interlaced and formed a high tunnel of greenery. At the river Darcy sat on her favorite rock and watched Jesse work.

"How's the baby?" he asked without looking at her.

"No better. Her cough sounds a little worse."

He muttered a curse born of worry and discouragement. Straightening, he glared at the river, but Darcy caught a glimpse of the wetness in his eyes.

"Have you found any gold today?" she asked in a softer voice.

"No, this damned river hasn't yielded so much as a sign of color in over a week." He ran his fingers tiredly through his hair. "Not even gold dust."

They both looked with concern at the river. It looked the same, gold-brown water racing with foamy white froth over the mossy rocks. But to Darcy's eyes it now appeared barren.

"You think the vein has played out, don't you," she said as a statement rather than a question.

"I don't know what to think."

Again there was a short silence. Then, "Will we move on?"

Jesse bit his lower lip and glared at the river. "Not yet. We can hold out a bit longer."

Darcy looked back at her husband. Even with the problem between them she loved him so much she ached. It hurt her to see him so unhappy. He had counted on the gold to make their life easier. In some ways he seemed to view the river as an opponent. For it to quit yielding nuggets meant that Jesse had lost. Darcy longed to hold him and tell him that she really didn't care about the gold. That she only wanted her small family to be happy.

That thought recalled the baby. She had been gone long enough. With a sigh Darcy slid off the rock. "Supper will be done in about half an hour," she said tonelessly.

"Fine." Jesse went back to his sluice box. He still hadn't looked at her.

Darcy hesitated, then turned and went back to the cabin. The gentle incline felt nearly as steep to her as it had the day Kathleen had started being born. She wondered dully if she, too, was getting sick or if it was only exhaustion. Probably the latter, she decided. She was never really sick. There just wasn't time.

She pushed open the door and went into the semidarkness of the cabin. For a moment she couldn't understand what was missing; then she knew. The silence was unbroken.

Quickly she went to the crib and what she saw made her utter a choked cry and grip the sides to steady herself. The crib was empty!

"Jesse!" she screamed. Running to the door she

cried out for him again. She saw him jerk to attention and start running toward her in long strides.

Unreasonably Darcy hurried back into the cabin and started searching for the baby. Although she knew Kathleen wasn't there, since the cabin's sparse furnishings allowed few obstructions to her view, she had to look anyway. Darcy peered beneath the bed, her heart pounding. Babies didn't just disappear! And she had been too sick to crawl away even if she had somehow been able to get out of her crib.

Visions of the bobcat that had once come into the cabin in search of food thundered through her mind. No! she screamed mentally. The baby was safe! She was here somewhere! She had to be!

Jesse ran through the door, his face pale and frightened. "What is it! What's wrong!"

"I can't find Kathleen! She's gone!" Panic coupled with exhaustion froze Darcy as she stared imploringly at her husband.

"Gone? Gone where?"

"I don't know!" she wailed. "She was asleep when I went to the river and when I came back her crib was empty."

"I'll look outside. Maybe Charley saw something."

Pale Moon! Darcy had forgotten them in her fright. Neither Charley nor Pale Moon had ventured inside the cabin since the night of their arrival, but their wigwam was right there in the clearing. Perhaps the Indian had heard something.

Darcy ran toward the wigwam as Jesse raced off to

locate Charley. Without hesitating, Darcy ducked under the flap and into the dim and smoky interior. What she saw brought a stifled scream to her lips.

Pale Moon had built a small fire in the center beneath the smoke hole. On the fire bubbled a pot that emitted a nauseating odor. Poised above the pot in the center of the steam was Kathleen, held in Pale Moon's grimy hands.

"What . . . what are you doing to her?" Darcy gasped, trying to keep her voice calm lest the Indian drop her baby into the boiling pot. "Give her to me, Pale Moon." Darcy edged nearer, ready to grab Kathleen should she fall.

Pale Moon glanced at Darcy but made no move to give her the child. Darcy cautiously held out her hands, but Pale Moon brushed her away. Tears were gathering in Darcy's eyes and her voice broke as she once again implored Pale Moon to give her the baby. The note of desperation in her voice made the other woman look at her once more. Then in a heavy accent, the Indian said, "Child sick." She nodded at the pot. "Medicine smoke."

"Medicine?" Darcy asked uncertainly. She sniffed. "What is it?"

Pale Moon nodded toward an empty whiskey bottle and a tin that had once held turpentine. "Onions," she added to the visual list.

Weak relief flooded over Darcy and she almost staggered. It was only a concoction to relieve Kathleen's congestion!

"Darcy! Is she here?" Jesse demanded as he entered behind her. "What—?"

"She's using the vapor to help Kathleen breathe," Darcy explained quickly. "I think she's all right."

Pale Moon silently gave Kathleen to Jesse but emphatically signaled that he was to hold the baby in the steam. "Her breathing does seem easier," he reported to Darcy.

Pale Moon went to a small drinking vessel and felt it with her hand. Satisfied, she waddled back to Jesse. Pulling a spoon from the pouch that hung at her waist, Pale Moon spooned some of the liquid into the baby's mouth. Darcy immediately moved in protest. Pale Moon glared at her as if she were the most incompetent of mothers.

"Boneset, honey, snakeroot tea," she informed Jesse, whom she obviously considered to be the wiser of the parents. "Drink cool. Drink hot she get sicker."

"What does the tea do?" he asked uneasily.

"Cool skin. Drive out devil." Pale Moon kept spooning the tea into Kathleen until she was satisfied the baby had swallowed a fair amount. "She sleep now. Give more later." The Indian pocketed her spoon and gave the small pot to Jesse.

He cradled Kathleen in the crook of his arm, where she slept easily for the first time in days. Already her skin was less flushed and he thought she felt somewhat cooler to the touch. "Her mother and I thank you," he said simply.

Pale Moon nodded almost imperceptibly and with more dignity than Darcy would have believed she possessed.

Jesse put his other arm around Darcy and took her

outside. As they entered their cabin—seeming suddenly spacious after the cramped quarters of the wigwam—Darcy took the baby and lay her cheek against the infant's forehead.

"She really is cooler," she said in surprise. "And she's breathing so much easier! Do you think she'll get over this now?"

"I think so. She seems past the worst of it." Jesse pulled back the dish towel from the crib so Darcy could lay the baby down, then covered her gently. "I think she'll make it now."

Darcy sank down onto her chair and buried her face in her hands. "When I saw Pale Moon holding her over the pot like that . . ."

"I know, Partner. I know. It scared me, too. But she was just trying to help. Maybe she really did turn the illness. Kathleen seems to be resting easier." He set the pot of tea on the table. "We have to remember what she put in this tea. Boneset, honey and snakeroot, I think she said."

"It's a wonder that concoction on the fire didn't explode. Turpentine, whiskey and onions!"

He grinned wryly. "That ought to loosen a cold if anything could. And she does seem better."

Darcy went to the crib and touched her baby's cheek. "She is almost cool now. I guess I owe Pale Moon an apology."

"She probably wouldn't accept it or even acknowledge it. Until a few minutes ago I would have sworn she didn't know any English at all."

Darcy longed to go to Jesse and lay her cheek

against his broad chest, to feel his arms protectively around her. But pride rooted her feet to the floor. Until he believed what she had told him about Charley, she couldn't go to him freely. Now not only Marlene but Charley stood between them. She turned away.

"I'm going to get some rest while Kathleen is asleep. It feels like I've been awake for days. Just let me sleep while I can and I'll get up with her during the night."

Jesse nodded. She looked so tired and vulnerable. They had both worried incessantly about their baby, but Darcy hadn't his physical strength. Jesse wanted to go to her and smooth away their differences, but he couldn't. Not when she had lied to him about his friend. And Pale Moon doctoring the baby had seemed to reaffirm their friendship and loyalty. Yet Jesse would have preferred to believe his wife in any circumstance. It was all very unsettling. Had Marlene not used the same ploy, he would have believed Darcy unwaveringly. Even to the extent of sending away his friend.

"Get some sleep," he agreed gruffly. "I doubt the illness is completely spent."

Jesse left her and went outside. The late afternoon sun was causing long fingers of verdant shadows to stretch across the grasses. A faint haze was blanketing the lower valley and turning the air to dusky rose. Far away he heard the call of a dove, then an answer in the woods behind him. Why couldn't his life be as simple as nature? he wondered. Because of women, he answered himself. Every time a man falls in love with a woman, he opens himself up to hurt from all sides.

He wandered morosely down to the river and dumped his sluice box. It was growing too dark under the trees to be able to see any longer. Besides, the river appeared to be barren anyway. Wherever the gold had washed from, it was no longer there.

He turned the box upside down to drain and pushed his shovel up under the overhang of rocks where it would be protected from the weather during the night. As he was returning to the cabin, Charley melted silently from the woods and joined him.

"Have you found your baby?" he asked as he fell in step with Jesse.

"Yes. Pale Moon had taken her to give her some medicine."

"Your woman worries too much."

Jesse walked slowly through the gathering dusk. Reluctantly he said, "Darcy tells me she talked to you the other day in the barn. Do you recall that?"

"I remember. I saw her go in and I went to see if she needed help with something."

His breath felt raw in his throat but he had to know. "And what happened?"

Charley was silent, as if he were wrestling with a problem. Finally he said, "You and me, we been friends for several years now. You looked out for me when I got frostbit two winters ago and you saved more of my foot than I had any right to expect. You've never turned away me or my woman from your hospitality. You are my friend. I will not answer your question." Charley gave Jesse a long look that damned Darcy more eloquently than mere words ever could have. Then he turned away and ambled toward his wigwam, where Pale Moon squatted beside a cook fire.

Jesse ran his hand over his hair and leaned his head back tiredly. Even in the face of his questions, his friend had not spoken against his wife. Yet Jesse had no doubts now that whatever had happened in the barn, Charley had not been at fault.

Turning his steps toward the barn, Jesse bypassed the cabin. He wanted time to think, time to ease his hurt, before he saw Darcy and her innocent, lying eyes.

Chapter Twenty-two

DARCY WALKED BENEATH THE TOWERING TREES, her footsteps silent upon the spongy ground. Last fall's leaves had mingled with those of years before to form a brown cushion of earth, which was still damp from the recent rain. A few of the smaller leaves clung to her shoes and the hem of her rust-colored dress. On her back she carried Kathleen in a sling that Pale Moon had shown her how to fashion. Since her illness Kathleen had been fretful, and only the warmth of Darcy's back and the steadiness of her movements soothed the baby. The sling also left both of Darcy's hands free to gather the wild greens for their supper.

Parting the underbrush, Darcy stepped out into a small clearing but kept near the woods where the sorrel grew. As she plucked the tender green leaves, her mind wrestled with a problem greater than food.

For weeks now the river had refused to give up any of its gold. Their last trip to Bancroft had almost depleted their hoard, and only a few nuggets remained in the leather pouch tied to the rope webbing beneath their mattress. Winter provisions for two had cost more than Jesse had expected, and now they had Kathleen to feed and clothe as well. The next trip down the mountain would see the last of the gold.

Darcy had gone back to panning in the last few days, although the water was still so cold it made her fingers aching and clumsy. By dark she was often too tired to stay awake and frequently went to bed as soon as Kathleen fell asleep. Jesse had tried to tell her there was no need for her to return to work when Kathleen kept her so tired, but she knew better. With both of them working the river they had twice as much chance of finding the gold. So she panned at every spare moment and ignored the tiredness in her bones.

What if the gold was indeed gone? she asked herself as she picked the sour greens. Would they move on to another claim? Or would Jesse leave the mountain altogether? She feared it would be the latter. Now that he had a family, Jesse had been feeling a great responsibility toward them. She could see it in the lines of his face when he gazed at Kathleen. Those worry lines had begun to etch his face much too often of late.

Darcy patted the crisp leaves and decided she had gathered enough for the two of them and some for Pale Moon's stewpot as well. She ducked through the underbrush, keeping the twigs well away from the sleeping baby. The forest was quiet and the path clear of brambles, as the dense overhead foliage blocked the sun so completely that neither bushes nor vines could grow. Darcy followed the slope of the land down to the low ground where she knew mushrooms to be plentiful. A red squirrel darted down a tree trunk to chatter at her before flicking his tail and racing back up the tree.

Over her head she saw a flash of scarlet as a cardinal and his mate flew by in search of a nesting place. She followed their flight with her eyes and sighed.

She didn't want to leave the mountain. After all this freedom and beauty she couldn't bear to face town life with its bustle and restrictions. Rarely was she ever lonely on the mountain, and she felt a sharing of its moods. Nor did she want to move to another claim, even if they remained on the same mountain. She had fought with Wolf Creek and sometimes she had won its gold. Elk Valley and the panorama of mountains beyond were hers now. And the cabin. True, it was small, and winter drafts blew through the miniscule chinks in its mortar and the chimney didn't always draw as well as she might like, but it was home. It was there that she had first loved Jesse. Those rough walls had seen the birth of her child and heard Kathleen's first cry. So much laughter and so many tears had sunk into the cabin that she couldn't bear to leave it.

Yet if Jesse decided to go, she would follow. They had had grave problems and his lack of trust in her was galling to a woman with as much inherent honesty as Darcy, but without Jesse, the mountain would have no meaning.

She knelt and picked the small brown mushrooms. If only, she thought, I could find some other way. There was only one possibility, and that was to farm the patch of ground beyond the cabin. The ground there was rich and relatively free of rocks. Would it be large enough, though, to support them? She had no way of knowing. And Jesse always teased her about thinking like a farmer. Maybe he would hate that kind of life. Although he had talked about it a few times, he had never shown any signs of really wanting to plant anything since she had known him.

Darcy stood up and turned her footsteps toward home. In a very short time the decision would have to be made or it would be too late to get a crop in the ground. She decided to talk to Jesse about it that night.

Jesse dumped the gravel out of the sluice box and glared at the wooden slats. Not a trace of gold! He straightened his aching back and rubbed his neck as he studied the river. The gold was gone. It must be.

He leaned his shovel against a large rock and climbed up to sit on the flat surface. Beneath his feet the river tumbled and frothed, its familiar voice loud in his ears. It was in spring flood now. If there was any gold to be had, this should be the time to find it. He drew up his knees and rested his crossed arms on them. A few days ago he had gone upstream, then downstream, trying to find any sign of color. There had been nothing.

He could no longer deny it. The gold was gone.

Jesse picked up a pebble and threw it at the river. Wolf Creek had won after all. He turned his head and looked past the wigwam to the small cabin up the gentle hill. Silver smoke curled from its chimney and drifted upward toward the cloudless sky. Soon night would fall and the tiny window would gleam with gold from the fire and lantern. Darcy was inside with their baby, doing the small tasks that made their life more pleasant. Before she had come up the mountain, it had been merely a shelter. Now it was his home.

He frowned. If only their marriage had lived up to its early promise. Things had been so much better before she had tried to come between him and his friends.

Darcy wouldn't want to move on, he knew. Her heart was here and she was the sort to put down deep roots. She had never before had the chance to call a place her own, her home, until now. He had tried to tell her they wouldn't stay here forever, but she had too strong a need for permanence for his words to matter.

He gazed out over the valley to the hazy vista beyond. If the truth were known, he had to admit to himself that he didn't want to leave any more than she did. Not that he had any great fondness for his enemy, the river, but it was comfortable here. He didn't look forward to raising another cabin and barn, to finding a claim that showed color *and* was flat enough to build a shelter nearby. He had been damned lucky to find this one.

With a long sigh, he tossed another pebble into the water. There was only one way to stay here and that was to farm enough land to both feed them and provide a surplus they could trade for whatever they couldn't grow. Once when he was a boy he had had a garden, a very small one. He had sown every kind of seed he could glean from his father's gardener, but within a month they had sprouted, withered and died. He still wasn't sure if it had been from too much water or too little.

And would Darcy like to be married to a farmer? For all his teasing he wasn't sure. After all, she had come all the way across the country to marry a prospector, not a farmer. What of all their dreams of the day they would strike it rich?

There was another possibility. One that he had deliberately overlooked until the other choices had been weighed. He could take his small family and return to St. Louis. He would be welcomed as the prodigal son and his mother would be beside herself over Kathleen. He couldn't, or at least wouldn't, oust his brother from inheriting the bank, but Jesse would always be assured of a job there. With a grimace he threw a handful of pebbles into the cold river. Darcy would be coerced into joining his mother's garden club and Kathleen would be pushed in her pram by a starched maid. The idea of his outspoken wife at a garden club meeting made Jesse grin in spite of himself. St. Louis wasn't ready for a woman as free-thinking as Darcy. Nor, he admitted honestly, could he return there himself. Not after the freedom of the mountain. Times might be rough, but at least he was his own man here.

Jesse glared again at the river. If only he could get out to the middle just once. If he could see under the raging water and know for sure, once and for all, if a fortune lay hidden there! But the water was far too swift. His feet would be swept from under him before he was ten feet from the shore. True, the river was swollen now with melted snow, but it had never been low enough to wade nor gentle enough to swim to the middle. Even if he did get there, the rapids were violent and he wouldn't be able to see beneath the mud and froth.

With one last sigh, Jesse decided to go tell Darcy about his decision. It was the only possible way. They would have to become farmers. He only hoped she had a greater talent for it than he did.

Darcy looked up when he entered and put down the pants she was mending. "Jesse, I need to talk to you."

"I have something to tell you first. Come sit by the fire and hear me out." He felt the unpleasant cautiousness arise that always seemed to color their recent conversations.

"But, Jesse, this is important!"

"So is what I have to tell you."

She let him lead her to the chair and sat down, but before he could speak, she said, "I think we should try farming that patch of land behind the cabin."

He stared at her. "That's what I was going to say to you!"

"You were? But you never even said you were

thinking about it! Why didn't you talk it over with me?"

"Well, you didn't discuss it with me, either," he pointed out. "What if I hadn't liked the idea?"

"But you do. You said so."

"Damn it, Partner, you just don't go around making up people's minds for them like that. I might have been set on pulling up stakes and moving on!"

"You weren't, though."

"But I might have been. Or I might have decided we should go back to St. Louis."

"And you work in your father's bank?" she said with a disbelieving laugh. "I don't think so."

"You mean you'd stay here? You wouldn't go?"

"I didn't say that. If you had your heart set on going, we'd go. But I wouldn't like it."

He looked across at her. The firelight played on the smooth curves of her face and her eyes were the deep brown of rich earth. A tendril of hair had escaped her braided bun and curled on her forehead. "You might like St. Louis a lot. As pretty as you are we would have more invitations than we could handle. Don't you miss shopping and visiting with other women?" Even though he would hate to return to that sort of life, he knew that he would if she wanted it. She had to be given the choice.

"I don't want to leave No-Name Mountain. I wouldn't fit into St. Louis society."

He smiled tenderly at her. "That's still the silliest name I ever heard for a mountain," he teased gently.

"I don't care. I still don't want to leave."

"We might find a better strike upstream a ways. Maybe even the mother lode," he suggested, determined to voice all their options.

"We would have to build another house," she said doubtfully. "The nights are still cold and what if it rains? Kathleen might get sick again." She left her chair and knelt at his knees. "Oh, Jesse, what have I done to you? When I came here this is how you said it would be. You didn't want to be tied down and burdened with worries. Please forgive me."

He cupped her face in his large hands and his dark eyes searched hers. "All you've done is love me, Darcy. There's nothing to forgive you for in that."

Tears brimmed in her eyes and he wiped them away with his thumb. "If you want to move on, Jesse, we will. We can make a lean-to until we get the cabin built."

"I want to stay here, too," he assured her. "I just wanted you to know all the choices."

"So we've decided for sure?"

"I guess we have." He grinned down at her and stroked the curve of her cheek. "We sure have a roundabout way of making decisions. Seems like we always start at the back and work forward."

She laughed and brushed the wetness from her eyes. "I guess we do at that." She stood and began to set out the plates for supper. "By the way, Jesse," she said casually, "do you know anything about farming?"

"Not a thing, Partner," he said cheerfully.

She sighed and shook her head. "It should be interesting, then, because I don't, either."

Chapter Twenty-three

DARCY SAT AT THE TABLE AND MADE OUT A LIST OF all they would need. A few apple trees would go along the back and maybe they could add some pear trees the following year. As for the vegetables, she hoped to find a variety of seeds at Fire Bluff. It would be a waste of time to go down to Bancroft. A plow and harness for the mule would be necessary. There was an old shovel in the barn that could be bent into a hoe, but it needed a new handle. Jesse could whittle one from a tree limb.

Darcy's forehead puckered as she studied the list. It would take all their gold to fill it. They might even have to sell Jesse's mule. It would bring more than Flower. Even so, it would be close.

She gazed out her open door at the yard. As always, the first thing to meet her eyes was the disreputable wigwam, and as usual she tried to ignore it. Charley Three Toes and Pale Moon seemed to have taken root in the clearing and showed no signs of ever leaving. Darcy had tried on several occasions to talk to Jesse about this, but his reaction was always the same—Charley was his friend and he was welcome for as long as he wanted to stay. Darcy no longer tried to tell Jesse about Charley's leering stares. Her husband refused to listen. She knew of no surer way to clear the room than to tell Jesse that Charley had been watching her again. Usually Jesse would get up and stalk outside and not return until Darcy was asleep.

She carefully folded the list and gazed down at the handwriting on the other side. Because of the scarcity of paper, she had used a portion of a letter written by Jesse's mother. The unknown woman's hand was firm and flowery, a no-nonsense penmanship that said the writer was never one to be caught unprepared. Darcy ran her finger over the ink and wondered about the woman she would probably never meet. Was she a pleasant woman? Would she be a person Darcy could turn to for advice about her problems? Most likely not, Darcy decided. Whatever her mother-in-law was like, she had almost certainly never been stalked by a half-wild man who had thrown up a wigwam in her yard. Darcy had never seen St. Louis, but she was positive this sort of thing wasn't allowed there.

And there was another problem. After all this time Jesse had not said he loved her. Oh, he had mumbled the words in a state of delirium when he was half-frozen, but never since. In all honesty Darcy had to wonder if Jesse had even meant them for her ears. Perhaps he had been reliving a memory of Marlene. Darcy felt a cold twist of pain at the thought. Now that the rift caused by Charley Three Toes lay between them, Jesse might never grow to love her. She knew she would never leave him, but she dreaded a lifetime of always knowing the memory of a past love kept them apart.

She leaned her elbow on the table and rubbed her forehead. He might never return her love, but perhaps she could save their friendship. If she could avoid Charley long enough, eventually he would go away.

"Morning, Miss Darcy," a nasal voice called from the open doorway. "Feeling poorly?"

Darcy turned to face Charley and carefully edged around until the table was between them. "I feel quite fine," she answered coolly.

He came into the cabin. "I seen you rubbing your head and I figured you might have a headache or something." He took another step closer as his eyes raked over her body.

"Jesse will be here any minute, Mr. Three Toes. I would appreciate it if you would wait in the yard."

Charley chuckled at her uneasiness. "Now, Miss Darcy, we both know Jesse's gone hunting. He thinks I'm hunting, too. What he don't know is that I circled around and came back here. By now he's probably reached the high meadow."

"I don't know why you would do a thing like that, but it really doesn't interest me." Darcy watched him edge closer and her pulse hammered in her throat. "Pale Moon may be by at any minute."

He chuckled again. "I'll say one thing for Pale Moon. She's obedient. I told her this morning I favored some trout for supper and she went off to fish for some an hour ago. She's not likely to be back any time soon. Of course, you know the best place for trout is way upstream above the falls." He took another step and only the table separated them.

Darcy felt the washstand at her back and she edged to one side. Charley stood between her and the door, but even if he wasn't blocking her exit she couldn't run. Not and leave Kathleen in her crib. She was afraid Charley would have no compunction about harming the baby in order to force Darcy to comply with his lust.

"You know, you sure are a pretty little thing," Charley said almost conversationally. "I ain't seen a woman like you since I came west. All soft-looking and ladylike. Tell me, Miss Darcy, are you really as soft as you look?" He put out his grimy hand and Darcy shrank away.

"Mr. Three Toes, listen to me. I'm your friend's wife. You can't dishonor him like this."

"Can't I? Jesse won't ever know, and if you're fool enough to tell him, he won't believe you. Seems like you ought to know that by now."

"You're not leaving me any choice!" Darcy cried out as her hand fumbled for her pocket. "Leave now! While you can! Jesse will kill you if you touch me!"

For an answer Charley laughed and snaked his hand out. His skinny fingers caught the collar of her dress and in two hard yanks he had ripped it to her waist. As she struggled to get away, Charley grabbed her chemise and tore it to expose her luscious breasts.

"Well, now, would you look at that." He gaped with lustful pleasure. "I ain't seen nothing that good in a long time." He held her easily as she fought to get free and to cover her nakedness. Her breasts bobbed with her efforts and the sight seemed to inflame him all the more. "Come here," he demanded, jerking her to him. He bent his head and bit her breast as she fought wildly.

Suddenly Darcy felt her hand fly free, and without hesitation she shoved it into her pocket and grabbed the knife she always carried. Not caring whether she killed him or not, Darcy jabbed at his ribs. He let out a surprised howl and turned her loose.

"Get out of here," she hissed in cold fury.

He touched his side and stared at the warm blood that came away on his fingers. In amazement he looked back at her. "You cut me!"

"I'll kill you for sure if you don't leave!"

Charley's expression turned to anger and he slapped her with the back of his hand. The knife flew from her grasp and clattered against the far wall. The sound startled Kathleen and she began to shriek at the top of her lungs.

"You don't never pull a knife on somebody that was Indian trained," Charley snarled. "When I get through with you, even Jesse won't know you. I'll tell him it was a band of redskins traveling through. He won't ever know the difference." He slapped her again, knocking her against the rough wall. "I think

I'll do you the way I saw an Arapaho done once. Even his own mama wouldn't have recognized him. That's after I'm through using you, that is."

As he lunged at her, Darcy screamed and dived for the knife that lay near the door. He missed but caught her skirt as she ran past, spinning her around. The material ripped as he threw her to the ground and hurled all his weight upon her. Pain made bright spots in front of her eyes as her breath left her, but Darcy stretched frantically toward the knife.

Charley forced her to her back, grinding her shoulders against the ground as he thrust his knee between her thighs. She kicked at him, but he slapped her again, stunning her. As Darcy felt him jerk at her skirt, she tried to claw at him, but he held her firmly down.

Suddenly Charley was lifted off her and slammed against the wall. Jesse pinned him there, his feet barely touching the floor. With Jesse's face only inches from his, Charley couldn't miss the murder lust in his former friend's eyes.

"Talk fast, Charley," Jesse ground out. "Because I'm about to kill you."

"Jesse!" Darcy gasped in hysterical relief. She stumbled to her feet and held the table for support.

"It was Indians, Jesse," Charley clamored. "I come up just as they was running off! I was just helping Miss Darcy up when you came in!"

"That's the worst lie I ever heard," Jesse growled low in his throat.

"All right! All right! You force me to tell you! Miss Darcy's been making eyes at me behind your back ever since me and Pale Moon come here. I come back to get the bullets I forgot and she motioned for me to come in here. She was all over me, Jesse! What else could a man do?"

"He's lying, Jesse!" Darcy cried in sobbing gasps. "Don't believe him!"

Jesse's eyes were like black obsidian as he tightened his hold on Charley. "Now who do you reckon I'm going to believe, Charley? A sniveling, backbiting turncoat, or my wife?" He held the man who was turning beet red from lack of breath, then yanked him toward the door. "Stay inside, Darcy!"

She watched as Jesse alternately dragged and shoved Charley toward the woods. Her lungs felt as if they were on fire from having had the air knocked from them, and the right side of her face was hot and swollen from Charley's blows. A throbbing ache made all her muscles tremble and her legs were suddenly rubbery. Slowly she sank down to the doorstep and sobbed into the remnants of her skirt, pulling her bodice together as well as she could.

A movement caught her eye and she looked up to see Pale Moon emerge from the woods. The women gazed silently at each other, Darcy's breath still coming in sobs, Pale Moon's eyes blank. Then the Indian tossed the fish she carried into the woods and began to pull down the tent. By the time Jesse came back, carrying Charley over his shoulder, she had almost finished packing the two scrawny horses.

Jesse strode across the yard and dumped Charley at her feet. He looked long at Pale Moon, then put his hand on her shoulder. It was a gesture of commiseration. Still Pale Moon gave no sign of emotion. Not even when Charley moaned and rolled to one side.

Without even a glance downward at his one-time friend, Jesse turned and walked back to Darcy. He stopped in front of her and their eyes met.

She gulped down her sobs and tried to read whatever lay behind his dark eyes. There was pain there, as well as something she couldn't understand. Then he held out his hand to her. The knuckles were cut and bleeding from contact with Charley, but his hand was steady.

"I'm sorry, Partner," he said simply.

She hesitated, then put her hand in his. "I'll forgive you, Jesse." She let him pull her to her feet and he took her into his arms. Thankfully, she laid her face against his chest and listened to the comforting beat of his heart.

"He won't ever come back again," Jesse murmured into her hair. "He knows that the next time I see him, I'll kill him."

Darcy looked across the yard to where Pale Moon was building a travois out of the tent poles. "He's not dead?"

"No. He may wish he was, but he's not."

"I never lied to you, Jesse. Not ever."

"I know that now. I'll never doubt your word again."

She closed her eyes and held him tightly. If he only meant that! If he would trust her, then she could wipe away the scars left by Marlene.

"Come inside," he said as he saw Pale Moon shove Charley none too gently onto the travois. "You need a cold cloth on your cheek." Gently he guided her back into the cabin as Pale Moon mounted her roan horse and rode silently away, pulling Charley behind his pinto.

Chapter Twenty-four

DARCY WAS NOT IN A GOOD MOOD. THE GARDEN PLOT was littered with dirt-encrusted stones, many of them still half buried in the ground. Even the bright blade of the new plow purchased at Fire Bluff failed to turn up the stones without a struggle. They had taken turns plowing, with Jesse working the rockier patches. Flower had not considered herself to be a plow mule and she periodically kicked her huge hoof back at the plow.

With a groan, Darcy pulled back on the leather reins and Flower flapped her ears warningly. "You take it for a while, Jesse. I can't go another step."

"All right, Partner. You take a rest and sit in the shade for a while by Kathleen." He poured a bucket of water over the freshly packed dirt of the straggly apple tree. Two other saplings stood dejectedly in their new surroundings. He dropped the bucket and wiped his sweaty forehead on his sleeve. "Go on and sit down now. I don't want you to wear yourself out."

She sighed and mopped her face with the tail of her apron. "I'm not resting until you do! I just don't want to plow anymore."

He took the reins from her and looped them over his body as he supported the plow's wooden handles against his hip. "Don't be so bull headed, Partner. We don't have to finish all this today."

"We are already late planting, Jesse," she said, barely controlling her temper. "Besides, if I sit down you'll keep on working until you drop. No, the only way I'll sit down is if you sit down beside me. And anyway"—she bent and began to gather the stones and threw them towards the woods—"the sooner we get those seeds in the ground, the quicker they'll start growing."

"You're a stubborn woman," he complained as he slapped the reins on Flower's rump. "I never saw a more set-in-her-way female in my life!"

Darcy threw another stone and glared at him. She was in no mood to be compared to anyone. "I may be . . . persistent, but at least I'm not as mulish as you are!"

He hauled back on the reins and turned to frown at her. "What's that supposed to mean?"

"Nothing. I don't want to talk about it." Darcy lifted her chin and tossed her head.

Jesse scowled but turned back to the plow. "Get going, Flower," he commanded, throwing his own weight against the handles. Flower laid back her ears and kicked at the harness. Jesse popped the reins and made an encouraging sound. The mule turned her head and bared her long yellow teeth. "Giddap!" Jesse added a commanding whistle for good measure.

"It figures you'd try taking it out on my mule," Darcy commented acidly.

Jerking back on the reins, Jesse wheeled to face her, his expression thunderous. "What is wrong with you! That stupid mule never has minded worth a plug nickel!"

"She minds *me*," she replied haughtily. "I guess she just doesn't like you."

Jesse went back to plowing with such a vengeance that Flower was temporarily subdued. Darcy followed them, gathering the rocks.

For days now she had felt this anger building. It had begun to grow when Charley had convinced Jesse that she was not to be trusted. In the days following Charley's expulsion the anger had dampened down. But then, perversely, it had bloomed again and she could no longer hide it or ignore it.

Ever since she had come up the mountain she had lived in the shadow of Marlene's memory. Every word of love she had spoken to Jesse had been balanced on the scales of the other woman's infidelity. Although she was almost positive Jesse loved her—certainly he gave her cause to think so—he refused to tell her. All because of the falseness of Marlene. Darcy was tired of being patient, and she was doubly tired of being rivaled by a ghost.

At the end of the none-too-straight row, Jesse

turned Flower and started another row beside that one. For a few minutes this put him face to face with Darcy and each glared at the other.

"I don't know what has you so riled up," he muttered as he passed her, "but I hope it clears up soon."

"Just think of it as the vapors," she snapped.

"Oh, no. With vapors you just faint on the couch or swoon a little!" He looked as if he would prefer for her to faint dead away for a while.

"Is that the way it's done in St. Louis?" she asked with acid sweetness. "I suppose that's the way your proper lady friends would do it?"

"Yes! And they would be damned feminine while they did!" He stopped urging Flower onward and the mule stopped at once.

"Oh, would they! And I guess you think I'm not feminine? Is that it?"

"Darcy! Darcy, what's gotten into you?" He shrugged off the reins and caught her arms with his hands. "Tell me what's wrong!"

"I love you! That's what is wrong!"

He gazed down at her and tried to make sense out of her words. "I know that," he said at last.

"Of course you do! I tell you! You never tell me!"

"That's it? That's why you're so mad?"

"It's a good reason! For over a year now I've seen you thinking about Marlene and comparing me to her, and I'm not going to stand for it anymore!"

"You've always come out best in any comparison I've ever made," he said without thinking.

Her mouth fell open and her words sputtered in

her anger. "You even admit it!" She threw down the rock she held, missing his foot by an inch. "You actually admit you compare me to her!"

"Now, Partner, I didn't mean that the way it sounded," he tried to explain. He had never seen Darcy so angry, and he wanted to smooth it over.

"Well, I don't care how it sounded," she stormed. "The point is, you *did* it."

He reached out to touch her, but she pushed his hand away.

"Maybe you would be happier if Marlene were here instead of me! Or maybe I can be like her and *that* will make you happy!" She turned on her heel and stalked from the field.

"Wait a minute! Where are you going?"

"To Prairie Belle's! I'll be back when I can compare with Marlene!"

Jesse hurried after her and pulled her around to face him. "That's crazy talk!"

"Maybe so. But at least then I will deserve your lack of faith!" She stabbed her finger at his chest. "Look how you accused me with Nathan! He's your best friend. Then you refused to believe me about Charley for the same reason!"

"Now, Partner, you said you forgave me for that."

"I said I *would* forgive you! I never said that I *had* forgiven you. But in time I will. Someday!"

"I've done all I can to fix that," he pointed out. "I made up with Nathan and half killed Charley. That ought to be good enough."

"Should it? That's only half the reason I'm mad. Mainly I'm upset because you don't love me. No matter what I do or what I say, you still haven't come to love me and I guess you never will!" Hot tears stung her eyes and coursed down her cheeks. "That's the main reason I'm mad and it's more at myself for wanting your love than at you for not giving it. I know I'm your friend, and Lord knows you're the best friend I ever had, but I can't help wanting more! I know you can't make yourself love me, but I can't figure out what there is about me that is so bad!"

"Darcy!" he interrupted her torrent of words. "Darcy, I do love you! How could you ever doubt it?"

She stared up at him. "You . . . love me?"

"Of course I do!" he said, glaring down at her. "Why else would I fight Nathan? Good Lord, he's twice my size! And Charley! He's little, but he's mean as a snake in a fight. He had a knife stuck down in his leggings. Would I act that crazy if I didn't love you?" He paused a minute, then added, "I would have fought Charley anyway, of course. No man has a right to force himself on any woman, but I wouldn't have tangled with Nathan!"

"You love me?" she repeated in wonder.

"I just said I did, didn't I? I love you!"

"Are you telling me that so I won't go to Prairie Belle's?"

"Of course not! That's the dumbest idea I ever heard of, though. Getting your husband back by working in a cathouse!"

"Well, virtue wasn't doing me much good!" she retorted.

"I don't know where you come up with such damned fool ideas!"

"You never told me you loved me," she reminded him.

"I did! The night you came after me in that blizzard. I figured you already knew it, but I wanted to tell you anyway. When a man comes that close to dying, he wants to get everything said that's on his mind."

Darcy stared up at him. "How was I supposed to know?" she demanded.

Jesse ran his fingers through his hair and gestured at the cradle beneath the nearby tree. "Well, for one thing, we had Kathleen."

"That's no sign of anything!"

"What about the way I can't keep my hands off you?" he challenged.

"That doesn't necessarily mean you love me, Jesse!"

He frowned down at her in frustration. "Well, I do, damn it, and that's all there is to it!"

"Oh, no, it's not, Jesse Keenan. I want to hear the words. Often!"

"I show you I love you every day and half the night!" he defended himself. "I've never been much with words, Partner. You know that."

"That's about to change," she informed him.

He stared at her. "Can we stop fighting now?" he asked after a minute. "I'm worn out from wrestling with that red mule of yours and you're far more stubborn than she is."

"Who are you calling stubborn?" she demanded.

"You. And you deserve it," he said with a grin. He put his arm around her and hugged her until she smiled in spite of herself. "I really do love you," he said experimentally.

"I love you, too," she replied softly, her voice catching on the depth of her emotion. "I love you so much."

He smiled at her and gently stroked the hair from her face. "Let's unhitch the mule and get the baby and go back to the cabin for a while. I could learn to enjoy this love talk."

"That's just what I was about to suggest."

As he lifted the baby, crib and all, Jesse said conversationally, "Did I happen to mention to you that I purely hate farming? It makes a person mean to work in the sun like this."

She put her arm around his waist and lay her cheek against his arm. "I don't like it, either, Jesse."

"Let's go put the baby down for her nap," he said gently. "I have some things I want to say to you. Like how much I love you."

Chapter Twenty-five

JESSE LOOKED PROUDLY AT THEIR GARDEN AND hugged Darcy. "Looks like it's going to grow in spite of us, Partner."

She nodded and bent to push aside the glossy leaves of a bean stalk. "There are already a few pods forming. The squash look good, too." She pointed at the squat bushes where bright yellow blooms in the shape of stars were beginning to give way to tiny vegetables. "I can't tell that the corn is doing much besides getting taller."

"It may fool us yet. For two people that didn't know one end of a hoe from the other, we've done pretty well."

Darcy nudged a clump of spear grass. "Speaking of hoes, it's your turn to weed."

He frowned. "Are you sure?"

"Positive."

He sighed. "I'll do it this afternoon. How about a swim?" he said to forestall the hated chore.

"I haven't gone to the swimming hole in days. Do you think it's warm enough for Kathleen to go in, too?"

"Maybe not. That wind is a little brisk for her. We'll take her next time."

"That's probably best. It's time for her nap, anyway. I think she'll be all right if we leave her here. Don't you?"

"Sure, we won't be gone long. She can't get out of her crib."

Darcy smiled in eager anticipation. "Let me put her to sleep and we'll go." She left Jesse and went back inside to get the baby fed and dry.

Jesse gazed at their garden. It had grown quickly and looked much healthier than he had had any right to expect. In fact he was beginning to think they might make a go of farming. Now if he could only learn to like it. Or to at least convince Darcy that he did. If she knew how much he detested tending the plants she would try to do it all on her own. Jesse suspected she disliked farming as much as he did.

His dark eyes strayed to the valley, now furred with the greens of summer. At least they would be able to stay in their home. That was worth having to hoe and haul water.

As always his gaze fell on his enemy, the river. If only its muddy waters had yielded the gold it had seemed to promise, life would have been so much easier. He had finally carried his sluice box to the barn and tossed it in the storage room. Darcy had been more stubborn. She had continued panning for gold off and on through the next two weeks. Finally she had given up, too, and was using the pan to carry feed to the four chickens Nathan had brought her on his last visit. Somehow it had seemed only just that the pan that had caught gold should now be filled with the gold of feed corn.

"Ready, Jesse?" Darcy asked as she rejoined him. They walked together hand in hand through the woods. "Before long we are going to have to swim in bathing costumes. Kathleen won't be a baby forever."

Jesse snorted. "You won't catch me in one of those striped jerseys! They look ridiculous."

"I think they're charming. I'll get me one with white cuffs and a pleated skirt."

"And you'll drown for sure," he predicted dourly. "All that material will take you straight to the bottom."

"At least I'll go in a stylish manner," she teased.

"No bathing costumes and that's final." He held aside a low-hanging limb and let her pass into the clearing.

The azure sky was mirrored on the pond's calm surface and grass spread like emeralds beneath their feet. Small white violets were sprinkled across its surface along with patches of pink and gold buttercups. The water tumbled from high above and splashed into the pond, sending lazy ripples to sway against the banks. Because the sun was out, a pale rainbow hung in the mist above the falls.

"It's so beautiful," Darcy exclaimed. "I always forget how lovely it is here." She sat down on the lush grass and pulled him down beside her. "Let's just look at it for a minute. I hate to disturb it."

Jesse leaned back on his elbows and watched the skipping flight of two butterflies. "There can't be a more beautiful place in all the world," he agreed. "I haven't done that much traveling, I'll admit, but I know what I see here. I knew as soon as I saw this place that I wanted to homestead here."

Darcy drew up her knees and wrapped her arms around them to rest her chin. "You know, Jesse, I've been thinking."

"Oh, no," he groaned, lying back in the grass. "What now?"

"We ought to build another room onto the cabin. Before long Kathleen will be a big girl and we need our privacy."

"You're right. When are you going to start building it?"

"Me! I just decide how big and where to put it."

"Is that a fact?" He grabbed her from behind and pulled her over on top of him. "What if I won't do it?"

She shrugged, her eyes mischievous. "It's privacy or abstinence. Take your pick."

"I'll start on it tomorrow," he said with a grin. "I guess you already know where you want it?"

"We should put the door opposite the fireplace and then when both fires are lit the rooms will be warm all over."

"I gather Kathleen is also to have a fireplace?"

"Well, of course, Jesse. You know how cold it gets

here. Then when the boys come along we can build another cabin the size of this one and connect them with a dog-run porch."

"The boys?" he asked.

"Our sons," she answered patiently. "When we do that, our cabin as it is now will make a proper living room. You see how well that will work out?"

He groaned. "I'm tired just thinking about it." He gazed past her and watched a cloud in the serene sky. "Maybe we could put in another window while we're at it. The cabin is pretty dark on cloudy days."

She lay her cheek on his chest and felt the rise and fall of his breathing. "You're so good to me, Jesse," she whispered.

"It's because I love you, Partner. You know that's the only reason I put up with you."

"Oh!" She ran her fingers over his ticklish ribs, catching him unaware.

He laughed and tickled her back as he rolled over and pinned her beneath him. He claimed her lips and kissed her with growing passion as his hands freed her hair. Pulling the loosened hair over her shoulder, he rubbed it against his cheek. "You always smell so good," he murmured.

Darcy ran her fingers down the line of his jaw and gently touched his lips. "I love you," she whispered as he took her fingertips into his mouth and nibbled them sensuously.

He kissed her palm and ran his tongue over the pink surface and down her fingers. "I love you, too."

Slowly she unbuttoned his shirt, kissing each inch

of skin as she discovered it. When she pulled the fabric from his shoulders and nuzzled kisses into the curve where his neck and shoulders met, she felt him quiver with excitement.

Jesse rolled over again so she lay upon him and began unbuttoning her dress. "We should have brought a quilt," he commented.

"I can make you forget all about the prickly grass." She kissed him, blotting out his thoughts for anything except herself and their love.

His hand cupped her breast, teasing her nipple to throbbing hardness, and Darcy sighed. She felt her breast swell eagerly beneath his knowing fingers, and she rolled to her side to let him have greater access to her body.

Jesse let his hands roam over her, removing the rest of her clothing as she removed his own. Her body was slender and her skin fine and delicate. As she rested her head on his arm, she let him look at her, touching her with a wonder that familiarity had not erased. Almost reverently he caressed the full curve of her breast, silvery white in the sunlight, and the dusky pink tip that strained toward him. Slowly, he let his fingers wander in the valley between and along the other breast that lay nestled against the grass and wild flowers.

"You're so beautiful," he said lovingly. "Sometimes it's hard to believe you're actually my wife."

"I'm yours forever," she answered. "Just as you are mine. We belong together."

He stroked her flat stomach and outlined the

undulation of her narrow waist and hip. Her thighs were firm and round beneath his palm and his eyes took in every inch of her unashamed beauty.

"I like to look at you," she said quietly. "Your muscles are so lovely. I can see them moving beneath your skin and I feel excited. You're like a thoroughbred, all lean and trim and satiny." She reached out to trail her fingers across his thick chest and along his hard biceps. Retracing her path, she touched his coppery brown nipples, which were as erect as her own. Slowly her hand wandered lower to caress his eager manhood. "I love the way you're made," she whispered.

Jesse could bear the tension no longer and he pulled her to him, his lips taking command of hers. Their kiss struck a fire in their souls and together they began to climb love's heights. He left her lips to pay homage to her neck, her shoulders, her breasts. Finally he took her coral nipples into his mouth one at a time and urged each to throbbing tautness.

Darcy murmured in her excitement and he flicked his warm tongue over her nipple until she knotted her fingers in his hair and put an end to his teasing.

Lower and lower his hand stroked her fine textured skin until he found the center of her womanhood. She allowed his fingers entrance and cried out as he touched the core of her being. Although she tried to draw him closer, he held back, letting his fingers and lips weave magic for them both.

When neither could bear it any longer, he raised himself over her and claimed her with a deep thrusting passion. Darcy clung to him as she matched her movements to his. Already she was feeling the hot glow of ecstasy as he moved deep within her. With a cry, she soared over the precipice and flew on wings of passion.

As the waves subsided within her, he once more began to urge her to another plateau, this one even greater and easier to attain than the one before. When he heard her sounds of pleasure, he let himself go and together they found completeness.

Darcy lay in the circle of his arms, her fingers lazily stroking his hair as she let herself float back down to the realities of earth. Dreamily she opened her eyes to find him smiling down at her.

"It just gets better all the time," he observed. "In another ten years we won't be able to stand it."

She let her smile broaden. "I'll take my chances."

"Are you going to lie here all day, woman? We came here to swim."

With a languorous sigh she looked over at the pond. "We did, didn't we?"

"I'll race you." Jesse got up and pulled her to her feet.

"It will be a slow race," she teased. "I can't seem to find my feet yet."

"Looks like I'll have to carry you." He swooped down and tossed her over his shoulder. Running to the pond, he unceremoniously dumped her in.

Darcy came up gasping at the shock of the cold water. "I won!" she shouted. "I got into the water first!"

Jesse dived in with her, his body making a clean arc in the air and slicing neatly into the crystal-clear water. He burst to the surface beside her. "Damn! This water's freezing!"

"Don't be such a sissy. I'll race you to the waterfall." Darcy swam off with clean, sure strokes that propelled her toward the far end of the pond.

Letting her take the lead, Jesse followed her, then used a burst of speed to overtake her and reach the falls first. When she swam to him, he pulled her into his arms. "I can stand on the ledge here. You put your arms around my neck."

She did as he said and let her bare body press his, her toes hardly reaching below his knees. The main body of the falls were beyond them and only a thin trickle fell onto their heads and left a dusting of diamonds on their skin and eyelashes. Buoyantly she floated in his arms, only her head and the top of her shoulders out of the water. When he kissed her, Darcy let the tip of her tongue taste the warmth of his mouth.

"You'd better stop that unless you want me again," he warned her huskily.

For an answer she let her hard nipples slide seductively across his chest, then wrapped her legs teasingly around his waist. "Is it possible to make love beneath a waterfall?" she asked innocently.

"Maybe, but we may drown in the effort."

Experimentally she positioned herself upon him and let him slide into her warmth. He caught his breath in pleasure and she laughed. "If you start to drown, let me know."

"It'd be worth it," he gasped as she moved sensuously around him.

The water supported them, let them float as if freed from gravity, and gave a depth to their loving that neither had experienced before. With a low moan, Jesse reached his peak and knowing that he did brought Darcy to hers. Simultaneous waves of pleasure roared through them and they clung tightly as they became one.

Darcy kissed Jesse and then laid her cheek next to his as they relaxed back into the world. "Are you still cold?" she murmured into his ear.

"Hell, no. I may never be cold again," he replied in a voice filled with love for her. He kissed her and gazed deep into her eyes. "I sure am glad you came up that mountain."

"Are you really?" she asked with the serenity of already knowing the answer. "Sometimes it seems as if I've caused you more trouble than not."

"Days like this make it worthwhile." He grinned.

"Worthwhile, is it? I'll show you worthwhile!" She grabbed a handful of his hair and ducked him under the water.

Swimming below, he grabbed her slender ankles and pulled her down, too. His lips found hers beneath the water and he kissed her as the pearls of their breath floated upward through the swirling masses of her dark hair.

Breaking surface, Darcy gulped in air and floated, laughing in his arms. "It's a wonder fish ever have babies," she told him. "You could drown kissing like that."

"Maybe fish don't kiss," he suggested.

"Then it's an even greater wonder that there are

baby fish," she retorted. "I'll race you to the far bank."

He took off with a splash and she watched him go. Chuckling under her breath, she swam instead for the rocks beside the falls. Carefully she climbed up onto the slick boulders, her hair molding her body as sleek as seal skin. Hand over hand she climbed, seeking sure footholds and raising herself high above the pond.

She had never tried this before and she felt a heady sense of adventure. Mist from the falls glazed her skin and she knew from Jesse's side of the pond she must be climbing through the rainbow. Carefully she slid onto the upper rocks where the water smoothed into the lesser falls. Not three feet away she could see the pale green of the swifter current round and swirl as it plunged over the drop. She sat down on the flat rocks, making an island of her hips, and let the water gurgle around her.

"Jesse!" she called out and waved as he reached the shore and looked back to gloat at having won. "Up here!" Even at that distance she saw his face pale.

"Darcy! Get down from there before you fall!"

"I'm not going to fall and it's really pretty shallow here. All the deep water is over there." She gestured toward the middle of the river.

"Be still. I'm coming after you." He dived back into the water and began swimming toward her.

Darcy laughed and tossed a pebble at him. It splashed a few feet away so she threw another. Then it occurred to her to see if she could hit the rapids below the pond. Selecting a larger rock, she hurled it. It arched far out into space and splashed into the white water.

"Look, Jesse," she called out. "I can throw all the way over there. Why is it I can throw farther from this high up?"

"Be still. I'm coming." He hauled himself out of the water and started to climb as rivulets coursed down his body.

"There's really no reason to worry," Darcy told him. "This is perfectly safe. I'm sitting on a huge boulder and it's as firm as the earth." She picked up a much larger rock and let it bounce down the falls in the swirling current. Glancing down, she reached for another. "Oh!" she exclaimed. "Jesse! Jesse! Come quick!"

"Hang on, Darcy! I'm nearly there!" He practically threw himself up onto the ledge where she sat.

"Look, Jesse! Look!" Darcy shouted, pointing into the water.

He splashed to her and grabbed her arms. "What is it, Darcy? What's wrong?"

She stabbed her finger at the water, too excited to speak. Jesse looked down quickly, expecting to see a snake, a widening fissure, anything but what he saw.

Beneath their bare feet lay a wide band of gold that coursed from the edge of the boulder to disappear under the undisturbed rocks and into the ground. His lips moved but no sound came out.

"It's the mother lode, Jesse!" she cried out. "We found it!"

Tentatively touching the broad stripe of gleaming

gold, he then hugged her to him. "I knew you'd bring me luck, Partner! I knew it!"

"Oh, Jesse," she sobbed joyfully into his neck. "We'll never have to plow again!"

Laughing and crying together, Jesse and Darcy knelt upon their fortune as the defeated river thundered past.